SORRY YOU'RE HAVING A BAD NIGHT

E.K. Robertson

E.K. Robertson

ISBN: 978-0-578-30610-0

*This book is a work of fiction. Unless otherwise indicated, all the names, characters,
businesses, places, events and incidents in this book are either the product of the author's
imagination or used in a fictitious manner. Any resemblance to actual persons, living or
dead, or actual events is purely coincidental.*

Manufactured and printed in the United States of America

Acknowledgments

Jamar, who has been everything I've needed on this journey. Thank you for your endless love, support, and your ear.

Sade, because without your words of encouragement, I don't know if I would've executed this year. You are a true friend, and I'm so thankful we crossed paths.

Darryelle, who lives the working writer's life we manifested many moons ago. Thank you for being a constant reminder of seeds planted way back when.

Nikki, whose excellent book recommendations prepared me for this journey, and whose smile cheered me on during the toughest times of my life. I thank God for you.

Stephanie, my angel. Thank you for your guiding light. Bless you, your children, and all those who had the pleasure of knowing you.

To everyone taking the time to read this novel, thank you so kindly for supporting me. Enjoy the story!

E.K. Robertson

Prologue
When Someone Learns Something...

The recording booth hummed with an electric buzz that sizzled from the grilles of the overhead mics, through the black mass of wires and into the four walls surrounding her. She'd been in this space many times before, but today's recording task gave her all the butterflies of a first encounter. Nervous, she grabbed and rattled a Chik Fil-A cup, filled mostly with her favorite type of chipped ice, and took a long needed sip. The cool water washed over the dry lump in her throat as she ran her fingers through the soft tangle of coils on her head. Her signature braids would be back by the end of the day, as soon as she wrapped this task in the bow it deserved.

She looked down at the script, on a stand in front of her. If she could have one successful read of it, just two paragraphs in size, she'd be grateful. No stumbling over the words and no awkward swallows of the tongue in between sentences, the latter of which she discovered was a true nuisance for the pirates at MysterPodcast Networks. Nevertheless, her recordings plunged through the sharp waters of sound mastering, and bobbed the treacherous waves of award winning audio engineering.

She hadn't been too rocked by the boat, one that she eventually steered into the victory of pure journalistic brilliance. Twenty seven colorful and controversial episodes of a story only she could tell.

The company agreed to take the project on, favoring the idea of conspiracy theories being explored within the black culture. But would it work? YouTube had its boatloads of goofy theories and even sillier, the people who made them. 'Is Tupac still alive?' theories to the Illuminati; it all oared the unforgiving oceans of social media.

But there were other opportunities to explore the storms of conspiracy and scandal. A chance to churn a sea just as eternal as politics. Here, was a story docked in the sophisticated narrative that made for the best of today's investigative journaling. Soon after its initial presentation, the network offered her a distribution deal, and agreed to fund her research and recording efforts.

As well they should. She presented them a tale as bittersweet as fruit ripped from the Tree of Knowledge of Good and Evil. Their insatiable appetites for true crime couldn't resist the hissing of any serpent's tongue. Neither could hers.

"Do you remember where you were the first time you heard about the Illuminati? What about that one conspiracy theory that made you question the world around you? I certainly have mine. And working in the entertainment industry, I've realized something. We *all* do! A plethora of stories circulating industry watercoolers, with rumors that big companies always put to rest as untrue, or six feet under. Black entertainment has its share of unsolved mysteries and conspiracy theories. And I present to you- a podcast willing to explore them.

"On season one of the Out & Industry podcast, we dig to the bottom of the scandals, mysteries and murders surrounding industry giants, with an inside look from the people who lived it. These are the stories that will haunt you forever, and make you question everything you thought you knew. So make sure you follow Out & Industry podcast, premiering Friday, July 2."

The host held a thumbs up to the control room, and the engineer pressed a button to end the recording. She grabbed the script, her water and exited the booth. As she joined him at the controls, she was unable to hide a cocky smile.

After replaying the audio, host and engineer approved a final playback and sent the file for mastering. She said her goodbyes, gathered her belongings, and exited Downtown Richmond's Regus Sun Trust Center.

As she stepped into the day, the last of a spring sun greeted her with its warmth. 10th and Cary buzzed with the moderate hustle and bustle of morning, and she with the excitement of a story that would set the industry ablaze.

One
June 17 | 5:38 am

The waters of the James River raged softly over Mayo's Island and Belle Isle. Bridges, highways and train tracks stretched towards Shockoe Slip, crisscrossing over the old faithful river as it winded its way through the city of Richmond, splitting it almost in half. There was an abstract metropolis of downtown buildings stacked like blocks against the orange turn blue ombre sky. A quilt of rippling clouds moved slow and steady against the textures of the cityscape, in the magnificent gentleness of dawn becoming day.

It was a view Evita Pitts would never grow tired of. She drank it in from the bedroom balcony with a caramel cappuccino, held snug in a wide coffee mug stamped with the monogram *Mrs.* Her 16th floor corner penthouse unit at Vistas on the James was located on the building's west side. The home in the sky offered an an intimate view of the city from its floor to ceiling windows that wrapped from one wall to another.

This was just one of three places she called home there in Virginia and her go-to, thanks to its panoramic views of a crane congested skyline; a subtle reminder that the city was always expanding. As life required.

Certainly a good thing for Richmond, a city where she'd come to enjoy her unforgettable 40s. It was her media mogul husband's hometown. A place where they were known, but not hassled. Doted on, but not disturbed. A low-key rather quiet lifestyle relative to the one lived in decades past. She found travel to be a breeze; whether she was careening Interstate-95 to the old and new luxuries of Northern Virginia (NoVa), or hopping a private jet to the bustling cities of Charlotte, Atlanta and Miami whenever she felt the need.

Still, it had taken much persuasion to get him there. It was Evita who discovered Richmond had a promising economic boom. She convinced her husband to put his money where his heart was when it came to giving back to the community, especially the ones that raised him.

So in 2019, the company packed their lives in New York and traded it for the city of Richmond. Two tough years of hard work held a tremendous pay off. Now, both the Pitts family and the business shared favor and clout in many political and social circles. Yes, the hometown hero and his trophy wife made good on their promise to advance the city with not just their connections, but also their funds. So much so that Evita was able to secure the Greater Richmond Convention Center to host the company's Sweet Sixteenth anniversary gala. It was a way to reintroduce them to Richmond society as economic pioneers.

Today, her role as wife and socialite meant she'd be spending the afternoon with two powerful women in business with her husband. Both of them in town for the gala. Evita had them scheduled for lunch and massages at the Jefferson Hotel. Two birds, one building. After her successful evening of daytime entertaining, she'd meet her husband for dinner at a white tablecloth restaurant like Fleming's Prime Steakhouse. Long after he concluded business in the boardrooms and offices, and she, in the life as a socialite wife. Both of them proud to host their friends and business family for the weekend ahead.

And with the reminder of a busy day, Evita went back inside the bedroom to prepare for the rest of her morning. Her husband was still asleep in their king-size aluminum canopy bed. By time he'd awake from his hard sleep, she'd be gone.

Evita took a long shower, an even longer dry off process, and slipped into an athleisure get-up. She followed up with a quick breakfast of grapes and buttered toast, and finally, a hurried dash out the door.

She was running behind and tried not to drive like it in her late model Range Rover. The buildings of downtown faded from rearview as the highway took her thirty minutes outside of downtown to the Henrico County estate in Chaffin's Bluff.

The property sat hillside along a bend in the James River, quietly nestled on two acres. It was a shot ripped from the pages of Southern Home. There was a columned wraparound porch, long paved driveway, and a backyard double deck patio overlooking the river and private dock. It touted six bedrooms, four bathrooms, and a black marble theme that reverberated in every room of the house.

Evita made it to the property at 10 a.m., much later than expected. The entire morning had been flanked by her sister's demanding text messages that begged to know when she'd arrive. After all, it wasn't her house who had the 8 a.m. appointment with a junk hauler.

Anya had been there since, as previously agreed. Her brown eyes peeled over Evita. "You seem a little relaxed for everything we've got planned today," she said. "Of all days, you had to junk the basement today?"

Evita had questioned her own decision to keep the appointment. But the project was two years overdue; the basement had been the dumping ground for Sam's personal New York offices. After his final pick-over, he ordered the clutter to be junked. And she did just that, locking in the first available appointment which happened to be today.

Anya continued, "You're lucky I was here. Where the hell were you?"

"I promise you I woke up early. But you know how long it takes me to get ready. I'm working on that." Evita's dark brown eyes met Anya's.

The sisters, though separated by seven years, were almost identical with their thick dark tresses and toffee brown skin. They had the same dark brown eyes, natural thick lashes and arched brows. The mild laugh lines in Evita's face gave her away as the older.

Anya, not yet 40, was the ideal little sister. She kept her head in the books and her life on the straight and narrow. After graduating from the University of Richmond, Anya found herself living a comfortable secure life as a busy housewife with a thriving family business of her own. A far contrast from the fast track to womanhood Evita stumbled down.

"Well, I'm glad you decided to show up. Now take a look at this," Anya said, shoving a stack of photos into her hands. She folded her arms across her chest. She had no idea where they were from, but figured, based on the addressee, it was urgent that they be seen.

Evita stared with wide eyes that moved slowly from image to image. She could remember the night as if it were a week ago, during a time when they were naïve to the success that awaited them.

"This is classic stuff right here. Where did you find these?"

"Something told me to go through that old file cabinet, the big ugly brown one. They were in an envelope addressed to *Sam's Eyes Only*."

"Sam swore he got all his stuff out of there. Come to think of it, that file cabinet may not have been from the main office. He must not have known it was there amongst the rubble."

"Where were these taken?" Anya wondered if Evita even heard her as the woman perused the photos.

"Our photographer LeVario took these at an industry party in '05, back when we were just getting started."

"Can you reach him? He may want them back."

"I would if I could. He died a week after the party. It was really sad." Evita winced, remembering the day she sent flowers to his mother. She kept to herself the dreadful detail that SamStar Enterprises was quickly forced to move on. Fruitful networking put the company on a trajectory towards success, the kind that didn't allow for the proper mourning of a family friend.

"Oh that's awful. How'd he die?"

"He committed suicide. We think it's because the boxer Hendrik Clary embarrassed him."

"You said what?" Anya was visibly confused.

"From what I remember, Hendrik didn't want any pictures taken, and LeVario flashed the camera at him. Hendrik punched him, and security dragged LeVario out before he could defend himself. Poor baby was only nineteen. Just couldn't handle the industry. I felt bad we invited him."

By the night's end, her husband and Dmitri were boarding a private jet, bound for Florida, where several deals and contracts were signed. She was left to console LeVario, who did not want to speak with her about the incident.

Within days, SamStar Enterprises had become the prime media distributor for Goode Records. The success had seen them through technology booms and digital takeovers, the tragic passing of Dmitri Goode, and most recently, the pandemic.

"But this is a sweet reminder of someone I almost forgot about," Evita said, flipping to the next photo in the stack. "We're lucky to have found these."

"With that being said, junk haul will be done in thirty minutes," said Anya, arms still folded. She wondered again if Evita heard her. Her sister's sole focus was on the pictures.

"Sam will be floored. Look at Kenny!" Evita showed Anya the photo. "He had to be about 13 or 14 years old here."

Anya paused, regarding the photo. "Kenny looks so goofy. And who's the girl?"

"Dreah McDonald. Do you remember her? She was a teen model back in the day. Eh, maybe you don't. You were in college."

"Definitely not my age group, but I should've known she was a model. Look at that gorgeous brown skin."

"Yeah that's because *we* worked on it. We were using all kinds of products until the hood put us onto African black soap," Evita laughed. "Miss Thang was our 2000s It Girl. Kenny had this teen rapper thing going on..."

Evita cackled at the thought of her son's short stint as a teen rapper, comparing it to recent years and all the accomplishments he'd made. Though Kenny's infatuation with being a teen rapper was but a moment, it exposed him to the inner workings of other industry career paths. And to that she was thankful.

"Mina wanted to put her in some of his videos and he did not like that! I tried to tell him it was just business, but the truth was, he had the biggest crush on Dreah and didn't want us to know. He always felt like Mina was putting him on the spot. Til this day he still doesn't like her."

"Eh, I don't blame him," said Anya, with a sympathetic shrug. "I don't care for her either."

Evita ignored the comment, instead choosing to reminisce over the photo with a forlorn expression. Everything about it took her back to calmer, safer times in the world. Dreah's smile sparkled at her. Bright brown eyes, a defined full nose, a clean smile flashing straight white teeth. Her hair was styled in a high ponytail, with the lower half falling down her back. She wore a chunky beaded necklace over a white crop top, and cargo capri pants paired with bedazzled peep toe pumps that one wouldn't be seen in today.

Her son Kenny was swallowed in an oversized basketball jersey, and a matching fitted cap that actually didn't fit at all. The wide brim was pivoted slightly to the left, sitting loosely over the du-rag and sports headband that covered his straight back cornrows.

"I haven't seen Dreah since she worked as Kenny's assistant a few years ago. That did *not* turn out well."

"What changed? Did they date? 'Cuz that'll ruin things," Anya said, as if she were a witness.

"No, no. That childhood crush stayed just that. Dreah became a part of our family. But she started lashing out, real bad. I guess she didn't want any part of the business anymore. Now she's all spiritual, into those crystals and shit. She's got a store too. Alchemia. Pretty sure that's the name. She made good for herself."

"Why don't you invite her to the gala?"

"That's actually a really good idea. I'm sure things have blown all the way over. It'd be a joy to see her face since she's been with us from the beginning. Why didn't I think of that?"

"Because I did." Anya touted a boastful smile.

"I'll have Tati take an invite to the store," Evita said with finality. She shuffled the photos into a neat stack, and placed them in their envelope. "I can't wait to show Sam. This will be quite the Father's Day surprise."

"You should convert them into a picture book. Something for guests to take home. Your first industry party? C'mon, you gotta admit that's pretty iconic!"

"You're just on a roll this morning." Evita gave Anya the side-eye; one that said she was impressed. "I'll turn that project over to Pia. She'll know just what to do. She's been killin' it with our creative endeavors. I just hope Kenny doesn't mind." She slipped the envelope into her Hermes handbag and turned back to her sister. "Are you flying with me to Atlanta tomorrow? We're picking up our *costumes* for the gala."

Anya quickly shook her head. "I wish. Daryl actually didn't have a tuxedo ordered so now we're both getting last minute fittings with a stylist from our social group. Not as highbrow as your people, but it'll do."

"Damn. I was hoping you could see this new jet. Maybe next time?"

"Definitely next time," Anya said, watching the junk hauler start his truck, his job complete. There was just the matter of collecting a signature from one of the women, whom he approached with a clipboard.

"Alrighty, all done. Just need one of you to sign here, and we'll authorize payment to the card on file."

Evita took the clipboard from him. "I'll do the honors. It's my card on file after all." She quickly signed and watched him go on his way, getting into the truck and stuttering down the driveway.

"I know we're having lunch at the Jefferson, but can we hit Perly's for a late breakfast? Lord knows I am not trying to host these women on an empty stomach."

"Now you should've known to eat something."

"Maybe I would've if I wasn't here at eight-o-clock in the morning. You owe me ma'am."

Evita looked at her Audemars Piguet watch and flashed an all-knowing smile. There was just enough time to catch a bite at Perly's and come back to the estate to freshen up. The car service would take them to the Jefferson Hotel around 2 p.m.

"Alright, let me lock up first," she said to her sister's delight. "And we gotta be back here by 1, no later."

Anya smiled naughtily and joked, "Oh *now* we want to watch the clock."

Two

June 17 | 11:03 am

Kenny stared smitten at his interviewee, a young lady he knew would be his assistant the instant she waltzed into Maya's Mexican Grill. She looked better in person, as the photos on her Instagram didn't do her the justice she was due. The moment she sat her slim petite physique across from him at a sunny lit table for two, she had the job. He would go through all the formalities of a standard interview. She, having both nothing and everything to lose, would navigate his questions like a true professional. She gave him hope; hope that would surely win his father over, in the same pleasurable manner she had overtaken him.

Pia was stunning, with unblemished brown skin and hazel eyes that sparkled like amber in the sunlight, lending its warmth to their window-side table. Her curly locks were pulled back into an elegant ponytail. Her baby hairs were modestly swooped, but certainly in place.

Sleek and sexy. I'd eat you all night, Kenny kept that thought to himself during the interview. He was secretly intimidated, struggling to remember this was on professional terms. He wondered if she shared the same hassle. He knew he was good looking, with pecan brown skin, caramel colored eyes and a taper fade with hair as thick as wool strewn about the top. He had his father's jawline, and prided himself on a full beard that was far better groomed than the hair on his head.

"So what are your credentials?"

"It's too late for that," Pia said with a bossy smile. "Especially since I had to remind you to ask about them. No, I'm kidding. I have my resume for you right here." She reached in her Louis Vuitton Onthego tote and handed him a copy.

"You also have the job." Kenny waited for her eyes to meet his. He analyzed the uncertainty on her face. *Please accept.*

Both her eyebrows were raised in contention, and finally, a satisfied smirk spread her perfectly oval face. "Thank you so much! I'm hype, really. When do I start?"

"The question is, how soon can you?"

That interview was in 2019, but felt like ages ago since the pandemic. Securing a job with SamStar Enterprises was the highlight of Pia's year. When the Florida native relocated, she had only a few thousand dollars saved and a fierce determination to make a better living. And here she was, two years later, working a dream job that afforded her an accomplished life.

By the top of 2021, hiring her became Kenny's best decision. Together they survived the pandemic, reinventing the rules as COVID-19 demanded. And they thrived. She adapted rather quickly to the new ways of doing business, at a time where the rest of the world had come to a standstill.

These days, Pia was consumed with the daily grind as his assistant. She worked hard to gain Kenny's trust, and twice as hard for his respect. She was empathetic to the plight with his father. Following the fiasco with the previous assistant, the son and young businessman was facing exile. She'd only heard pieces of the story from a few coworkers, but knew enough not to make the same mistakes of the former employee. Specifically, badmouthing the boss and his son.

Last minute planning for the gala found Pia teaming up with Tati the publicist, whose job was far more tedious than her own. She was the daughter of a distinguished banker, one who'd come from a long line of black banking in Petersburg. When she wasn't monitoring public image and opinion, Tati was about her advancements- socializing and rubbing shoulders with the new generation of wealth in Richmond.

Pia was a Miami-transplant; one who left everything behind in Florida for a more subdued life. It was the complete opposite of what most adults her age were doing, but it had a great dividend. And with motivated coworkers, the decision became a no-brainer. Pia liked working alongside the equally kept-up Tati, who shared her same appetite for luxury and efficiency. The publicist was fast becoming the best friend she didn't think she needed.

When Pia got the call from Evita about a last minute project for the gala, Tati was gracious enough to drive her to the downtown restaurant and delicatessen where the woman was having breakfast with her sister.

Evita and Anya were exiting Perly's when Tati's white Mercedes Benz rounded into a free space behind Anya's black 2020 Audi. Both had run into a bit of luck that Thursday morning with the open parking spaces. Evita was first to spot them, and hurried over as Anya roared the Audi to life. She leaned into the passenger window, carefully looking behind her at the line of vehicles slowly crawling the one-way Grace Street.

"Good morning Evita!" Pia greeted.

"Hey Pia! Tati." Evita gave a nod to the publicist, enthusiasm diminishing at the mention of her name.

"Mrs. Pitts," Tati replied, just as flatly.

Evita reached into her Hermes, removed an envelope and handed it to Pia.

"Thank you for taking this on so last minute. It'll be a miracle if we pull these books off."

"I agree. I'm sending the images to be formatted, then to a local publisher. They've agreed to push our order to the top of the list, and for what we're paying, they better come through," Pia advised, placing the photos in her purse.

Evita grinned and wagged a finger at her approvingly. "I really like you. You'll have to join us for breakfast soon. You'd love this place!" Then, she turned flat eyes on Tati and added, "The store is called Alchemia, on Franklin. Just tell her Evita wants her there *if* you run into trouble."

"Certainly," Tati replied with a sheepish grin. "Anything else before we go?" She reached for the radio, ready to turn it up before Evita could even answer.

Evita looked at Pia as if she were going to remind her of another last minute task. "Nope, that's all. Pia, I'll listen for your call later."

They watched Evita's woman-about-town stride carry her into the passenger seat of the Audi. Tati cut the radio on and it squawked at them with the voice of a morning show host.

"This morning's question is: Ladies, are you gay because you're really gay, or has today's female rap culture influenced you to explore that part of your sexuality? I'm Cece the Talkative, and we'll be back in five. Keep it locked!"

Tati popped open the roof to the Benz. It reversed, folding open above them as cars sped down the one-way. Once she had a clearing, she too sped away from the curb and into the street.

"You're wrong about Evita," Pia said.

Tati knew the comment wasn't coming from left field. "I stand by every statement I've ever made."

"I like her so much. She's cooler in person than what she lets on social media! A real girl's girl, for real." Pia exchanged a look with Tati as the car purred to a stop at the red light.

"Well as you saw, she still keeps it short and curt with me. I don't know what I did to her. She barely says hi."

"Oh no, be clear. She *won't* say hi to you. That sucks too 'cause I like both of y'all. Maybe y'all just didn't vibe."

Tati begged to differ, saying, "I'm a publicist. I don't give a fuck if I vibe with Evita Pitts or not. I'm here to work. She just never liked me, and there's no reason why."

"She likes me." Pia's face rose in a childlike smirk.

"I'm sure she does likes you, seeing all the work you put into the gala on her behalf! She probably wants to hire you for herself."

Pia fondled the ends of her ponytail, a thoughtful expression etched on her face. "I'd hate to do Kenny like that, but I sure would for the right amount!" She laughed, mostly because it was true.

The car zipped through green lights, away from the tetris of downtown until they arrived at Alchemia, a holistic healing store in Richmond's vibrant Fan district.

"You're listening to 104.3 with Cece the Talkative. We're back, and let me tell y'all something. Cuz y'all been blowing my mentions up since I announced today's question. I'm asking because some of y'all girls

really ain't gay. Y'all just into girls 'cuz they make it look cute, but when it's time to get down, you get up. Keep it-"

Tati shut the car off and lowered her D&G sunglasses. Her high-yellow skin burned just a tinge, as she absorbed the heat of what was fast becoming a heated afternoon, complete with the inconsistent breeze of southern summers. She never cared for this type of heat. And heat like this just days before the official start of the summer solstice worried her of temperatures to come. She ran her fingers through a sharp shoulder length bob as her green eyes peeled over the neighborhood.

As she opened the door and exited the car in one perfect motion, excitement turned Tati's face. She realized where they were. "I follow this store's Instagram. I've been meaning to come here on my day off but I didn't know it was right here."

Pia joined her on the sidewalk, staring up at a large custom neon sign of the company's name. It buzzed above the glass door of the storefront window, which was lined with LED light strips flashing purple and pink.

Wind chimes on the door's other side pulled the clerk's attention as they pushed through in the store.

"Hey ladies! Welcome to Alchemia. I'm Dreah. Are we looking for anything special today?"

The two women didn't look like her typical crowd of youthful progressives and artsy fartsy hipsters. The type of people on a quest for everything from crystals to herbs. And based on their awe, she knew it was their first ime.

Paper flowers dangled from the ceiling on invisible hanging wire, surrounding firework chandeliers that dangled ad dazzled amongst the floating garden. Three of store's walls were covered in artificial grass mats. There were three long bookshelves on the left wall. All three rows were dressed with books ranging from astrology to alternative medicine. Beneath the shelves stood three antique white dressers, with shelves pulled out in intervals to display other products. A clear display case of an endless supply of crystals sat in the center of the room, like that of a jewelry boutique. Two pink tufted chaises sat along the right wall. They were surrounded by gaudy vases of silk peonies and eucalyptus.

On that wall hung a photo of Dreah draped in a gold and white silk kimono robe, and adorned in a jeweled crown.

"Yes, this is definitely the store!" Tati looked around in amazement. Instagram posts didn't do it justice. "You've got the most instagrammable boutique in Richmond right now! I'm excited to be here."

Dreah couldn't help but smile bashfully at the comment, no matter how many times she heard it. She looked around the store with the admiration of self. She put everything she had into it. She stepped from behind the register, approaching them with two mini wire shopping baskets. "Thank you so much. Take all the pics you want, and all the time."

"I sure will. This is right on time. I need a new numerology book. Do you have any?" Tati asked as she took the basket from Dreah.

"Yes, of course. Just got two in last week. One gives lots of biblical references." Dreah led her to the appropriate shelf.

"And crystals!" Tati looked over her shoulder at the rainbow of crystals shimmering in the display case.

"Do you know what you're looking for?"

"Pyrite, if you have it."

Dreah's face registered her surprise. "Ahhh. Fool's gold. You sure you want that?" She wondered if the slender beauty knew what to do with such a stone.

Tati wouldn't spare her imagination any longer. "I sure do. I'm a leader type with a lot going on career wise, so I need my energy protected with everything I'm about to walk into."

Dreah turned to Pia and asked, "Is she a Leo?"

Pia shrugged as the three woman shared a laugh.

"Virgo actually. And before y'all say I'm a perfectionist and I'm competitive, let me just say, you right!" Tati shrugged her shoulders and smirked at them.

"Would you like the stones in a necklace? Waist beads? Or do you prefer it as is?"

"As is, of course!" Tati answered as she panned over a selection of books. She thumbed through pages as Dreah crossed over to the center of the room and removed the cluster of pyrite from the display case.

It shimmered like gold in a treasure box. Dreah regarded the stone for a brief moment before saying, "You be careful with this thing here. And what about you? You into any of this stuff?" She turned her attention to the other customer as she placed the pyrite stone beside the Square stand.

"Oh no, no thank you. I'm just here for her." Pia threw a nod to Tati and took a seat on the chaise lounge. She wondered if Tati remembered the reason they had come to the store. And it certainly wasn't to shop. "Looks like we'll be a minute so don't mind me."

In less than five minutes, Tati was knee deep in shopping- her basket filled with sea moss, teas, natural soaps and body butters, and essential oil candles.

Pia took Evita's photos out of her purse. Now was a good time to see exactly how many photos they were working with. But while flapping them onto her knee during a count, the photos slipped off, fanning out on the rug beneath her.

"Oh dear!" Dreah said when hearing the shuffling of photos. "Let me help you with that." She quickly hurried to the spot in front of Pia where the photos lay scattered. It took her just a second to realize their origin. "Where did you get these?"

Tati and Pia exchanged looks. Neither knew who should answer that. But the publicist stepped in with her confident smile and produced the formal invitation to the gala.

"I'm so sorry. I never got a chance to introduce myself. I'm Tati Hines, publicist for SamStar Enterprises. I have for you an invitation to our Sweet Sixteenth Anniversary gala, Sunday at the convention center. Here, this is for you." She turned the envelope over to Dreah, now standing and staring at her with cold eyes narrowed in slits. She remembered what Evita told her about running into trouble.

"I was sent by *Evita*, personally. She wants you there."

"So you're a publicist for SamStar and you were sent to invite me to their party?" Dreah was genuinely stunned. She knew her relationship with the company ended on a bad one. She wasn't sure if this was a joke, or a peace offering. An opportunity to let bygones be bygones, and the past be the past. She turned to Pia and asked, "And who are you? Where did you get these?"

Pia also remembered what Evita said, and answered back, "These belong to *Evita*. We're turning them into a picture book. If you can come Sunday, you'll receive one in your gift bag."

"Who needs the book when I was there?" Dreah meant the question to be rhetorical, and that's exactly how it was received. She thumbed through the rest of the pictures gathered off the floor. A pensive look came over her face. "I'm sorry, and who are you again?"

"I'm Pia, just an assistant."

"So Evita *finally* got herself an assistant." Dreah snickered and looked at the photos with more scrutiny, soaking in every detail of the image before turning to the next.

Pia handed her the remaining photos and said, "I'm actually *Kenny's* assistant, just doing Evita a last minute favor."

Joining her on the chaise, Dreah continued observing the photos in reminiscent fashion. "Evita was always a nice lady."

Tati and Pia exchanged looks right after she said it.

With the flip to another photo, Dreah winced, bringing the picture closer to her face. She bore squinty, scrutinizing eyes that couldn't pull away. She paused a moment to gather her words.

"I think I should hold on to *this* one." Her leg bounced in an anxiety filled way as she spoke. "This photo caused a lot of controversy back then and I don't think anyone who's made it through that shit storm wants to relive it."

Pia wondered if Dreah knew her bouncing shook the entire chaise. "I mean, these are Evita's. She felt it was good enough for the book. I just can't let you keep it."

"Well hold on, hold on," Tati butt in. "What's the picture? If it's linked to old controversy maybe it needs to stay out." She held out her hand, beckoning for the photo.

Dreah looked on with a blank stare that shifted nervously between the two women. After muttering to herself, she turned the photo over to Tati.

The picture was of a bald man in a long-sleeve button down shirt and baggy designer jeans. A king's crown titled on his head, and on his arm, an exaggerated woman in lots of makeup and a fur lined sequin gown.

"I'm not sure what the problem is here. I mean, this guy looks pissed, but this woman looks fabulous. Also like she could be a man," Tati noticed.

Dreah pulled the photo back into the fold of her arm. "First things first, that woman is Zsarina Gambino. For Hendrik, it wouldn't have been a good look to be seen with a transwoman."

Tati and Pia knew the name Zsarina Gambino and her decades of work for the LGBT+ community. She was a revolutionary icon, complete with the surgeries needed to make her more feminine, more of the true self she most identified with.

Dreah moved on, "I don't think this is appropriate to have in the book, with all the controversy it caused. Hendrik doesn't need his name brought up for this in 2021."

"Ain't it the Age of Aquarius? I mean, what's it to him?" Pia couldn't understand. Her sarcasm said as much.

"*Exposure* and enlightenment are two different things."

Tati agreed with Dreah, whom she turned to, saying, "Look, you're talking my language. I need the least amount of work possible after this weekend. Keep the photo and give it back to Evita on Sunday, if you come. If not we'll get it Monday."

Dreah was thankful, appearing thoughtful as her mind ran on a tangent not congruent to the conversation. She returned the rest of the photos to Pia and met Tati at the sales counter.

After payment, Tati looked at her watch. "Shit! Pia it's 12:12. We need to get going. Dreah, thank you so much. I'll tag the store on Instagram. Pleasure meeting you." She grabbed her shopping bags and started for the door. "And it's a casino theme so wear your absolute best on Sunday!"

With a wave, Dreah watched the women hop into the Benz up until it pulled away from the curb. Then, she turned her focus back to the photo, staring at it more intently now.

And this time, it stared back at her.

Three
June 17 | 8:16 pm

Samuel Pitts was a true business mogul in every sense of the word. Shrewd in all his ways, logical and calculated. A man of true finesse. He stood a stark 6'3, with even deep brown skin, a well-groomed goatee and smooth bald head. He was chiseled with a strong jawline to compliment fairly built biceps, triceps and quads. A far cry from the days of youth, but solid for 53, nonetheless.

The storied Virginia Union University graduate touted degrees in Music, Bachelor of Fine Arts, and a Master's in Business Administrations. A musically inclined frat brother who had always been methodical about his college experience. His underlying love for visual arts is what kept him motivated in the classroom. The same motivation had taken the graduate to Atlanta, granting him opportunities to create music for late 80's acts, and helping to orchestrate the sound for the best in R&B, Soul and Urban pop. A career that, by the mid-90s, had thrust him into a high rise in the concrete jungle New York.

He was a young father and husband then, and a bit more settled into the gritty melodic sound of late 90s hip hop. His goals for the genre included giving rap artist a variety of sounds, instruments, and vibes. A three to four minute symphony of a day in the life. The talent had prospered him time after time.

By the turn of 2005, the mountain goat producer stunned the business world by announcing the arrival of SamStar Enterprises, a new digital media distributor for black entertainment. There were doubts, and many ill comparisons to BET, MTV and UPN. But he was focused on the world beyond- the infinite mass known as the internet.

How to do I make money on that? The answers to the question garnered many complications, and included coaxing the best and brightest employees to his company. People who were already equipped with field knowledge of what would make him successful. The president of an urban TV network, a former Google CFO, and several software developers who once programmed codes for Apple and Microsoft.

It took the company several years to develop the software necessary to provide a one of a kind streaming experience to consumers. But that's just what they did.

Sam was relentless in encouraging industry friends to invest in his company. He left meetings feeling inspired by business partners and employees who had a vision that he, as a CEO, was willing to trust in. It took a lot to make employees feel valued, he knew that. But it also took a lot to make profit. They knew that.

And SamStar Enterprises earned its profit, millions by millions. Year after year. The business had branded and developed several entities; including their own streaming platform, a publishing company, and a casting and modeling agency.

Sam enjoyed the twists and turns of life, especially as it took him into an opportunity to move back to his hometown. He felt *almost* political, paying dues to local businesses and funding campaigns that best suited him. While uncertainty plagued them the first year in 2019, 2020's turnabout did him proud. His son Kenny hired a new team and proved himself to be quite the heir to his throne. It was a well-earned change of opinion.

A few years prior, Kenny felt cursed with being a rich kid spoiled by the perks of the industry. Well-traveled and well-off, sitting on a college Business degree that had afforded him nothing but a disrespectful assistant, several failed projects and the pressure of being in a generation to which the hard-knock life was lost.

By the age of 29, Kenny fixed that. He presented his father with new streaming content ideas and hired fresh, innovative millennials to power them through the pandemic. Kenny's brigade of strong young men and women were encouraged to speak their peace in the fight for reinvention at every level COVID-19 demanded.

And it all happened in Richmond, where he sourced from local talent and media pools, saving the company money and almost doubling its earnings in bi-yearly reports.

Sam looked forward to their meeting at the penthouse to review some last minute gala details. He enjoyed the place as much as his wife, who added the luxurious touches that made the place their own. It was a far contrast from the big southern estate on the hill, where the cicadas' song never ended, and you could hear them from any room in the house with an open window.

That home, however, had its pros. Like the private dock that gave his Viking 64 Convertible boat access to the James River. Or the double deck patio where they entertained their closest friends on autumn nights under the warmth of barbecue pits.

Still, it failed in comparison to the comfort of the penthouse suite, where he found himself intoxicated by the view of a city on the edge of economic promise. A handful of planes twinkled like early evening stars as the sun hung out over downtown. Just another ten minutes until its descent over the west. The winding highways were scarce with traffic, speckles of red and white lights zipping to and fro. A flock of birds flew in formation towards the clock tower of Main Street Station, where each one landed on its own perch in synch with the others.

Sam looked from the window to the television, enjoying the last of a Yahoo Finance clip, then lowered the volume as Kenny turned key into the home.

"What's good pops?"

The two men bumped fists and Kenny joined his father on the sofa to lay out his business updates. It wouldn't be a long conversation, but having it in person always seemed more appropriate than a standard phone call.

"I just got word from my assistant that mom's books have been sent for print with pick up for Saturday night. Production management is putting together the last of the press kits and gift bags... Pia's overseeing that. And it'll be an all-nighter so I gave her the company card for breakfast, lunch and dinner. Whatever it takes right?"

He chuckled, catching his breath a moment. "Pia will report to me Sunday morning, unless we run into a problem before that. And you're sure you don't want a Father's Day tribute video shown at the gala?"

"One hundred percent."

"Then my work for today is done."

"I love to hear it. I know this ain't been easy, but your team is gonna knock it out the park. I can feel it. Shit like that keeps me confident." Sam looked his son in the eye, meaning every single word. He never spoke unless he did. "And I really like that Pia for you. She's exactly what you need."

Kenny grinned, showing just a glimpse of his perfectly gapped teeth. The kind that were straight enough to do without dental correction. He knew what his father was implying. He came to expect this type of praise ever since Dreah's firing. Which was actually more than the standard firing of an employee because they were once the best of friends. Both were bratty industry teens raised in the lap of luxury. But having her as an assistant quickly fizzled into a bad idea. She was constantly dropping assignments and there was too much tension in the workspace. Their personal relationship eventually suffered. By time Kenny realized it was over, all he could do was turn the matter over to his father.

"I don't think I ever asked, but where'd you meet Pia?"

"Same place this generation meets all its new employees." Kenny grinned. "She slid in my DMs." He was the only one chuckling. "I made a job post on Instagram, and she was interested in the position."

Sam's face was tight with disappointment. There were many things he disagreed about with this new generation, and garnering employees from social media was one of them. "So no business resume? No interview? No background checks?"

"*Of course* I got alladat. Relax old man." Kenny laughed at his father's scowl; laughter always disarmed the man's disdain.

Sam was hard on his son, but also compassionate. They were his pride and joy. He didn't mean to come off like an out of touch prude, but there were things about business Kenny needed to know. He dropped his frown, figuring there were things he ought to know too. Especially when handling his oldest son.

"Well, I'm glad it worked out."

"Me too. She needed it bad. The company she previously worked for was involved in a bank fraud scam. She got out just in time."

"So now we got a scammer on payroll."

"Sure dad. I'll just hire any damn body."

Sam waved his hand dismissively, Kenny's sarcasm not lost on him. "You know better. *Slid in my DMs,*" he snorted mockingly. "Only you'd hire a girl who admitted to bank fraud."

"Nah she's innocent!"

"That's what they all say."

"It's not like she handles the money."

"You gave her a company card to make purchases with. She handles the money." Sam threw his hands up, finally annoyed with his son.

Defending his honor, Kenny countered, "But I see what she purchases online. And I look at that shit every day. Shawty not getting over on me. I got an accountant for an accountant. You know I don't play."

"I trust you. Always have, believe it or not." Sam nodded, agreeing after all. He regarded his son's attire. "I see you're dressed up. What's the plan tonight?"

Kenny stood, making this his cue to leave. "I'on know just yet. Waiting for this pretty little analyst to hit me back but she's playing games. She's childish."

Both men stood, and grabbed each other in a final hug. Sam showed him to the door.

"I'll call you tomorrow morning before we take off. You be safe out here, son."

Before making his leave, Kenny looked around the penthouse. The sun was just setting behind the downtown skyline.

"I gotta get me one of these," he said, standing akimbo. Then, a better idea. "How long will y'all be gone again?"

"Stay out my house while I'm in Atlanta. I know you like to pop up when we're out of town," Sam chuckled with a slap to his son's shoulder.

As Sam opened the door to let Kenny out, in walked the younger and wilder of his two sons, Grant. He was hands down the most popular amongst the Pitts, finding fame via YouTube and Instagram. At 22, he was known for viral pranks, videos and even had a song making rounds on Tiktok with a dance to match. His money was not contingent upon the success of SamStar Enterprises, therefore he had a more laid back approach to the family business. It was barely an approach at all. Not when he made millions just being his loud, exuberant self for the sake of vlogging and social media.

It also helped that he was good looking. Fair skinned with sepia brown eyes and a baby face that could charm women of all ages. Unlike his big brother, his face was free of any kind of beard. Just a trimmed goatee framing a mouth of appropriately sized veneer implanted teeth. His shoulder length mane was pulled into a neat low ponytail.

"Big dawg!" Grant greeted upon entry, a phone in hand as he recorded content for a future vlog. "Guess who I'm bringing to the gala this Sunday? Wait, before I announce it, y'all be sure to like, share and subscribe to the AccessGRANTed YouTube page. Okay, okay, back to the question."

Sam slammed the door and crossed into the living room, returning to the solace of the sofa, and the view. "Beats me Grant. I don't have time for your lil' pranks," he said in his usual huff. He loathed his son's need to share just about every detail of his life with *fans*.

"Yeah guys, this is dad being his normal grumpy self. They love you, dad."

"They gon' love when I put my foot up yo' ass, too. And what I tell you about recording in my house? Turn that shit off!"

"Sheeeeeesh, this dude. He's got the best view in the city and doesn't show it off. That's alright. That's what I'm here for. Be right back."

Grant walked over to the window, and started recording a Tiktok video. The skyline was in perfect view behind him as he fired off a list of names, "Monica, Jada, Erica, Nia, Brianna, Sheena, Amina, Jalisa, Gloria, Keisha, Nisha, Frida, Talisha-" He stopped recording, having run out of another name to say.

"What are you doing?" Sam looked on, his face wiped with confusion.

Grant paused the recording to explain. "I'm making a Tiktok. For some reason, I do serious numbers when I film in the penthouse. I think it's the views."

"Remind me to take your key."

"I'll add text speech later," Grant murmured to himself. Then, he suddenly remembered his announcement. "Oh yeah! Guess who ya' boy got to be his date this Sunday night? I'll give you a clue! She's fine, she's a model. I know, they all are but the kid really outdid himself this time."

Grant waited for a response that would never come. He ran his hands over his ponytail in a dance and said, "Super Vixen Sienna!"

"That's not funny Grant."

"I'm not joking."

"And you're not taking Sienna to the gala."

"She's getting on the jet as we speak!"

"Grant, are you dumb? She's almost twice your age!"

"So? She's 40 and looks betta than my exes. Built betta too." He licked his lips as the half-naked pictures of her Instagram came to mind. He spent half an hour liking every single one in efforts to get her attention.

"Grant I will snatch you up by that dumbass chain around your neck! You're not bringing her. That's final."

"No you won't. This shit is 24 karat gold!" Grant was offended, really. "And why you coming at me? Like I'm not my own man or something? One of my checks is twice Kenny's salary. You need to show me a lil' respect. I ain't even livin' off you and mom."

Sam loved his sons very much, but for the life of him, he couldn't figure out how they were so vastly different. Kenny was more settled and calculated towards life. But Grant was a different kind of millennial. Obsessed with himself, to the degree that Sam thought the boy was void of respect for others. Grant flossed his riches in ways that made his father sick. He would never understand this brazen infatuation with money. He liked his wealthy lifestyle a little more refined. Where the assets spoke for themselves.

Grant raged on, "And what do you mean that's final? Who are you to tell me who I can bring as my date?"

"I'm your father, that's who. And don't fucking forget it." Sam stood up and crossed over to the stocked minibar to pour himself a suddenly needed shot of cognac. "Don't embarrass your family and bring Sienna to this gala."

There was a knock at the door, then it slowly turned open. Kenny announced himself in the foyer.

"I forgot my damn phone." Kenny had no idea the heated moment he'd just walked into.

Grant screwed his face to his father and replied, "That's my woman, and we'll *both* see y'all Sunday."

Kenny waited for Grant to exit the penthouse before turning to his father to ask, "What the hell's going on?"

Sam shook his head, still brooding. He took a second shot and mumbled an expletive under his breath. Kenny had to repeat the question two more times before he finally answered.

"Why didn't you tell me he was serious about Sienna?"

Kenny sucked his teeth and answered, "I didn't know she would actually go on a date with him."

"Well this is more than a date. He wants to bring her to the gala. While I'm away, you tell that knucklehead she bet not step foot in the convention center this Sunday."

"What's wrong with Super Vixen Sienna? Other than being an industry pass around who got rich off writing a groupie tell all?" Kenny was silenced by his father's cold glare.

"You read that shit?"

"Hell nah but c'mon, I know a *little* something."

"We should've never published her."

An exasperated sigh escaped Sam. He hated that book. But he'd been skewed by lust in the thick of an affair, unable to realize his own exploitation in the matter. When readers matched Sam to the pseudonym lover of Sienna's escapades, it ruined him and Evita's marriage for a long time. Took a whole year to recover her affections.

Sienna was the perfect femme fatale. Sexy, smart, stylish. A real sexpot to the sensual side of him that wanted pussy at his beck and call. She had the then 40-something year old right where she wanted him, and he let the opportunity to make better business decisions regarding her fall by the wayside. Long and pricey affairs from Vegas to the Caribbean Islands, where he flew the model in for weekend rendezvous. Nights that ended in him releasing all his sexual inhibitions and business frustrations on and into Sienna. Until times changed and the tides turned in favor of his wife, whom he was ready to be faithful and devoted to.

"I don't want to see my son walk into my event with Sienna. I swear she's just doing this to piss me off. She doesn't even know Grant."

"I mean, he does have two million followers on IG. She could be doing it for clout." Kenny found his phone hiding between the sofa cushions and pocketed it. "Look, I can't promise anything, but I'll talk to Grant. I'm sure no son wants to date a woman his dad smashed. Then again..."

Kenny shrugged and made his final exit, while Sam slammed the cognac top on the counter and poured himself a third shot.

Four

June 18 | 7:06 am

M ina sat on the jet, patiently awaiting the Pitts' arrival. She was an almond-eyed bombshell with luminescent beige skin and voluptuous hair that gave lots of body in her signature silk-press. These fortunate looks had brought her the affections of a new suitor, one much younger than she. And he, a naïve still wet behind the ears love pup, had no idea the full-fledged woman he happened upon.

While Mina enjoyed the idea of being a cougar, she wasn't prepared for the mentality of a 20-something fresh out of college, still finding his way in the workforce. The twenty five year age gap was not sold on her as he bored their dinner with corporate world conversation. She, being a well-off woman of a certain age, just couldn't relate, having never succumbed to the American dream (or falsity) of devoting half her life to a company, letting them decide when she could and couldn't take off, as the government reached its never ending claws into a biweekly paycheck. No, that wasn't Mina. From early on she took her gift and her career into her own hands.

Mina was from New York, a round the way girl with bold attitudes towards business and love. She worked her way from the underground ballrooms of 80s drag culture to the brazen world of 90s hip hop fashion. The intricacies of ballroom couture equated to long hours working on projects for several picky "I know what I want and what I won't wear" performers. But the young Mina balanced her time as best she could between the Fashion Institute of Technology and New York's underground festivities.

When Mina met her, Evita was a junior at South Bronx's Roosevelt High School. This beautiful young socialite-to-be taking the grimy clubs of the city by storm and surprise. At least when her fake ID worked over the bouncer. Sure they had questions, but she was a beauty- worth risking all fines and termination.

Evita made connections with promoters and event managers who provided her access into more affluent parties. At a

New York Fashion Week party in 1990, she bumped into Mina, now working under a prestigious designer.

Soon after, Evita the newest industry muse and Mina the up-and-coming stylist, ran in social circles of only the rich and famous. One legendary party after another. Including an album release party in '91 where Mina introduced Evita to a hot producer named Sam.

Come spring of 1993, Evita became Mrs. Samuel Pitts and Mina was fast becoming the go-to stylist in black music. After SamStar Enterprises launched in 2005, she headed the company's modeling agency and her own fashion clothing line. Who would've known the girl who bled her fingers to the bone over a sewing machine for acts like Zsarina Gambino, House of Je Ne Sais Quoi, would become one of the premiere black stylist of the 90s and the 2000s? She was celebrated by today's generation for contributions to fashion that would be replicated forever more.

So when the company moved its headquarters to Richmond, Mina too packed a bag and headed south of the Mason-Dixon Line. She now led a team responsible for styling talent acts and produced fashion based content for SamStar's streaming service.

For the gala, she linked the Pitts with a black stylist out of Atlanta, and was asked to take a flight down for the final fittings. On the new "toy" that made Evita giddy. But now on the jet, she sat alone in her thoughts, still playing out the memory of the night before.

All the talk about her date's dilemma reminded Mina why she said no to the two engagement rings offered her, and yes to a life free of kids and a man. She lived her best life while making herself the highest priority. She enjoyed the opportunities, connections and privilege granted to her by a fabulous career. Nothing and no one would interrupt that.

Once her date shut up about his life as a Genworth financial analyst, Mina lured him to the bedroom under the sultry sounds of Sade and the scent of peony cashmere scented candles. Her experience knocked the young man's socks off, riding him in true cowgirl fashion that proved she wasn't new to the rodeo. He flipped her on her back, and cupped both breast in his hands. *Nice and supple,* so he thought, aroused even more at their plumpness. Tits firm for affection, with a style of sex that rose in pressure and steamed like a natural geyser. She was the last of a dying breed, and the beginning of a new. Mina felt him pulsing inside her, and tossed back and forth under his exaggerated expressions of ecstasy and the open window.

A surprise rain began to pelt her townhome, in Libbie Mill Midtown. The deep blue sky was suddenly bruised with bouts of lightening and corresponding cracks of thunder.

The lovers ran cool as a gust of wind blew through the window of the third floor loft and in between their bodies. After a hard earned climax, she released him to the side of the bed that wasn't her own, and checked the weather on her phone to see the random thunderstorm wouldn't last into the morning.

Sure enough, Friday morning had arrived and the only thing delaying the flight was Evita's tardiness.

When the couple arrived, Mina was surprised to find another employee would be joining them on board. She watched as Pia tossed a large duffle into the nearest seat.

"I made sure we had a little food this morning. Hope y'all don't mind seafood *this* early. My friends at Crab Du Jour hooked us up," said Mina.

Sam chuckled, saying, "I actually do mind but Imma let you ladies do ya' thing."

Minutes later, all were seated- Sam near the front and the ladies in the comfort of the plane's rear. The jet lapped the tarmac of Hanover Air Park, prepping for take-off and clearance. Soon after, the jet ripped from the pavement and soared into the sky. Once they were coasting high over Virginia, Evita poured herself and the other women glasses of champagne.

"Pia, I can't thank you enough for these past couple of weeks. You had my back yesterday, while I entertained those uppity women who are gonna make my husband even richer," Evita said, finding the latter quite funny. She paused a moment to catch Pia's eyes. "I know I put a lot on your plate, but you manage to get it done. You deserve this day trip. I know Kenny wasn't too happy about it. He called me, fussing of course, but Sam smoothed it all over this morning."

She handed the two women a flute, and turned to face Pia again. "We got you an 11:30 appointment at the spa in the hotel, which you are going to love. Wait, have you been to Atlanta?"

"Believe it or not, this is my first time."

"Even better. Wish we had more time but make sure you relax and get yourself some retail therapy. Just use *my* company card, the American Express. It's been a while since I used it. I'm sure they're wondering where I've been."

"*Whew*! Pia, what did you do to earn all this?" Mina fanned her hand around them.

"She's done the damn thing, that's what! And a cheers to that and a toast to a successful gala!" Evita raised her glass and clinked it against the others.

Pia indulged in the most expensive champagne she'd ever had, and stared at the charcuterie boards and seafood boils before them. Her first time on a private jet and she felt so accomplished, even if it wasn't her account footing the bill.

"Does Tati know you're flying out?"

Pia reached for a small clear plate and picked over the spread. "Yeah, she's picking up the order from the publisher later on tonight."

Evita shook her head with a frown, distaste on display. "She could certainly take some pointers from you. If it were up to me, she wouldn't even be our publicist. But Sam insisted we hire her. Her father is the only reason she's here, if you ask me. He and Sam are good friends.

Evita turned around to see if Sam was awake. As expected, he was not; he was known to fall asleep in the air, often knocked out before the jet took off. She grinned and turned her focus back to Pia and Mina.

"I personally think the bitch is the type to sleep her way to the top."

"Oh relax. That girl don't want Sam. She's too prissy. And some of these millennials *actually* believe in hard work. Ain't that right Pia?" Mina tore open a steamy bag of seasoned, buttery seafood. Complete with boiled eggs and chops of cob corn and sausage. She slid on the plastic gloves and asked, "Are you even 30 yet?"

"27. I need to be half as accomplished as y'all in that time. Or at least on my way."

"I'm sure you will," Evita replied.

Cracking at a lobster tail, Mina continued, "Did you ever work as a model? I know *all* the girls are these days."

"I'm good just doing what I do as an assistant. That's all."

"You got to SamStar a little late in the game. Didn't she Evita? These assistants come in around 20 and 21 years old. All inexperienced and what not. I like that you got a little seasoning to you."

"Shit. If she's seasoned, what are we? Stale?" Evita joked.

Mina rolled her eyes to that. "*We* are the flavor. Make no mistake about that. I just like to pick the brains of these new girls. See if they're on what we *used* to be on." She winked at Evita.

Evita threw the look to Pia. "Basically she's saying we walked so you girls could run."

Pia raised her glass. "Well somebody had to, and we're thankful y'all did!"

After landing in Atlanta, Mina and the Pitts took a car to the designer's studio, while Pia and the luggage were taken downtown to the Ritz-Carlton. They booked three suites next door to each other, and Pia's job as an assistant still required she put their bags in the appropriate room. When she entered hers, she threw her shoes and duffle aside, and jumped on a most comfortable king sized bed, taking in the views of the downtown skyline.

Life is good, she thought, as the blessing had not escaped her. Two years ago, she could not have fathomed her life as an assistant being this fulfilling. In a business that found her learning on the go, and figuring it out on the spot, she was successful. She'd been determined and her life was in a phase of reward. She smiled at the critical thinking skills she foolishly believed were a thing of junior college past. Her job as Kenny's assistant found her using them every day.

But there was no time to rest, or reflect for that matter. She hurried down to the spa, and later to the upscale shopping mall, Phipps Plaza.

Come 7-o-clock it was time to meet the Pitts for dinner at the hotel's AG Steakhouse restaurant; the establishment carried a vibe that winked at modern Atlanta luxury.

Pia dressed into a sleek black spandex jumpsuit and Bottega heels, items purchased earlier in the day with Evita's AmEx card. She found only the wife in the exclusive Hideout Corner, a reserved booth with curtain for additional privacy, in a room already perfectly discreet.

"Hey you!" Evita greeted. She stepped out of the booth to give Pia a hug. A red satin slip dress fell just above her knees, and hugged her curves with a sensual embrace. "Sam's running a little behind but let's get started with a drink. I'll order a bottle of champagne but feel free to get whatever else you want."

Pia grinned, excited. She hoped it would be the same champagne they had on the jet. She took her seat in the round of the booth and asked, "How did the fitting go? Do we have a winner?"

"We do! A few alterations here and there because *somebody* didn't stick to their diet- but we will be the best dressed in the building." Evita appeared smug as she handed Pia the bar menu.

When their server approached, Pia ordered a top shelf Long Island. Evita laughed as the drink's name took her back to the freer times in life. She decided to get one too, saying,

"Haven't had one of those in forever. Make it two, each!"

Thirty minutes later, the ladies were two cocktails in, full of appetizers with champagne still chilling on ice, and no sign of Sam. Pia was seeing the side of Evita who trusted her not only as an employee, but also as a friend. She watched as Evita looked over a thread of text messages.

"This is so frustrating. He's always busy in Atlanta. Getting up with old friends and whatnot. But it wasn't supposed to be all this on a simple one day trip."

"Where is he now?"

"Says he's leaving a friend's new studio but I wouldn't be surprised if he was crushin' wings at Magic City."

"Then more fried green tomatoes for us!" Pia shrugged and reached for the appetizer.

"I wish I could be that chill about it." Evita rested her hand on top of Pia's and continued, "Being wife to this man ain't been nothing but hell and back. I wish I could tell you *half* the things I let slide for the sake of business and image. Don't get me wrong. We have our moments of heaven on earth. I love Sam and I'd do anything for him, for *us*. But it took a lot for me to get here. I use to tolerate things that I damn sure wouldn't allow today."

Pia didn't wish to pry anything open but the oysters on the table. So she listened, as Evita pranced over stories of Sam's old sins- giving attentive gestures like a head nod and the occasional screw face in the vein of 'I know he did not!'

"...But Sam knows what I'm about now. It took a long time, but he knows I'm not the little girl I use to be. And there wouldn't be a SamStar Enterprises if it weren't for me. Just saying.

Evita poured the bubbling champagne into their flutes, though Pia was almost certain they didn't need it with the Long Islands kicking into second gear. Pia took the flute from her though.

"Oh listen to me. Just rambling. I'm sorry girl. And I got to be careful with that. You keep bringing up the past, it'll show up." Evita tapped her glass, swirling the champagne. "Make sure you sip and try the oysters. You taste the sea even more."

"I don't know if I have it in me. And kudos to you 'cause it takes a strong woman to forgive a man who disrespected her over and over. And still let him lead? Couldn't be me!"

Evita sucked her teeth and laughed. "Don't do that. I know what it means when women say that. It means you think I'm stupid."

Pia quickly refuted that. "No, it couldn't be me because I have a fear of commitment. Not because I think you're stupid."

"Oh it can be you. If you truly love a man, one day it'll be you. One day, you'll walk away from another instance, ready to completely and totally forgive him." Evita shook her head, stunned by her own patience. "And you gotta forget the past every time he runs late for dinner."

Their cackles were interrupted as a server brought a peach and white bouquet to the table. Its arrival took both women aback. Roses, alstroemeria, hypericum berries and lisianthus with pops of dianthus and babies' breath in a large square vase. The arrangement was so fragrant and thoughtfully crafted. The sort of things that made women whip out their phones out and record a video for social media. Then, Evita received the text from Sam apologizing for falling behind schedule.

"The man sure has his ways," Evita laughed as she fiddled the peachy cream roses. "It does pay to be by his side."

"Flowers will do it every time. Women love them," said Pia, also pleasantly surprised by Sam's gesture. She understood the little things meant so much in relationships, even without plans to get into one of her own.

Evita fondled the ends of Pia's ponytail, dropped her fingers down her thigh and swirled them at the young woman's knees. The two made eye contact and for a moment, Pia thought Evita was flirting with her.

"You know what else this woman loves?"

"Money."

"Good one." Evita smirked naughtily, then continued, "Every now and then, I fancy the touch of another woman while Sam watches."

Kinky. Pia's lips pursed in a way she hoped didn't appear judgmental.

Evita went on, "We usually do it Atlanta, at the swingers clubs. So you being invited is *absolutely* by design."

Pia's brows furrowed, judgmental now. *Swingers clubs?* But she stayed silent as Evita continued her proposition.

"No I'm not inviting you to a swingers club." She had read the thought as it registered on Pia's face. "I also want to make it clear that your professional life is not threatened by what I'm about to ask. And I will put this out there one time, and one time only."

The women leaned closer into each other, as if sharing a secret that no one else should hear.

"I just see you as hardworking and determined, beautiful inside and out. Someone who knows the rules and when to mend them. I like that about you. Which is why I trust you'll keep whatever happens between us."

Pia leaned in closer, the smell of Chanel on Evita's neck intoxicating her even further. The anticipation was building, and she watched as Evita's mouth formed the words,

"Would you like to join us in our suite tonight?"

It was asked with the type of bravado that just came with age. Evita, like many other rich and modern 40-somethings had it going on. Bodies still in decent shape, some with the help of surgery, others with healthy diets and consistent workouts. The woman was wealthy, healthy and the manifestation of a vision board. And Evita knew this.

Her youthful effervescence was working its magic on Pia. Exposing the charisma that made her devilishly attractive. And while Pia was intimidated, she was also turned on by the invitation. She'd never been with a woman, and something about having her first experience with Evita Pitts (while Sam watched) rattled the muscle between her thighs.

Pia's mischievous grin was infectious, finding its way to Evita's waiting gaze.

"Hmmm, okay, I'm in."

But Evita wasn't new to this. She looked back at Pia with an expression that asked if she was sure, to which a more assured nod was returned.

"Good evening ladies."

The deep, rich voice of Samuel Pitts took both the women's attention and breath. Though Evita was startled, she didn't show it, and instead rose to greet him with a hug and kiss. Pia smiled awkwardly as the couple adjusted themselves in the booth. Servers immediately followed with entrees.

"Excuse me, we haven't order yet." Evita looked confused as steak, salmon, halibut, and an array of sides were placed on the table.

"I took care of it when I dropped off the bouquet. A little bit of everything. Is that ok?" Sam posed the latter question to Pia.

He wrapped his arms around Evita's neck and kissed her ear. This made her blush and swat him with a bashful hand.

Pia quickly nodded her head. "Yeah sure. I'm down with *all* of this," she said with a gesture towards the food. Though she very well meant the two of them. The couple together were stunning, and a charge of energy she was suddenly ready for. "Pass the salad, please."

Evita handed it to her and turned the conversation back to her husband. "So, a new studio tour?"

"You should've seen this studio and soundstage. We want to buy a few sessions for some upcoming projects. But all it did was inspire me for what we can do in Richmond. Then I had to pick up your flowers, of course." He looked thoughtful, casting concerned eyes on his wife. "Why? Did I miss anything?" He looked back and forth between the two women with a suggestive grin.

"Champagne. But here's enough to fill your glass." Evita poured the last of the bubbly in her empty flute and gave it to him. "Finish that off." The instruction rolled off her tongue like a command. *Foreplay begins now.*

And Sam did as told, finishing the glass in one swallow while keeping his eyes locked on his wife. She felt the bulge in his pants, and he flashed a flirtatious smile. He set the glass down and turned his attention to Pia.

"Kenny told me you're from Miami. What brought you to Richmond?" Sam cut into a glistening pink salmon filet.

"Economy really. I was down and out after the company I worked for tanked. The owner went to jail for bank fraud, and I just needed a restart. I heard about Richmond through a Facebook group and made my way up."

"Sounds like you go after what you want." For a moment he stopped eating, placing his elbows on the table and cupping his large hands under his strong jaw.

"I'm aggressive with my goals, in a good way though."

"That could *only* be a good thing. We like driven people at SamStar. You can never be too aggressive, right baby?" He nudged

Evita who forked over a piece of halibut and ignored him. "Any plans for moving up in the company?"

"Well Kenny's got me next in line for production assistant. But working with Evita's event coordinator makes me want to stay on the fun side of things."

"I think you should go for both. You're *that* good. So it's just you in Richmond? No family?"

"Just me. The rest of the family's back in Miami."

"We're looking to host our next summit on South Beach."

"See, that's what I mean about staying on the fun side of things. Maybe I can come on as an event manager."

Sam replied, "The sky's the limit here at SamStar. You can do whatever you like with hard work," said Sam, grinning. "Your reputation already precedes you. Keep it up, young lady."

"Enough about work. We got plenty of time for that!" Evita cut in with a dismissive wave.

Sam agreed a change of conversation was needed. "So what were you ladies discussing before I got here?" He ran his hands over Evita's thighs. Foreplay back underway.

Evita and Pia traded laughs before the wife decided to speak for them. "The usual. Men, money, mayhem. You know how we do."

"Nah I don't, that's why I asked," chuckled Sam. "You got plans later tonight, Pia? Y'all wanna hit a club or something?"

"We do have plans, and none of them include a club. Pia and I are well over our drinking limits- thanks to your failure to show up on time. I think we'll retire to the suite," Evita answered. "I figured you were at the club already with one of your rapper friends. But the studio is a better place to be, I guess."

"*We* guess," Pia added.

"Cut it out. And Pia, don't take sides. You don't know this woman like I do." Sam's dark eyes twinkled in a smile.

When the trio finished as much of the food as they could, Sam grabbed the vase of flowers and said he'd take them to the room. Evita and Pia stayed behind to pack their leftovers in to-go boxes, then took the elevator up to the suite's floor.

"Guess I'll get changed and meet you in a few?" Pia asked, key card in hand. "Lingerie?"

"Actually," Evita began. "I think we should wait. I'm sorry, but I can't go through with this tonight."

Pia was silent, unsure if she should be happy or upset at the sudden cancellation, far more sudden than the invitation.

"You sure?"

"Yeah, those Long Islands did me in."

But Pia sensed another reason for the change in plans. "You know I'm not offended, right?" She would do anything she could to make it less awkward than what it had become.

"Good, because I want you at SamStar Enterprises for a long time." She brought her hand to Pia's flushed cheek, and ran her fingertips along her collarbone. "Goodnight."

Pia laid gentle eyes on Evita, admiring the red dress that gave its lusty assistance to her glistening brown skin and made her all the more desirable. Shame she wouldn't be sticking with the offer presented. Pia would've done anything she said.

"Goodnight," she said with a coy smile. "If you change your mind, call me."

Five
June 18 | 9:52 pm

Evita placed the suite keycard on the kitchenette countertop and sauntered into the bedroom, where Sam was getting undressed for a shower. He could sense her frustration creeping to the surface, and knew a verbal altercation was soon to follow.

"What is it Evita?"

"A studio tour? You sure about that?"

"Positive, and don't give me no shit about it either. You and Pia make nice?"

"I cancelled those plans so don't get excited."

Sam sighed. "Damn. I was looking forward to that."

"Is that why you were so interested in her at dinner?"

Sam scoffed, unsure about where his wife was going with this. He refused to end their brief time in Atlanta on an argument. "Let's just shower and go to sleep."

"To hell with this Sam! Every time we come to Atlanta it's always some shit. I could've went to this studio as well, if it was business related like you say. Don't I have a say in these upcoming projects?"

"Evita, are we really doing this right now? We just had a wonderful dinner. I got you flowers, for cryin' out loud. Don't mess this up."

"Why didn't you tell me about it?"

"So this is about you not coming with me?"

"You don't view me as an equal and that pisses me off."

"Because on paper we're not!"

"You wouldn't be where you are today without me. Don't forget that. I made you! But all people see is you. I gotta sit back and watch all of Richmond celebrate what you do for the city. And they don't know you didn't even wanna be here!"

Evita thought back to a conversation they had before the big move. One where she fought to convince him that SamStar Enterprises could do wonders and numbers in Richmond. He was so comfortable bouncing from New York to LA (and draining funds into overly priced projects) that he couldn't see the vision. The vision of where they were today.

"You ain't give a rat's ass about Richmond until I showed you the potential gold mine you were gonna miss out on."

Sam rolled his eyes and pulled the tie loose from his neck. "Here we go again. You always bring this dumb shit up you're your drunk. What do you want Evita? More stake in the company? You want ten, fifteen million? A divorce so you can walk away with half? We don't have a pre-nup so you can tell a judge all about what you think you've done."

Evita threw her heels at him, missing him by inches. "What I *think* I've done? I know damn well what I do. I was there when you were a has-been producer, stuck making beats for no-names and nobodies."

"I woulda made it *with or without* you. You broads were a dime a dozen!" Sam roared in retort. He couldn't show any sign of weakness, any sign that her words offended him, hurt him deeply. He stuck out his chest, continuing, "You think you made me? Okay, then I *saved* you. Fair trade."

Evita replied with a wicked smile that chilled his blood, and what she said next worried him even more. "No Samuel, I saved you. If things played out the way we *didn't* want them to, where would you be? What would've become of your legacy?"

"I don't think like that."

"Well you should, especially the next time you wanna show up late to dinner."

"Now you just wanna argue, and make me feel a way about God knows what," Sam muttered as he slipped back into his dress shirt. Forget the shower. Now he just wanted out of there.

"Sam, I want respect. I want recognition. I put in work. You know how hard I go for us. I would clean a crime scene if I had to!"

Sam scoffed, finding her statement to be a complete exaggeration. He was incredulous at the turn of the night's events. He knew humility could help fast-forward them to the end of discussion. Just like he knew all the sacrifices Evita made in supporting him.

"Well you'd never have to get your hands dirty, especially as my wife. You didn't have to do what you've did for me, but I'm grateful baby. I don't want to argue either." He planted a kiss on her forehead. A gentle one, but to Evita it felt patronizing.

He stepped around her, saying, "Run yourself a bath, by a new handbag, do whatever you need to do to feel better. We have an early flight tomorrow morning, and on Sunday we have a gala to host." When he was at the door of the suite, he looked back to firmly inform her, "I'm going to the bar. When I get back, this better be over. Do I make myself clear?"

Evita ignored him, her only reply a heavy eye roll. What more was there to say? The sensuous mood of the night had plummeted to an emotional low, and she couldn't fathom who was to blame. The Long Islands? Sam's tardiness? Was it his attentiveness to Pia? Or her foolish insecurities?

The answer wouldn't come to her as quickly as Sam left the room. She slipped out of the little red number and ran herself a much needed bath. Suddenly, as she sank into the warm water, the only voice she wanted to hear was that of her sister's. She reached for her phone on the sink countertop and dialed.

Anya answered quickly. "Hey sis. How's the A?" She knew Evita was well over her inebriation limits when the reply was a tearful run-down of the night's events.

But Evita stopped abruptly when it got to the part about Pia. Too embarrassed to admit the twinge of jealousy she felt when Sam addressed Kenny's young hot assistant, whom she'd just propositioned for a ménage a trois.

"Evita, are you still there?" Anya sounded annoyed at the sudden break in story.

"Yeah, sorry. He was all in the face of this *lady* I was talking to at the bar." Half-truths would suffice for now.

"A lady you were talking to? This better not be that freaky ATL shit. Evita, I thought we were beyond this. You remember what happened last time you invited some random hoe into your bedroom."

As if it would make the story less painful, Evita lied and said, "She isn't random. She knows us both."

"And this is why you're sitting in the tub mad. And where the hell is he? At the bar? You better hope he's not with her!" Anya sucked her teeth, internalizing her sister's anger.

Evita winced at the dreadful coincidence of Sam and Pia laughing it up at the bar while she drowned herself in tears and bath water.

"I always tell you this shit is a bad idea. I don't care if you like it, nor do I care if he *just* watches. You're the only one who loses in the end."

"Anya, you don't understand this lifestyle because Daryl doesn't put you through no shit." Evita had done enough comparing to know. Daryl had given up late nights with the guys early into the marriage. He'd been a most patient man, spending most of his time with Anya and their daughters.

Sam, however, had taken his time moving beyond late night studio sessions and social gatherings with his fellows. As recent as this year, he still spent most nights entertaining and mingling with clients ranging from politicians to celebrities.

Anya begged to differ. "Daryl's a man. He still steps in it from time to time."

"Yeah and you'll be right there to clean it off his shoe when he does."

"Well that's better than him getting into the marital bed with shitty ass shoes on. And then wining to my sister about it! You went out there to get your dress for the gala and now you're crying in the tub over him showing another bitch attention. Make it make sense."

"Spoken like someone truly out of touch. Just 'cause shit went down perfect for you-"

"Perfect for me?"

"Yes! Someone who plotted since we were kids on having the same baby daddy-"

"Husband. Get it right."

"Whatever. My point is I don't like the shit you're saying. Especially when I came to you to vent. I didn't even ask for your funky ass advice."

"Damn it Evita. I know we're different but you're still my sister. Hell, I *am* you! I love you and want you to love yourself enough to not put up with Sam's shit."

"You're definitely *not* me. And I'm sorry I called."

Evita abruptly ended the call, one she shouldn't have placed to begin with. As she started to get out of the tub, she heard the door to the suite open and shut. Sam was back, and so was her need to stay in the tub a little longer. She listened to the sound of shoes shuffling off, the unzipping of pants and a belt hitting the floor. Then, moments later, his footsteps as he entered the bathroom.

She closed her eyes just as he came in; she felt his figure move past her. The squeak of the shower handle almost opened her eyes, curious as to what he was doing. But then, his footsteps neared the edge of the tub. Evita looked up to find him dressed in nothing but his erect manhood, which waved at her temptingly. He stroked himself and looked at her with a hot lust that drove her to submission.

"Get out," he commanded softly.

Evita wanted so desperately to say no, but couldn't move the muscles in her mouth to speak it. Couldn't bring herself to refuse him. He was so big and powerful, not just in stature. But in the business overall, and in the marriage. One of the guys who did right by most of the promises made in his life. Promises to her and their sons. And to the empire that kept them secure in a world of privilege and luxury.

She unplugged the bath and rose to her feet. Sam squeezed her ass, dripping in suds, and stuck his finger in the hole of her warm, waiting center. She pulsed hot for his erection pressed against her thigh. The heat from the previous argument seemed to drain like the water in the bathtub, whose slurping sounds diced through the silence.

The couple were entangled in a wild and passionate kiss- the kind all about the business of love-making. The kind pulled from deep, requiring lots of blind trust and attention. Heads moving side to side, eyes closed, while the lips lock in a war of silent words. Words that said '*I love you, I need you*', '*Don't ever let go*' and '*Fuck me now*'.

Sam lifted Evita's slender frame onto his and carried her into the shower, all set to serve its purpose with a big rain showerhead and Plexiglas wall. In a sudden motion, he brought her glorious hole down on his bulge, holding her mounds with all the power of his big hands. She felt so helpless, yet protected, in his arms.

Under the stream of running water, Evita squeezed him with her throbbing muscle, and ran erotic kisses down his face, neck and chest. She clenched his shoulders with a desperation that told him don't stop. And for almost thirty minutes, he didn't, as he rocked his erect fullness in and out of her. Couldn't stop until his power rushed to climax, and burst inside her. She met him halfway with a swell of her own and exhaled vehemently.

"You have nothing to worry about anymore. You know that right baby? I love you. I owe you everything." He set her down on wobbly legs, the orgasm still rippling through her. Then he placed that gentle comforting kiss on her forehead. "Now, we shower. Big weekend ahead."

Evita nodded in agreement, and knew the argument from earlier in the night would not be had again. Despite years of not feeling appreciated and the shortcomings of marriage infidelities, Evita knew her marriage today was a solid one.

Later on, in the big king sized bed, they laid together in bliss as downtown Atlanta flickered outside the window. Evita calmed herself as Sam pulled her into his big build. There was nothing like that feeling of being held through the night, even as they slept. He knocked out first. She soon followed after a mirage of thoughts played out in her mind, reminding her to forgive him totally, and forget their past.

Six
June 19 | 10:15 am

Daryl and Anya Carver were Richmond royalty. Married ten years, the late 30-somethings were highly regarded by an inner circle and surrounding community of realtors, developers and bankers. They were largely responsible for helping other young men and women secure funding for business and real estate purposes. Wildly adored on social media, the Carvers used their popularity to build a successful online empire based on black love, equity and generational wealth. They lived in an ornate modern Tudor home in a family oriented neighborhood in the East Parham district. The college sweethearts were the parents of two girls, ages 5 and 7. When they weren't networking and mentoring, they were often vacationing the Sea Islands of South Carolina, and other beachy towns along the east coast.

This Saturday morning came to them with a gracious heaping of sunlight, spilling in through the kitchen's large bay windows. Anya soaked in the tranquility as a small terrier puppy, the only distraction, nipped at her ankles.

"Stop it Gino."

She spent a few more minutes aimlessly wandering the house, the kind one does when unsure of how to start the morning. Anya could feel boredom kicking in on what was yet another day in a perfect life. She decided to make busy with breakfast, fed her daughters and later went to her husband's office with a tray of her efforts; sausage patties, waffles, eggs and an assortment of fruit. He thanked her with a kiss on the cheek and a gentle smack to her behind, which she sat along the edge of his desk.

"What takes you this morning?" she asked, watching his eyes dart at the desktop's large monitor.

He was so pensive and focused, normal traits for the 6 foot tall, sinewy Daryl Carver. He was a sharp man with a light brown complexion, a clean, always groomed beard and low Caesar fade. He stood up from the desk and came towards her with open arms. Arms as open as the Shenandoah Valley, where they often took their daughters for bike rides and mountain hikes. Arms that were loving and powerful, and now swaying her in a hug.

"The United Casino Group got an update on our proposal. Just over half a billion dollars approved. And guess what? Carver Realty might secure a few million of that, along with some infrastructure contracts that'll keep us busy and paid for years to come." He kissed her face with all the confidence a successful man would. He felt on top of their little world. A man on his shit.

Anya took his hands and twisted herself out of the hug. Now, dancing face to face with him, she replied, "All of this sounds lovely but how did we get mixed up in this casino mess? Especially with *our* reputation. A lot of people who look up to us are against it."

Since its early whisperings, the proposed casino put a foul taste in Anya's mouth. Gambling of any kind was, for her, a pungency that rotted the city of Richmond and its people. She hated everything from scratchers to the mega millions.

"Well unfortunately for them, what they think is a bad look is actually a goldmine for the city. Their moral compass is not ours to go by. Banks don't exactly specialize in sympathy."

"But we do expect banks to consider community opinion. Dear God! Have you seen the news? Now they wanna tear down the Coliseum." Anya couldn't help but consider the other economic projects that moved the needle of moral compass.

"Should've been did that! Richmond's spent enough years wasting good space."

"Space that's occupied by the homeless. It wasn't enough to rebuild when they showed up. But now that the Mayor has a new economic plan to make himself look good, they're being forced out? And just what is the city doing about its homeless population?"

"There are resources in place to help."

"Well the response has been piss poor, if you ask me."

"And I didn't ask you. Shit, they better get in on this money if they want a roof over their heads."

Anya didn't like that response, nor his sudden lack of compassion. Surely the fault of exaggerated gains promised by the casino. Her face registered her discontent, and her folded arms were like those of a disappointed school teacher.

Daryl paid her scorn no mind, and mimicked her frown, which brought a smile to her face. It didn't last though.

"This is good for business, bad for the brand," she said with a pout of her small mouth.

"You wanna know how I feel? People are gonna drink, they're gonna smoke, and they're gonna gamble. You can't save em all baby."

"I'm sure the jails are gonna love it." Anya rolled her eyes and turned away from him.

"They plan to expand and invest in addiction programs and mental health facilities in the local area. That's all we can do. And you? Try not to take it so personal."

"That's a little hard to do when you're a community activist. Christ, Daryl. What about *our* people? Those who oppose the casino?"

"The city's gonna turn with or without them. I'm not here to debate what's morally right, Anya." Daryl hugged her delicate frame from behind. "And it's not a matter of *if* Richmond gets a casino, it's a matter of *when*."

"The same communities we serve will be impacted the hardest. They're already tearing down public housing and displacing families. What's next? More gentrification?"

"Which is exactly why black folk shouldn't depend on the government for housing in the first damn place. And those areas need a revamp, to tell the truth. The city is rebuilding and people can either get with the program, or move."

Anya sighed and pulled away from him. "How did we got mixed up in this? Why us?" Now she was facing him, staring into his perfect face with pleading eyes.

"What do you mean why us? I'm the real estate banker! I had to jump on this when it was presented to me."

"And just *who* presented this to you?"

Daryl sucked his teeth and stared at her with a look of contention. "Didn't I tell you this already?"

Anya firmly shook her head. "No! You just said United Casino Group reached out to you but you never told me who it was. And I want to know who thought we were a lock for something like this. Do people not know who we are and what we do?"

"Hollup! Whoa whoa! Since when have you known me to turn down a lucrative project for the sake of community service?" Daryl asked with one sharply raised eyebrow.

"Oh please Daryl! We've listened to communities make the plea for why a business should or shouldn't be in a certain area. Like those skill games in convenience stores near school zones."

"That was one time, and skill games are out come July anyway. A casino is coming, and that's why when Tati-"

"Tati? The publicist?" Anya poked out her hip. Her face was screwed in a confused glare. Tati was a woman already lacking favor with her sister, and now, with her.

"Woman, will you let me finish?" He laughed to charm her, and it almost worked. "Yes Tati, the publicist who gave us the invitation to the gala."

"I'm familiar with the publicist. Go on..."

"Her father's a partner, and since SamStar's endorsement, she thought now would be a good time to-"

Anya wrung her wrists. "I knew it! That man's always involved!"

"What are you talking about?"

"It's no coincidence the theme for the gala is casino night. Sam's gonna bribe half the town for the upcoming vote!"

Anya paced the floor as she looked at the gala invitation package, still sitting on the bar cart in the office's corner. A beautiful black velvet box that contained a formal paper invite and plus one ticket, a complimentary bag of casino chips, a slot machine voucher for $500, and a bottle of SamStar's sponsored Cognac with two martini glasses.

Daryl sat down to start his breakfast. He knew to quiet down when it came to conversation about their famed brother in law. Most of Anya's animosity and resentment was on behalf of her sister's pain. But Daryl knew not to speak on other marriages.

He just made sure to stand tall as a faithful and focused head of his household. The truth was, he refused to judge Sam Pitts. Every man had his marital woes; and money certainly magnified the typical quarrel to degrees he couldn't imagine. At least not yet.

"I should ask Evita what she knows about this."

Daryl couldn't let that one slide. "Stay out of Evita's relationship with *our* business. I told you what I told you as my wife. Not for you to go prying information out of your sister."

"Daryl, that's my-"

"I won't ask you again." His voice was firm and unwavering.

Anya sighed, agreeing for the sake of peace. "Fine. You're right. Besides, Evita's mad at me. She and Sam got into it last night, and I wasn't of any comfort. I hope everything's okay with her."

Daryl remained silent. *No speaking on other marriages.* His golden rule to live by.

Anya continued, "Anyways, I'm sorry. I don't mean to fuss. I just want us to be on the same page with our vision for this family." She massaged his shoulders with a soft and delicate touch.

"C'mere you." Daryl stood up and pulled her into his embrace. He hushed her simmering fears with a strong kiss that lasted minutes, while fondling her firm and supple breast in his hands.

Anya knew his erectness was calling, and quickly freed herself of the robe to let him inside her. He hoisted her on to a bare spot on the large desk, accidentally knocking over a pencil holder. She looked to see what it was that fell, but he turned her face back to his wild gaze. A gaze that showed he yearned for her and only her. She recognized it before and, the dutiful wife she was, always responded in kind. She spread her legs, he entered her with ease and pumped himself heartily.

"I'm gonna take care of you for the rest of our lives. You hear me?" Daryl grunted.

"Yes Daryl. Yes I know." It was a whisper.

"I need you to believe me baby. Believe in me." He repeated it over and over as he built himself to climax with each tender stroke.

Anya's legs trembled under his the weight of his power. She knew she had to tell him what he wanted to hear, needed to hear. "Yes baby. I believe in you. I believe in you... You always take care of me." A lot louder this time.

"Oh fuck yeah. That's right, tell me that shit. You feel so good," Daryl moaned as his release drew nigh.

Anya matched his peak, the aftershock of an orgasm chilling the nape of her neck, and travelling down her spine and into her toes. The two collapsed over the desk, taking a few moments to breathe their way out of the lingering ecstasy. Daryl pulled up his jogger pants as Anya refastened her robe and combed her wild hair behind her ears.

He regarded her, his loving wife in all her natural morning glory. Just as beautiful as the day they first met. But worry still sat behind her eyes. He could see it, feel it. He suddenly felt sorry for her, and the strong need to reassure her of his truth.

"I got us, woman. Don't stress yourself, or my little one in there." He eyed her belly and took a bite of cold sausage from the breakfast plate. It'd gone cold during their tryst.

"Let me warm that up for you and check on the girls." Anya couldn't help but smile as she planted a submissive kiss on his lips and sauntered out of the office with his plate. He grinned too, thankful and proud, as she made her exit.

Anya always knew how to make him feel like a king. She exuded a femininity that lent itself to his feeling appreciated, with charm and care that graced their home, their children and the business. Because of her, life was relatively simple and easy in ways he was careful not to take for granted.

If only he could get her to worry less about her sister. He noticed the emotional strain that befell Anya ever since their relationship took off in 2011. The year he proposed.

Back then, Anya had expressed so much joy over her sister's delight at the engagement announcement. She was in elementary school when Evita up and married Sam. A sisterhood already strained by an age gap became practically non-existent after that. Her big sister being married didn't come as the fairytale her favorite Disney movies made love out to be. Anya convinced herself Sam took away the only sibling she had. She was forced to feel life through the experience of being an only child with a single mother who, through no fault of her own, fell short of several marks.

But when it was her turn to walk down the aisle, Anya had found her fairytale romance becoming a reality. She had no idea how to relate to the big sister she barely talked to outside of holiday family gatherings. Gatherings that often took place in the Pitts' center hall colonial home in the suburbs of Staten Island.

Evita stepped up and offered to pay for everything from the venue to the wedding coordinator; abiding by the traditional rule of 'the bride's family pays for everything'. The big sister certainly had the funds to do it. Back then, the idea didn't sit well with Daryl. But he didn't voice that, as Anya saw nothing wrong with her sister's generosity.

But the years following found Anya emotionally indebted to her sister's marital matters. Especially the ones magnified by money and media. There was a continuous 'feeling worried for' that plagued both of Anya's pregnancies, and threatened to affect this third one. Stress of any kind was never good on his wife, something he knew from her anxieties towards college exams. She was emotionally fragile in ways he sought to protect. The delicacy of compassion could easily drive one to a state of codependency.

And Anya didn't need to rescue her sister.

Daryl knew she needed to be rescued.

Seven
June 20 | 7:50 pm

Dreah sat at the vanity, lining her lips with a final coat of the blackberry lipstick that paired well with her satin chocolate skin. It'd been so long since she put on a full face of makeup and a fancy dress, settling on a white modern flapper dress made of fringe and shimmery lace. Atop her head sat a classic mid-ponytail with just enough hair left out around the edges to frame the face.

Just three days before, she couldn't have imagined she'd be attending the gala. Now, the night was here, and her nerve to show face was wearing on her heavily.

She retrieved the picture of Hendrik and Zsarina from the wedge of the mirror and stared it over. Her mind ran to and fro, not exactly landing on one thought in particular, but absorbing an array of them all at once. She reached for her selenite crystal, going through a number of breathing techniques as she prepared for the clarity and enlightenment the night would surely bring.

Growing up under the SamStar spotlight was lonely at times, difficult and traumatic in parts. She'd been privy to so much and made to suppress even more as a young teen model, surrounded by adults drunk with the power of fortune and fame.

The latter year's crash-and-burn with Kenny only complicated the matter. The two always played down their attraction to each other, as they'd grown up like family. But when the fast developing years of adolescence came about, Dreah finally felt in position to take charge of the one thing she hadn't been in control of. Her sexuality.

She and Kenny made love in a college dorm room, an act of both freedom and rebellion for the then 19 year olds. They would spend the next ten years regretting that decision. Especially Dreah.

The twenties saw them through failed romances, four years at Morgan State University, and quickly thrusted into the working world of adulthood. All the while, Dreah was left unable to speak on a brokenness that haunted her everyday life with traumatic memory.

It grew in intensity from 2016 to 2019, during the years she worked as Kenny's assistant. She was nowhere near capable of being is assistant, and struggled from day one. It wasn't just the physical act of balancing his and her schedules (and needs), but also the mental act of balancing emotions. Hers especially, a tangle of thoughts and feelings she hadn't been willing to explore. The ones she ignored in college, while experience life on her own for the first time.

Dreah didn't know a breakdown was imminent, as she fell into an endless cycle of triggers, time after time and task after task. After one too many drunken tantrums (ones where she threatened to expose the dark secrets of SamStar Enterprises), she was approached by Sam in July of 2019, and paid rather handsomely to go away.

The pandemic forced her to deal with questions that needed answers. Could she forgive her past self for not knowing any better? For not knowing what was safe and who was not? Would she follow her passion to be her own boss? Right there in Richmond? The same city she saw as a fresh start for all when SamStar initially relocated. Having found some of the answers, she used the severance pay to open Alchemia.

But the more personal issue of forgiveness had been left unresolved. It wasn't until just recently that Dreah was willing to confront the past in whatever ways the universe would allow her. To be honest, she wasn't completely surprised when two SamStar employees came into her store. A nod to the age old principle of *be careful what you pray for, you just might get it.*

Of course the universe, with its karmic resolve, would gift her an opportunity to confront those who needed it. Life was funny in that way, especially in a year like 2021.

Back in March, a cherished customer confided in her about a podcast idea she had successfully pitched to networks. "*Unsolved Mysteries meets the entertainment industry.*"

At first, Dreah wondered if her SamStar testimonies were enough to satisfy the ravenous host. It took some time, and self-coaxing, but Dreah divulged the mystery of LeVario's suicide.

As the story went, the young photographer planned on exposing a married athlete as gay, having the picture to prove it. Samuel Pitts caught wind of this, and asked to meet with him. But the day they were supposed to meet, LeVario committed suicide by jumping out the window of his Brooklyn apartment. The pictures were never found.

That is, until sixteen years later when a little sister nosed through the rummage of an old file cabinet. One that stood as inconspicuous in the basement as it had in Sam's former office.

But Dreah was privy to another part of the story, one that hadn't been told to the public. When she happened upon the infamous photo of Hendrik and Zsarina, she knew things were falling into place. Another blessing from the universe. Yes, her redemption was drawing nigh.

An incoming text from her Uber driver lit the screen of her phone. Dreah looked at herself in the mirror one last time, making sure everything was in place. She spritzed perfume at the base of her throat and fastened her heels. She placed the photo and selenite in her clutch, slipped on a face mask and out the door.

When the driver brought her to the convention center, Dreah knew there was no going back to the safe confines of her Scotts Addition apartment. The cozy loft sat along Marshall Street, in the midst of restaurants, breweries, and rooftop bars. The neighborhood had coddled her through quarantine and self-assigned isolations.

Dreah had her ticket scanned by a doorman on the first floor, and took the escalator to the second level's grand ballroom. In the pre-function area, a red carpet had been rolled out for SamStar and affiliates. A variety of media outlets and pushy photographers lined the carpet, excited to snap the photos that celebrities and locals alike would share and like hundreds of times over.

Dreah entered through ballroom B's doors, and found that ballrooms A, B and C had been converted into one giant casino floor. The roar of jazz music pierced her ears, her heart thudding with every horn blow and sizzling high-hat. The sheets of overhead lighting were dimmed just perfectly. The ambiance transported her to a time and place reminiscent of 1960s Vegas.

An event of this magnitude had never been seen in Richmond; the casino theme had been masterfully executed, with the power of SamStar Enterprises on full display. At the top of the room, a sturdy makeshift stage had been built against the wall. The house band tested its strength, serenating guests with popular jazz numbers before a small checkerboard dance floor. Seating tables had been speckled on both sides of the stage and lined the walls of the room. A tea light candle in a holder lit each tabletop.

Ballrooms A and C sweltered under the flash of slot machines, lined in rows of 6 by 6. The high pitched blend of gaming music and ca-chings pushed against the jazz that screamed from the stage.

In between those two rooms, Ballroom B was littered with Baccarat, poker, blackjack, craps and roulette tables. Dealers shuffled their cards, making them dance before excited players. Roulette wheels clucked in their spins as crowds cheered for red, black, even or odd. Bar and food tables were set up in the four corners of the room, and girls in flashy showgirl costumes balanced drinks and tip jars on trays in one hand.

For a moment, Dreah felt bad about what she came to do and started to second guess her strategy. Maybe somethings were better left unsaid, and unchallenged. She rounded the room, coming back to the door in which she entered. What would she do now? She started to test her luck at a slot machine, but quickly decided against it. She'd be testing much of her luck later into the night.

So, Dreah walked the room again. This time, looking more intently at who was in attendance thus far. She hoped to see Evita first. Ready to bear her soul to a woman who once served as a second mother. Even in the time she worked as Kenny's assistant, the woman defended her in ways that only a mother would. In ways her real mother had not.

That motherly love is what led Dreah to protect Evita from the truth all these years. She had already been going through the occasional storms in her marriage. The last thing she needed was the thunder of a scandal that would ruin everything she had left.

But once they arrived in Virginia, Dreah realized that protecting Evita from the rain had only gotten her drenched. Drenched in sorrow and regret. She did the only plausible thing at that time, which was to disappear out of sight, out of mind.

That is, until the storm found its way to Alchemia, and drenched Dreah all over again.

Eight
June 20 | 9:09 pm

Super Vixen Sienna rose to fame during the wild times of the 2000s. She was the exotic looking beauty with an ambiguous look, one that said she was *mixed with black*. Tanned skin, narrow nose and a luscious black mane that reached her perfectly sculpted booty. She was blessed with the sought after look wanted by every video director and casting agent she auditioned for. It got Sienna in the good graces (and bedrooms) of many powerful men.

After earning her keep as a top video girl, her thirties found Sienna depressed and no longer industry most wanted. She had become nothing more than the memory of a good time to the same moguls and rappers who once clamored for her attention.

But Sienna would rise to the top again in 2013 with her lessons of courtship in a tell-all guised as a self-help book. 'Super Vixen to Super Villain: Either Way, Get Yours'. SamStar Publishing had a best seller on its hands. But the intimacies revealed in the book quickly rotted the business relationship, and she never completed a sequel.

Royalties kept Sienna paid in full until her social media platform rose in the latter years of the decade. Everything from commenting on The Shaderoom posts to appearances on reality TV brought her a new following. Her naturally fit body (still tiptop at 41) and nostalgic looks were being praised every post. Capitalizing on this new fame, she opened up a boutique for curvy women, inspired by looks from the 2000s that were once again the latest fashion trends.

Recently, the young Grant Pitts contacted her with a flirt-filled DM, one she had to entertain. He had 7 million followers on all his platforms combined, so being seen with him anywhere in the world was a plus for her. She'd do whatever it took to stay relevant among this generation of fans. Besides, they paid better than those of days past.

And Grant's significant bank account was enough to keep her courted and entertained. He was always energized, bouncing through the day with endless vigor. A vigor that spilled into the bedroom. He had impeccable stamina and fucked her with all the strength and pizzazz of a porn star. He also had a fetish for pulling hair and smacking ass. She couldn't wait to get her nightly dose of him after the gala.

At times, Sienna found herself annoyed that Grant recorded every moment of their day. This included the airport pickup. He flew her in from LA on a private jet, and immediately took her shopping in NoVa at a galleria in Tyson's Corner. She never had to reach for her wallet when he was around. Another turn on that kept her at his beck and call.

And now here they were, on the highest floor of the Marriot hotel, overlooking the downtown district as Grant recorded them.

"We're about to leave the room and head over to the gala. And I already know it's a movie." Grant made sure to lower the camera on Sienna's backside as they left the suite. "My woman lookin' good as hell, per usual."

Her perfectly dolled up face was framed by long tresses that fanned out in waves. Her sleek black mermaid gown was littered in Swarovski crystals, and paired with Giuseppe Zanotti stilettos. The real diamonds on her neck and wrists danced in the reflection of light. All of it purchased on Friday's shopping spree.

"*Period.*" She gestured an 'off with her head' swipe at her neck.

Grant let out a wolf whistle several times over. "She know what she doin' to me y'all. And Imma let her do it!" He chuckled and turned the camera back on her.

Sienna blew a kiss and said, "Guys it's my first time in Virginia, and he's making it so hard to leave. Imma have to get him to come to LA."

"I'm already out there every month."

"Then it's time for you to move," she said, switching her hips. Hips that he zoomed in on as they moved down the hallway.

"The convention center is just across the street. We're gonna head over and get back with y'all in a few. Be sure to like, share and subscribe to the AccessGRANTed channel. And make sure you turn those notification on."

Grant stopped the recording, and took a moment to review his date. She was a dream. A wet dream. The fantasy of all young men. Certainly, he had seen her shouted out in social media; appreciation posts for 2000s baddies who still had it going on. She was holding rank as the epitome of top tier over 40. And he managed to shoot his shot, making nothing but net.

The very thought of her being a few years younger than his mother never crossed his mind. He didn't care about her past, at least what he heard of it. And he didn't have the energy to read her book, or any comments that spoke ill of her.

Grant was infatuated with the beauty business mogul who surprised him by egging on his advances, flirting back with him in ways that made him act quickly. He'd spend the remainder of their fling doing what he could to make her happy. Money seemed to handle much of that.

They took the Marriot bridge entrance into the convention center. On the second floor, the flashing lights and the red carpet were calling them as loudly as the needy photographers. Grant made sure to cuff Sienna's plump behind for their debut as a couple. Individual shots followed, where they catered to the calls of photographers with a variety of poses and model faces.

But the warm welcome was short lived, Sienna noticed under the hard glares of many of those inside the ballroom. Yet, she reveled in the audacity it took to show up with a date 20 years her junior, while looking better than the 20-somethings in attendance. *You better hope you look this good when you're forty!* She wish she could've told them directly. Her defiant smirk would have to do.

A few topnotch men in building were the same ones she used to work for. But it was a new era now, one where she was self-made and accomplished in her own right. The playing field was leveled and she could stand toe to toe with their bank accounts, and the power of multiple generations behind her.

Look at Timothy, with his thievin' ass. I see you came to Richmond but yo' ass is still missing in LA! Her face bore an all knowing grin.

Another person, another memory. This time, her face puckered in disbelief. *Damn, she still working these parties? Girl get out of bondage. It's better ways out here...*

"What's wrong baby? You ok?" Grant asked, the light of his video camera blinding her.

"Damn Grant! Do you have to record *everything?*" She pushed the camera away from her face.

"Watch the lens!" He stopped the recording and carefully inspected the lens for a smudge. "You looked upset so I had to ask. I know people lookin' and hatin'. But I don't give a fuck. You mine tonight."

Sienna blushed, answering, "I'm fine baby. You make me feel so special. That vial won't be the only thing hanging from your neck later tonight."

Sienna ran her hands along his black and gold paisley designer shirt, and down the seam of his perfectly tailored matching dress pants, hemmed just above a pair of black and gold Jordans.

Grant was instantly aroused with her touch, and almost ready to call an audible back to the Marriot. To the suite where he'd tackle her with every ounce of his aggression, prepared to work every muscle in his body, tongue to penis, just to see her orgasm. The very thought of what awaited them caused an enlargement beneath his slacks.

"I'm just sayin', we can bounce." His expression and tone suggested that was now the better idea.

"Nah, we're here already. Let's have fun."

Grant surrendered. "Okay then baby. Now fix ya' face and check in with the Youtube family for me." He pressed record and held the camera on her.

Sienna became mildly annoyed, but quickly smiled, saying, "You're a mess... What's up Youtube! We have just arrived and as you can see, the theme is casino night. I got my chips in my purse and I'm ready to bet it all!" She shook her purse at the camera.

"Guys, it's a whole casino in this convention center!" Grant panned the camera over the room. "We got the slot machines, the tables. Definitely bout to hit that baccarat. That's where the ballers go. I got the bands with me. Bands for the lady. We bout to win some bread, right baby?"

Sienna didn't have time to reply as she looked up to see Samuel Pitts reaching for his son's neck. Another face she didn't care to see. This became her moment to escape; and as the men argued, she hightailed it to the nearest bar and food station.

"Hey Sienna."

The voice was calm, in an eerie but friendly manner. In a way that reminded Sienna she didn't have many allies in the room. She quickly about-faced to see who this was.

"*Dreah?* Long time no see. How are you? Still gorgeous as ever, that's for sure!" She embraced her in a hug that suggested she was elated to have her company. Another rebel in the building.

"To be honest, I don't know what I'm doing here," Dreah answered with a nervous chuckle and removed her face mask.

The coverings were just now becoming a thing of the past for those who were vaccinated, and represented a certain level of cautiousness to those who opted to wear them. Tonight, it had allowed her to blend inconspicuously into the party.

Sienna grabbed her drink from the bartender and spun back around saying, "I can imagine. I like your dress. Right on trend. Did you come with anybody?"

"Hell no. I wouldn't bring anybody to an event like this. Not with what I'm about to do."

Sienna's eyebrows rose suggestively as she took a sip of her cocktail.

Dreah noticed the look and asked, "Why that face?"

"What face?"

"The one that could be a shady real housewives GIF."

Sienna snickered, almost losing the liquid in her mouth. She locked eyes with Dreah and said, "C'mon girl. It's me you're talking to. We know what this industry does to women like us.

And last I heard, *you* made it out. So what's going on? What are you doing here?"

For the first time that night, Dreah felt seen and present. Felt like she could trust Sienna, too.

"You're gonna think I'm crazy."

"Aren't we all?" Sienna laughed. "But real talk, if there's something going on with you and you wanna talk it through, I'm here as like a big cousin."

Dreah smiled, regarding the comment and the kind authenticity radiating from Sienna as strong as her Tiffany & Co. perfume.

"Okay, I'll tell you. But let's sit down."

Dreah took off faster than Sienna could keep up. But keep up she did. And at an empty table, beneath flashing lights and roaring jazz, Dreah showed her the picture of Hendrik and Zsarina, and began her story.

Nine
June 20 | 9:31 pm

Grant flared his nostrils as he cut the video camera off and handed it to his mother. He pulled away from his father's grip, saying, "Get the fuck off me! Let me go! Ma, what's with this guy?"

Sam's face was contorted in rage that boiled beneath the surface of his velvet red and black tuxedo. He was prepared to make an example out of Grant, even if it meant kicking him out of the party, literally, in his Gucci loafers.

"What did I tell you? Is this a joke to you?" Sam aimed a fist of condemnation at him, but thinking better of it, then lowered his arm.

Evita appeared unfazed at the quarrel between father and son. She handed the camera back to Grant and said, "Work it out as men at a later time. But not here, not tonight." She pointed her finger between them both, meaning just what she said.

Grant hated to disappoint his mother, and grabbed her in a lazy one arm hug. "I'm sorry mommy. And you look beautiful." He kissed her forehead and spun her around for a 360 spin of her sequin trimmed cocktail dress with a feathered hem. It was red in color, long sleeved with a plunging neckline, and paired well with her Chloe Strass snake-wrap stilettos. Her hair was perfectly straightened for the event. What was a mass of wavy curls earlier in the day was now Dominican style pressed hair flowing down her back.

Sam flushed hot at his son's disobedience. But the firm voice of his wife was soothing, and of reason. The night was bigger than a rift with his son over Sienna. At least for now.

"Alright, I'll eat this. Take the pics, the video, the YouTube- do whatever you need to. But after tonight, that's over. Whatever you think you got goin' on with this bitch, dead it," said Sam crossly. "You embarrass the family doin' shit like this."

Grant wasn't having it. "What I do for my brand has nothing to do with y'all. My mom ain't got shit to say about this, so why do you?"

Evita shook her head, quickly disagreeing. "Nah baby. You should not have brought a woman your dad cheated on me with to our gala."

"What do you mean cheated? Is *that* what this is about?" Grant's voice was elevating once again and Evita had to remind him to keep it down. He regarded her disappointment, then turned his angry glare onto his father to ask, "Why didn't you just tell me?"

"Didn't you talk to Kenny?" Sam remembered delegating the chore to his oldest before the trip to Atlanta.

Evita considered her husband's pensive stare with great concern. There was something in his face that she couldn't put a finger on.

"No, and for what? He wouldn't have been able to stop me. But you-"

Sam pushed his son in the chest. "What about me? Boy I'm your father. You should've listened and obeyed my word when I told you don't bring her. You're wrong for that. Got me ready to kick yo' ass."

Evita stood in front of her son, her back to her husband, who was inching nearer to Grant's face.

"Go find your date. Get out of here before your father does something we all regret," she said warningly, eyes unable to meet his as they bounced from the floor to the people walking around them.

Grant looked his father up and down, and turned on his way, disappearing into the crowd, growing more and more flamboyant with the arrival of guests.

Evita waited a moment before turning her collected anger onto Sam. "Why didn't you tell *me* he was bringing Sienna? Even I could've made him cancel that."

"How Evita?" Sam's voice was thick with sarcasm. The embarrassed kind though, and she knew this.

She added to his shame by answering, "By telling him the truth. Miscarriage and all."

"Alright Evita. I ain't tryna go back into the past. We both know that was a mistake."

"Yeah damn right we do," she quickly spat in retort.

The embarrassment that had befallen the couple was Sam's fault. His fault their youngest son had walked into their gala with a former side chick. His fault the odd pair had made a mockery of romance on the red carpet, just before it was his and Evita's turn to display what a solid union looks like.

But Evita refused to lose composure, at least what was left of it. She would, however, wound him with her emotion. Using the same knife that stabbed their marriage to stab him now.

"I hated myself, Sam. But I forgave you while praying God would forgive me for the things I said about Sienna and her baby. Do you understand how fucked up for me that was? How could you let Grant show up with her? Of all people?"

Sam started to speak, but she elevated her voice over his saying, "You had a chance to stop it, and you turned it over to our oldest son. Like some business project?"

"I personally told Grant don't bring her. He defied me."

"You shoulda told him *why*. He's not the type to order a book and read some fuckin' hoe tales." Evita stopped shy of another insult. "Why didn't you tell Grant the truth?"

Sam swallowed hard as she covered all bases in a field of past transgressions. For all his wealth and accolades, she knew how to keep him buried in regret. In moments like these, he couldn't understand why she stayed married to him. This led to nonchalant responses whose purpose was to deescalate.

"Kenny was supposed to handle it. Clearly that didn't happen."

"Shouldn't have been his job to begin with."

"I know, Evita." Sam wrung his hands, visualizing them clasped around her mouth. *Just shut up already.*

"Now you got him in here looking stupid. Can you imagine what our friends are saying?"

The chorus of a winning hand followed by the cheer of another crowd brought them back to the importance of the night.

"C'mon my love, this shit is small in comparison to what we're here for. And our son is right. You look absolutely beautiful." He kissed her hand and released it gently.

"I know I do..." She blushed, a smirk pursing her lips. "Sam, just do better. For the love of family, do better."

He accepted that with a firm nod. "Guess I'll make my rounds now. Then I need to find Mayor Myles. I'll see you in a few." There was his signature kiss to her forehead, the tender kind that dismantled her. And with that, Sam slid past home base, and right into the smiling faces of a nearby crowd.

Evita was to herself but a moment before the rapid shoulder tap from behind. She spun around and stared in disbelief at Dreah. She almost forgot she sent an invitation to Alchemia.

"You made it!"

Dreah took in her hug, a powerful squeeze that made her feel loved and appreciated. She inhaled the Chanel perfume, its crisp flowery scent melting her back to the days of high school when Evita would wake her up with a pleasant smile and song. She didn't want to let Evita, or that memory, go.

"And you're teeth are still perfect! Are you sure you never had braces?" Evita thought back to when Mina first introduced them at a photo shoot. It was one of her first questions.

"Nope, never," Dreah replied in the same coy fashion she had back then. She tucked her clutch under her arm and wondered where to start.

Registering the caution on Dreah's face, Evita said, "I know this is a lot for you, but I'm glad you came. You will always be a part of our family. You hear me?"

"Thanks Evita. I appreciate that, coming from you especially. Is Kenny here?" He was another one Dreah needed to talk to, and now it may have been in her best interest to see him first.

"Not yet. You know he's got a whole team to run these days. I'm sure he'll be here soon. By the way, speaking of Kenny, I never got a chance to tell you how sorry I was about you being let go. You never answered my calls."

"I was really hurt back then. I was wrong to ghost you."

"I just swore y'all would work it out as brother and sister. But you being fired? Unacceptable."

Dreah titled her head, inquisitive now. What had Evita heard? Because that wasn't accurate. "Fired? I wasn't fired. I was actually going to quit. Sam gave me a severance package."

An approaching waitress offered them champagne. Evita took two glasses and handed one to Dreah, saying, "Oh, I could've sworn I heard... oh hell, it's doesn't matter. What matters is you showed up, and I appreciate that."

"When I found out you personally invited me, I figured I had to. Besides, there's a conversation I've been meaning to have with you..." Dreah's throat was suddenly dry. She took a swig of the bubbly, hoping it'd help.

"What conversation?" Evita smiled, but it was weak.

Dreah stared down at the stilettos on her feet; at first it seemed like a good idea to wear them, but now she worried if they were strong enough to support her. She'd have to stand tall and solid in both the heels, and her truth, throughout the night. She didn't how many people she'd have to swear her accounts to, but she did know she would do it as many times as necessary. And if anyone deserved to know her truth, it was the woman who sent the rain her way three days prior.

Dreah was fourteen when she met Sam's wife. She found the woman to be beautiful, youthful and in tune with her budding career as a young model. When Dreah moved in with the Pitts, they had given her a stable home life. One that had been stolen from her.

Evita's worry was rooted in her eyes, which tried to read the now deadpan Dreah as she reached in her clutch and whipped out a photo. Evita took the picture into her hands and reviewed it. Embarrassment sunk in her face.

"Oh no. How did I miss this?" She knew it was amongst the photos found in the basement, and hoped it hadn't been sent for print with the others.

Dreah stifled that concern with, "I took it from those girls when they came in my shop. Have you ever seen this photo?"

"Not this one. I only flipped through a few of them. There were so many. But I was so excited at the thought of a picture book, I just gave them all to Pia to get the book done."

"So Sam's never seen this photo?"

"Isn't this the photo that got LeVario kicked out?"

"It got him more than kicked out. It got him killed."

Dreah's tone was now cold and matter-of-factly. She asked Evita to look closer, particularly at the background. Evita casted her eyes on the image, this time dragging her line of sight from one corner to the other.

There in the top left corner, Evita saw it. Her mind's eye processed that part of the photo, bringing the scene to life in an almost cartoonish fashion. All of it spooked her, and at the sound of her gasp, Dreah snatched the photo away.

"Wait!" Evita reached for it, but it was too late. The photo had been placed in the confines of a shimmery clutch. But the image was still etched in her mind.

When Evita spoke again, she kept her voice as low as she could without being drowned out by the jazz floating above them. "Dreah, what the hell you were doing in Dmitri's lap?"

The outfit had been a dead giveaway. She helped Dreah decide on the white crop top and capri pants. And she knew Dmitri's flamboyant lynx coat from anywhere. He was known for his grandiose array of furs. PETA enemy #1. Chinchilla, sables, minks and the infamous white lynx.

"Doing what I was told to do."

The open ended answer didn't satisfy Evita one bit. She was prepared to spar back with questions far more direct than the answer she'd been given. In a firm motherly voice, she asked, "*Who* told you to do that?"

Dreah's eyes bounced across the room before meeting Evita's waiting gaze and answered, "Sam."

Evita too looked around the room, which was now swallowing her whole in its grandeur. The party suddenly felt void of excitement, the room sucked of its oxygen. A desolate land where just the two of them existed. Where a vortex of truth threatened to snatch the rose-colored glasses right off her face.

"Excuse me?" This came out with a twinge of defense. Evita grabbed the base of her throat, pushing out words that she couldn't believe were being said. "You're telling me my husband told a fourteen year old girl to sit on a grown man's lap and let him feel her up?"

"Yes I am." Dreah didn't blink, not until Evita threw the empty champagne glass to the carpeted floor and it shattered at their feet.

A nearby waitress, seemingly disgusted with the actions of Sam's wife, rolled her eyes and paged the janitorial service for cleanup.

"Dreah if this is some sort of joke, I'm not amused."

"It's not a joke. LeVario was killed because of this."

"LeVario committed suicide." Evita tried to sound firm. In what took only a few minutes, Dreah had sent her over a cliff, plunging head first into the choppy waters of a sea of doubt.

Hendrik's love affairs with transgender women were taboo amongst industry folks. And most certainly, no one wanted it on camera. The fact that a photo existed at all because of *her* photographer wasn't lost on the Pitts' social circle, who began to distance themselves as soon as the next day.

Evita learned that Dmitri had been informed about the scuffle in which his top biller acted *"out of character"*. Just mere association with the intrusive photographer could muddy up the new friendship between her husband and Mr. Goode. Sam convinced her they had to let LeVario go, but the young man offed himself before Sam could break the news. Up until now, she had always assumed his pending termination, combined with the shameful manner in which he was thrown out of the party, played a factor in his suicide.

"He wasn't gonna talk to Sam about Hendrik. He was gonna ask about me and Dmitri."

"Dreah, just a damn minute." The words escaped in a stiff whisper. Her mind babbled with questions she was afraid to ask. Questions that may have wrongfully put guilt on Dreah, and not the institution to whom it belonged. *Why didn't you tell me? Why didn't you give me the opportunity to protect you? Why are you bringing this up now?* She fought to maintain her stance as the room spun rampantly around them. Her mind bounced from the year 2005 to the present day. How had she totally missed the signs? And just

74

what were the signs supposed to be? Infidelity was one thing, but pedophilia and sex trafficking was another. "I'm sorry I'm at a loss for words."

Dreah recognized the perplexity in Evita's look. That inability to ask questions, though they weighed on her face. An expression that wavered from confusion to guilt. She grabbed her hand, daughterly now, and said, "When I saw myself in that photo, I realized something. I don't have to protect Sam anymore. *We* don't have to protect him."

Evita took her by the shoulders and held back her tears. For some reason, it didn't feel appropriate to burst into a crying fit. "No you don't. And you never should've. I'm sorry I wasn't there for you. I wish I had known. How could you hold all of this in?" Evita couldn't fathom the level of despair Dreah must've endured.

"I never would've shared this with back then. I actually felt bad for you."

"Me, why?"

"Sam and Mina mentioned he had to marry you after you got pregnant with Kenny." The words never faded from Dreah's memory. They were said when Sam successfully convinced Mina to put the girls on birth control. For *"just in case"* reasons.

The thunderous boom of another revelation rippled through Evita's body. "You're scaring me."

"They used your story to scare us. This was an entire operation, Evita. I was foolish to take a payout two years ago when I promised Sam I wouldn't say anything. But this isn't blackmail, not this time around. This is my truth, and he needs to pay for this."

The statement chilled Evita's blood as she put everything together. Did Dreah plan on confronting him there at the gala? Too many thoughts to sort through. The thuds of her heart accelerated as the pain of truth rose in the pit of her stomach.

A janitorial party of two were walking over to clean up the broken glass. Evita grabbed Dreah's arm and quickly led her to a table on the left side of the room.

Concerned for both of their safety, she said, "Listen to me. You cannot do this tonight. There are other ways we can go about it. And I promise to help you."

"Yeah, like going public. I just wanted you to be the first to know."

"*Public?*" Evita clutched diamond necklace at her throat. The sharp pain had made its way to her chest. Her head slumped forward as she struggled to catch her breath. Just as sudden as the pain arrived, she fainted, eyes rolling into the back of her head as she went down. The side of her head grazed the metal nail of the stacking chair leg. Blood appeared at the fresh cut above her chin.

"Evita? Evita!" There was no movement, and no response. Dreah put aside the reason she was there and exposed herself to call for help. "Excuse me! Somebody help me!"

Guests were staring at her, concern etched on their faces as calls for help echoed off their lips. The request journeyed through the nearby audience, yet no one knew what to do except gawk. Anya caught wind of the commotion. Upon the realization that the woman on the floor was her sister, she hurried over, casting unsympathetic eyes on Dreah. She turned around to find Sam and Kenny approaching.

"She fainted. Help me get her to the restroom," Anya said, thankful for their timely arrival.

"Mom! Mom, wake up! What's wrong with her?" Kenny's voice cracked with panic. He looked up to see Dreah staring back at him. "*Dreah?*"

But Anya, Kenny and Evita started to disappear from view, as well as the rest of the ballroom, as she was dragged away from the storm by Samuel Pitts.

Ten

June 20 | 9:42 pm

Now outside the ballroom doors, Sam unhanded Dreah and watched with trepidation as she turned to him. He thought Sienna's appearance was immoral, and now, here stood a presence most unwanted. He had no intentions of letting her back inside.

"What did you do to my wife?" Sam's steely eyes didn't mask his rage. It magnified it.

"I told her the truth."

"The truth about what?"

"Things that happened behind closed doors."

Sam sucked his teeth, cursing himself. He always thought he lacked the ability to get Dreah the kind of help his family tried to provide. Even with a loving home environment, private school education, and the promise of a successful modeling career. Dreah's problems were far more insidious.

It was Diondra McDonald with whom the relationship first began. Back in 2003, the 26 year old waltzed into Mina's modeling audition with her 13 year old sister in tow. Dreah was only there because she threatened to tell their grandmother that she was being left home alone, while big sister Diondra trucked all over the city trying to be model.

Samuel Pitts was also in the building, with a team specifically assembled for what was Kenny's short lived rap career. Dreah had the type of pretty needed for upcoming video shoots. She was also his son's age, which made for an appropriate lead girl. The audition was no longer about Diondra, who with her chocolate satin skin and deep almond eyes, was the blueprint of her sister's beauty. But Dreah had stolen the show, and the hearts in the room.

Every other adult could sense the severity of Diondra's jealousy. She objected to every plan for Dreah, until Sam and Mina promised her future work as well. Sam sensed the beginning of a tumultuous time, and not too long after signing them, that was confirmed.

Diondra revealed to him and Mina that she was actually Dreah's mother. A few months later, she agreed to let her daughter live with the Pitts on a long term basis. *Family discord* named as blame.

"Dreah, why didn't you get professional help with the money I gave you? You're clearly still not well if you showed up tonight to attack my wife."

"I'm *very* well, and she fainted. I didn't attack her!"

"So what the hell are you doing here?"

"I have proof that you set me up with Dmitri Goode back in '05. When you and Mina groomed me for sexual exploitation. And I know you had LeVario killed because he caught on to your secret pedophile club."

Sam took this in with a chuckle. "I take it you were there when LeVario told me he had a photo of Hendrik and Zsarina."

"I don't think it was about them at all. Why would you have him killed when everybody knew Hendrik was on the down low? You wanted us to think it was about that." She tucked her clutch underarm.

"This is real sick of you Dreah. You know that? The man is dead. I'm insulted, *just a little,* that you think I had something to do with that."

"Because it's about everything else in the photo! Damn it, I remember sitting in Dmitri's lap when Hendrik punched LeVario. I never knew he got *us* in the shot."

Sam took a step towards Dreah, his face twisted with a foul composure that ran her blood cold. "You got this wrong sweetheart. LeVario jumped the day he was supposed to show me those photos. A photo which never turned up."

"That's odd, considering I have it."

An incredulous smile spread Sam's face. "May I see it?"

"You're wife saw it, and that's good enough."

"Now why would you do that?"

"She deserves to know you trafficked me from exec to exec to help SamStar Enterprises move up in the industry. And the media's gonna know it too."

Sam chuckled menacingly, saying, "Dreah, who's gonna believe you? Your own mother was prepared to tell the state of New York you had an issue with *lying*. Thankfully, my family welcomed you into our home, with open arms at that. So for you to come here tonight with this shit is highly disappointing."

"Diondra didn't know how to be a mom, and nobody told me I was her *daughter* until it was time for family court. By then the damage was done."

"Your mother didn't want you."

"We agree on that. She practically sold me to SamStar. How much did you pay her?"

"We gave you a home."

"No, you preyed on me!"

"Dreah, you're crazy. So crazy that you'd come to the party of the man you claim abused you." Sam waved dismissively.

Dreah stayed poised under his poor attempts to gaslight. She'd had enough time over the years to process her reality. No one, not even Sam, would make her question her experience.

"The photo is proof that Dmitri Goode assaulted me. And if he were alive today, I'd confront him too!"

"I don't believe that. Where's this proof you allegedly have?" Sam took another threatening step towards her.

"Catch it on the Shaderoom." Dreah spoke through a clenched jaw, shoving him out of her way.

She had Sam right where she wanted him. Shaken up. If the allegations saw the light of day, it would be a complete blow to his reputation. They both knew it.

Prideful, Sam couldn't let the conversation end like this. There was too much at stake. He sighed, and hurried in front of her. He appeared apologetic as he said, "Dreah, wait. Listen, you're not crazy. I was wrong to insult you, but, it's very clear that you need *help*. I can make sure you get the help you need this time around."

"The only insult is you acting as if this never happened!"

"Because you're wrong Dreah. Especially if you think I had something to do with that. Dmitri did what he did, and I'm sorry you were put in that position. But I didn't know that happened. I brought you into my home. You should've told me."

"You're sick." Dreah rolled her eyes, and tried to sidestep him. He grabbed her arm, holding her against her will.

"Don't go public with false accusations. What exactly do you get out of it, huh? You getting paid? You think you're getting revenge? What if you're actually getting yourself hurt?"

Dreah swallowed the lump in her throat. Something in her spirit told her not to test Sam. Her best bet was to make it out of the party alive. "And just who is gonna hurt me?"

"Shit happens Dreah."

"Are you threatening me?"

"I just asked a question." Sam's grin was thoughtful, and suggested much. He let go of her and straightened his tuxedo coat. "Look, Dreah. How much money do you need right now? Give me a number, *any* number. Just like last time."

"My silence can't be purchased!"

"Your silence can't be purchased but guess what can? Your business, your building, your name." He looked her up and down, that once thoughtful grin turning vicious. "Imagine not being able to step outside your home without having to go through me."

"You don't scare me, and you can't pay me to go away this time. In fact, you just might have to kill me."

Sam thought about killing her. Wanted to wring her neck right there on the spot, but instead, he kept his hands to himself. And his composure. He was oddly calm when he said, "I'm asking you to leave, and don't make any more trouble about *dead* matters. If you know what's best for you, you'd go home."

"Just buckle up, Sam. This isn't over."

Sam's grip was back on her arm, this time more firmly. His eyes searched around them for a security guard- one who would personally see to it that she was removed from the premises.

Dreah did the only thing she thought she could do. Scream. Scream until someone in the foyer agreed to intervene. She thought Sam would drag her to the exit himself, but thankfully Kenny came to the rescue she desperately needed. He pushed his dad aside and said,

"I got it, I got it! Dad, let me handle it!"

Sam snarled, "Like you were supposed to handle Grant?" He watched as Kenny ignored him, quickly moving Dreah around the corner and out of the foyer.

Sam turned on his heel, deciding it was best to be with his wife than left alone in his wrath. He wanted to aide her with all the care of a loving husband. He went first to the nearest ladies room, bumping into Anya just as she made her way out.

"Wait! She's getting herself together," Anya said, pushing him back out the door.

"Is she hurt?"

"She's fine. But Sam, what's going on?"

"She didn't tell you?"

"I haven't asked yet. Who was that woman?"

Sam shook his head dismissively. "Kenny's old assistant."

"Well what did she want?"

"It's none of your business."

"Sam, Evita's my sister. We're family. I mean, she passed out for Christ's sake. Did this chic at least tell you what happened before that?"

"Anya, what I'm trying to say is this is a personal matter. One that I need to talk to my wife about first."

Anya studied him, looking him up and down and sensing the frustration of a husband who was only concerned about his wife. She could understand that. "Of course."

Sam saw that his tone offended her, and said, "I'm sorry Anya. I don't mean to be short with you. There's a lot happening right now, and I can't function without knowing if Evita's alright."

"I get it, I get it. I know this is a big night for you both. When Evita's ready, I'll tell her you're looking for her. Go ahead, handle business. I'll make sure she's good."

Sam's smile was gracious, hinting at just a fraction of his appreciation for his sister-in-law's cooperation.

Eleven
June 20 | 9:59 pm

In the privacy of the Governors Room, Kenny prepared himself to be a protector. Of what? He didn't know. All he wanted right now was Dreah's trust and cooperation. Her pain stabbed through him when she burst into tears, collapsing in his embrace. Her frightened eyes found that his were soft and sympathetic, like the days when they considered themselves family.

The comfort of Kenny's arms bound tightly around her as he said, "It's gonna be okay." He looked around the room, which had been provided with two tables with four chairs each, and a standing mirror.

Dreah found that hard to believe; she knew he wouldn't believe it either once she revealed the reason she was there. But how? They had such a complicated past. From her time as his childhood friend, and definitely as his one-time lover and assistant.

"Kenny, I'm sorry."

"Don't be sorry. My mom said you wanted to see me. Tell me what's up. What's wrong?"

"She didn't tell you?"

"Not sure if she remembered. That fall knocked her out pretty good."

"How is she now?"

"She's fine. What about you though?"

Dreah swallowed. "I'm worried about what I have to tell you. This entire conversation scares me."

Kenny chuckled rather nervously. He shrugged his shoulders and said, "C'mon Dreah. We're not exactly strangers. We were *once* the best of friends. What's on your mind?"

"What did your father get you for your 15th birthday?"

The question came out of left field.

That confused look on Kenny's face fell flat, now pondering a moment in time that he had long forgotten. He didn't have an answer to give her, not one he wanted to say out loud anyway. In fact, he couldn't speak at all due to a numbness that hung in his throat, and clenched the muscles of his mouth.

Dreah registered the inability to speak, as it wore on his face. She followed up with, "Mina was wrong, and so was your father."

"No! Don't do that. This ain't about me. This is about you, not me! Tell me what the hell you're doing here." Kenny didn't appreciate her bringing up his trauma. Stemming from the days of adolescence when he learned that careers were riding on his ability to generate revenue. Something the teenager didn't do, and eventually saw his star (and childhood dreams) fading because of it.

"Kenny, before I tell you, remember that back then- I didn't know any better. I was just fourteen. My mother was under the impression that I'd be better off with your family..."

Kenny nodded, softer eyes now. His expression, full of yearn, told her he could handle the truth.

She continued, "...And our handlers would tell me in order to get gigs, I had to do stuff. They made me do things..."

Tears fell from Dreah's eyes and she closed them. For all her healing, she still struggled to voice the abhorrent actions of sexual deviancy. Actions no young girl should have to take.

Kenny pleaded with her, "Do what? Do *what?*"

"Mina said all the young girls in the company did it to get ahead. I realized years later that the only thing that got ahead was SamStar as a company."

Her statement suggested enough. Kenny hung his head, as if it would stop him from mentally spiraling down the rabbit hole of her accusations.

"At the industry parties, we were instructed to let Sam's friends cop a feel, give them a quick peck... In private space, it could be oral sex. Mina said it was okay because it wasn't like *real* penetration. Just making a man feel good."

Kenny bristled, nose twitching at the mention of Mina's name. So this was the conversation that had befallen his mother. He folded his arms across his chest and harnessed all of his energy there. And there was a lot of it. He felt it by the multitude; rage, disappointment, embarrassment, disgust, confusion, fear. It stiffened his fingertips and he balled his fist, fighting to urge to throw the chair in front of him.

It was as low as it got for a father's son. He (and Sam) thought their days of doom with Dreah were over. She wreaked havoc during her last days with the company, in 2019. In her aftermath, two destroyed offices, a wrecked company Jeep and several other employees who came to Kenny with the ultimatum. *"Either that crazy bitch goes, or we do."* By time Kenny handed the matter over to his father, his employees were gone and so was his first business role as a digital media strategist.

Of all the reasons to reunite with Dreah, why over abuse allegations? At an event celebrating sixteen years she'd been a part of. A party his team helmed at the command, clearly impressing everyone in attendance.

What emboldened his ex-assistant to come here tonight? It didn't make sense to Kenny. Surely, it couldn't have been intentional. She wasn't *that* vindictive about their ending. That's not who Dreah was. Was it?

She, oblivious to his mental dilemma, went on. "I thought about telling you in college, when we got intimate. I wasn't the virgin you thought I was."

Kenny realized what she was confessing to. "Was it my dad?"

"Dmitri Goode."

"I'm heartbroken for you. I hate that you went through that alone. Are there other victims?"

"I can only name three girls who were catching flights every other month, like me. But I don't know where they are or what they're doing. This is just about me."

As if that's supposed to make it better. Kenny's arms dropped to his side. He moved closer towards her, asking, "How long was this shit going on?"

"'Til I turned 17."

There was a desire to respect her truth even though it wasn't his own. Her experience with Sam had been the opposite of his experience as a son. There was no way his loving, albeit firm, and supportive father could be a pedophile.

Kenny waited a moment, straightening the bow tie to his black slim-fit shawl collar tuxedo. "So is that why you're here? To confront *everybody* with some personal shit?"

"I'm here because I need to make amends and right my wrongs with you! I was wrong to take my frustrations out on us. The person I was mad at was your father. And I should've gotten the professional help I needed back then instead of working for you. But I've forgiven myself for not being there for myself in the ways I needed to be protected. I never asked for this lesson, but I figure damn it- if it's mine I'm gonna learn it. As for your father, he has no idea what's coming. I've said my peace with him as best I could."

"I don't know if I'd call it peace. Especially if you confronted him about all of this." Kenny remembered the rage plastered on his father's face just moments before they turned the corner and high-tailed it to the Governors room.

Dreah turned away from him, suddenly unable to match his gaze as she admitted, "I know that's your family but, please understand this is personal. I promise you, this isn't about revenge."

"Or attention?"

"*Attention?*" The question set Dreah aback.

As Kenny pondered her accusations, and what they would do in the media spotlight, his father's rage became warranted.

"Dreah, I'm all for women's liberation but this is my father we're talking about. You understand the position this puts me in, don't you?"

"Well get used to it. I'm going public whether you like it or not."

Kenny froze at the word 'public'. Surely she must've known what she was saying, what she was doing. She had to have known that her plan was far from rationally thought out.

"You're talking many years ago, Dreah. My father clearly isn't that man anymore.. He's changed, and we've forgiven him." Kenny swallowed, wondering if she could hear the lack of confidence in his voice. He hoped the beads of sweat accruing on his forehead wouldn't hint to her how nervous he was. Nervous for his father, the company and everything they were getting ready to do in Richmond.

"Who is *we*? I can't forgive somebody who isn't sorry, and Sam isn't sorry! I don't give a damn how many years *ago* it was. It's my truth to tell. If he doesn't like it, he can sue me. And he better be careful with that."

Dreah looked around to make sure they were still the only two in the room, and retrieved the photo from her purse. She held it, saying, "Sam thought he was doing the right thing by giving me the money I needed to turn a new page in life. And let's be clear, Kenny, I did just that. But your new assistant walked into *my* store and I came across a photo that changed everything."

She handed it to Kenny, who glanced it over. His eyes bounced from Hendrik Clary, hugged up with Zsarina, then to the VIP section behind them, where the Dreah of his childhood dreams sat in Dmitri Goode's lap. He knew it was them by the outfits.

Looking more intently, he noticed one of Dmitri's hands cupping the round of her behind, while the other groped her barely developed chest. When his face registered the photo's incongruence, she took it from him. He thought about tussling with her for it, but decided against the idea.

Dreah's plight was bearing ridiculous and immature. There were ways to start a scandal, and ways to avoid one. She wasn't giving anyone the chance to approach this in the professional, legal matter it required.

"You have no idea what you're getting us into."

The hairs on the back of Dreah's neck rose, as the air conditioned room suddenly became cooler than preferred. She moved quickly towards the center of the room, and then towards the door.

"I'm afraid my only option is to find out," said Dreah, and she bolted out of the room.

Kenny started to chase after her, but he couldn't be bothered. What would that look like? Him chasing Dreah in his four thousand dollar tux. No chance. He'd see her later; he was sure of that. He started for door but was startled silly as Grant burst into the room.

"My bad, I thought it was empty," Grant said. His glassy eyes flittered all about the Governors room, never meeting Kenny's waiting glare.

"It's about to be. I was just leaving." Kenny looked at Grant's palm, where the vial necklace dangled from between his fingers. "I'm sorry about dad. It's my fault, actually."

"What happened with that?" Grant wiped his nose and looked behind him. Then he stepped fully into the room and made sure the door was closed.

"Dad slept with her back in the day. I know you not big on reading, so you probably never even seen her book."

Grant shook his head. "It don't even matter now. Bitch got me stuck." He imagined her on all fours, ready for him with her wet tongue and wetter center when they made it back to the hotel suite. She was the perfect fuck doll. He look around with approval. This room would be absolutely perfect for getting a quick nut in.

Right now, Sienna was having the time of her life at the Blackjack table. He was just with her, until nature and a boner called, followed by the curiosity of a private room where a girl had just stormed out.

"Who was the shawty leavin'?" Grant asked as he latched the necklace around his neck. "That's you?" He wondered if the lady's stormy walk off was rooted in rejection. And who rejected who.

"Nah nah nah," Kenny said with a dismissive wave. "Hell nah. Just my old assistant."

Grant answered. "Oh ok, respect. That's a balcony over there right?" He pointed to the doors on the other side of the room.

Kenny chuckled, "Yeah man. What's up?"

"Look, you gone be in here long?" Grant took out his cell phone and started up a text Sienna.

"Nah I'm outta here. Mom will be back later. He purse is in that chair under the table. Keep an eye out." Kenny opened the door to leave, unclear if he should go looking for Dreah, or tend to his mother. Her fainting spell really bothered him.

Now he was certain Dreah's revelation is what sent her over. He bristled as a chill blew through the foyer. The AC felt on full blast. He felt the strong urge to get back into the ballroom and hurried down the hall, damn near skipping to ballroom B's doors. He shuffled to a halt as Sienna appeared at the top of the hallway

She regarded the Kenny, smacked with a foggy look as the color drained from his face. He pulled his lips back in a nervy smile and nodded at her as they crossed paths.

Caught his brother? She wondered that and then some, daintily teetering past Kenny. "Have a good night," she said in a sing-song way that ran his blood cold.

Kenny turned the corner, while she switched forward to the Governors Room. He was certain the chill that preceded her was appropriate.

Twelve
June 20 | 10:05 pm

Daryl enjoyed the company of Tatianna Hines for several different reasons; not only was she was attractive, she was a young woman full of ambition and hell-bent on success. The latter he didn't see coming. He later realized he should've. The daughter of a prestigious local businessman, she exuded an attractive confidence in every room she walked into. Including his kitchen, when she first came to him on a rainy morning back in March.

Anya had been asleep, after a serious fit of what would later be confirmed as morning sickness. Nonetheless, Daryl was happy to take the gala's invitation box from the publicist. He'd been awaiting its arrival since the official announcement was made back in February.

"Allow me set it up for you," the spitfire said, gently lifting the box away from his waiting and open arms. In turn, he gestured her inside where she placed the box on his kitchen bar top. She took her time opening the large two fold gift box and removed its contents. Once the contents had been aesthetically placed in front of the box's black velvet exterior, she snapped a picture with her cell phone.

"For the 'gram."

Daryl chuckled at that. "Ah, yes. Can't forget the 'gram."

"And *now*, the introductions. I'm Tatianna Hines, publicist for SamStar Enterprises." She stuck a confident arm out, and matched his responding handshake just as firmly. "It's nice to meet you. I've learned quite bit about Carver Realty and the businesses with your wife. I love the brand. It's giving power couple goals. Can I just say, I'm a fan?"

Daryl nodded, both impressed and flattered. "Thank you Tatianna."

"Call me Tati." She gestured towards the invitation display. "This here is your official invitation to the SamStar

Enterprises Sweet Sixteenth gala. It's a black tie affair, Sunday June 20th at the Greater Richmond Convention Center."

Tati pulled a folder from her work bag and handed it to Daryl. She continued, "What I have to say next would've been twice the pleasure to present to you and your wife, but I'm just as happy to talk with *you* at this time."

"About the gala?" Daryl was confused.

"No, Mr. Carver..."

"Call me Daryl."

"Daryl." A delicate smile parted her lips. She casted thoughtful eyes on him and continued, "As you know, Richmond is turning a new page when it comes to entertainment and tourism. We're one of the major cities off Interstate 95 that hasn't reached its full potential. For far too long, we've let other states outbid and outdo us. That is, until now. My father, Vernon Hines, is on the United Casino Group commission board. And he's looking for young innovative investors and businesses to partner with. Seeing all you've done for Richmond, we want to *personally* extend an offer to you."

Daryl eyebrows drew together in a stare of intrigue. She paused a while, as his expression led her to believe he had questions. Instead, he waved her on. "Continue, please."

"Economic growth opportunities unlike anything seen before. But we need the power of local businesses to make that happen. We're presenting our budget plan in a community hearing, and we'd like you to be there. This will give you an opportunity to see what it is my father and his associates are going to do for the city."

"This sounds really good, but why me?"

"What do you mean why you? *You're* the real estate banker. My father asked for you by name. We want to bring you into the United Casino *and* the Vernon Hines family. Samuel Pitts has given us his endorsement. Why not have another hometown hero on the team?" Tati's enthusiasm was enticing, intoxicating. She made it hard for him to say no.

And why would Daryl do such a thing? The board meetings and community hearings opened his eyes to a reality he never thought possible for Richmond. He was ready to be a part of history, and totally indebted to Tati for the opportunity.

Upon arrival at the convention center, Daryl (unlike his wife) agreed the casino theme was timely and appropriate. He found the décor of the foyer exceeding his wildest imagination. He smiled, impressed, as caterers rowed trays of covered dishes down the long hallway and into the ballroom. One stopped at the bar and food table in the pre-function area. He chuckled, impressed that food and beverage hadn't been limited to the ballroom only.

Daryl looked rather dapper and vintage in a slim brown tweed tuxedo suit. Anya, was elegantly made up in a mauve off-shoulder flare gown, belted and bowed just below her breast and loose enough to cover her burgeoning belly without looking like an improper fit.

After obligatory photos on the red carpet, The Carvers made their initial walkthrough of the ballroom, shaking hands with known friends and making new acquaintances. The casino theme came to the delight of all- except Anya, who wore her disappointment behind a face mask in disgusted silence.

She saw Tati approaching from the other side of the room, and pulled her husband towards the doors and out to the safety of the foyer.

"I'm going to the restroom babe."

Daryl watched his wife dash to the nearest restroom, and grabbed a drink from a nearby table. Now alone, he found himself loitering the foyer, still crowded with photographers, press and media outlets, and guests who needed to escape the flashing glitz and glam of the ballroom.

Dressed in a blue fringe midi dress, Tati approached him with a martini in one hand, and charisma leading from the other. She complimented him, saying, "It's good to see you! Lookin' sharp, brotha!"

"And look at you Miss Lady. I like this dress, I like it a lot," Daryl said, looking her up and down in a way he wouldn't have had Anya been present.

"So much to celebrate tonight, and a few new faces to introduce you to. My father can't wait to finally meet you face to face. It's the ultimate Father's Day gift," Tati giggled the latter.

"It's truly an honor. My wife and I are excited," Daryl said, needing to remind himself of her. He didn't know how long Anya would be in the restroom, and hoped she'd quickly hurry back to his side. He couldn't wait to introduce the two women. He looked at his watch, as if it were going to tell him how long she'd been away.

"Oh wow, it's 10:10," Tati said, his actions having prompted her to check the time on her phone.

"Something special about that?" Daryl's face housed a curious smirk.

"I've been obsessed with numbers since I was a kid. They play a heavy role in my life. Especially synchronicities. As a matter of fact, I've been seeing them all weekend. Today alone? I caught 11:11, 2:22, 4:44 and I just caught 10:10! I take it as a sign that I'm on the right track career-wise, and maybe this casino *is* going to happen. The universe has our back."

"Well I'm having quite the time selling some folk on it, but *most* of my people are ready to vote yes. I'm not gonna waste my opportunity with these infrastructure contracts. There are too many mouths to feed in my line of work."

"We wouldn't want it any other way. Cheers to that?" Tati held her champagne flute before him, and he gently knocked his against it.

Hoping to never see the restroom again, Anya hurried through the foyer to find her husband. She'd been back and forth all day. *A symptom of the pregnancy,* she was sure.

As she approached her husband, she didn't expect to find him slapping shoulders with Tati, of all people. A flirtatious grin parted Daryl's lips and revealed his handsome smile and perfect teeth. Tati was just as dazzling, her green eyes ogling him with fond devotion.

Anya screwed her face in an inquisitive stare as she approached, praying Daryl would make eye contact with her. But she quickly traded the expression for a forced smile, telling herself she wasn't insecure and this was nothing more than a simple conversation between man and woman. Her heightened emotions were just a symptom of the pregnancy. But, she couldn't be sure of that.

"Anya baby. C'mere! I want you to meet Tati." Daryl extended his arm towards his wife the moment she came into view.

"The publicist, right?" She extended her hand. Tati responded in kind. "Lovely invitation to a lovely party."

"I can't take all the credit. We have a super creative production team. Seeing what they've done tonight just takes my breath away," Tati said, placing a hand over her chest.

"Yes they really captured that casino vibe." Anya hoped the sarcasm wasn't too thickly laid on.

She figured it might have been when Daryl cleared his throat to say, "You know, Anya and I have a mentorship program for local youth. Someone like you would be a great role model for the girls."

Agreeing with him, Tati nodded enthusiastically. "I've been telling myself since quarantine to get more involved in the community. I'd love more information on that. Maybe we can set something up."

Anya's retort was brusque. "I'll look at the roster to see if there're any spots available for new mentors first."

"I'm sure you can pencil her in somewhere, babe. Seeing as though her father is Vernon Hines," Daryl said, his words teetering on the edge of braggadocious.

Anya cut him a cold glare. Tati caught wind of the unspoken stiffness between them and wished to make the introduction easier to withstand.

"Hey, if no spots are open, I'll wait it out. My family is all about doing the work. Hopefully something opens up down the line."

"There'll be plenty of mentoring opportunities if this casino gets approved." Anya tossed her scrutiny between Daryl and Tati.

"We don't want to get too ahead of ourselves. There's still a vote in November, but if this gets the greenlight, the possibilities are endless," Tati replied, her tone far more amicable than Anya's.

"Endless you say? Tell me about it! I told Daryl the other day that addiction destroys our communities. He mentioned there's a pledge to aid Richmond with resources. But we won't know that to be true until it happens, right? The city can barely handle its problems as is."

Tati drew a blank, not exactly sure how to respond to the gruff in Anya's tone. Then, a bashful grin spread her lips. "I take it you're not for a casino coming to Richmond."

Daryl disguised annoyance with a wide grin, wrapped his arm around Anya and said, "Don't mind my wife. She's just more emotional than usual because of the baby."

"Daryl!" Anya gasped, offended. But she wouldn't fuss with him yet, certainly not in front of Tati. She turned to the publicist and said, "No one knows I'm pregnant. We're making a special announcement so please-"

"Anya, I get it. You have no need to worry. My lips are sealed." She drew her fingers against her mouth, as if zipping it shut. "But, please, let me be the first to say congratulations. Now, I'm gonna get back to this party. Mrs. Carver, it's been a pleasure officially meeting you. Daryl, see you inside."

Tati threw a solemn nod to Daryl, and made her much needed departure. Anya watched as the young beauty left the foyer, her satin blue Manolo Blahnik's clicking into the ballroom.

Anya turned her unpleasant focus on her husband. Her eyes narrowed in slits that threatened to slice him apart. "What the hell Daryl? Why do you have to get so damn friendly and run-of-the-mouth when you drink?"

"Why do you have to be so rude when you don't?" Daryl countered. He casted disapproving eyes on her, moving them up and down her frame. Her beauty had fallen short against the attitude from moments before.

"Well Evita doesn't like her, so why should I? I don't care to know that girl. In fact, I don't care know *anybody* who's linked to the United Casino Group."

"Anya will you calm down? You're stressing yourself and the baby out. I'm not having that. If you ain't feeling the gala, a driver can take you home."

"Don't be an ass, Daryl. I'll leave with you!"

"Then play nice. And as my wife, you know better. I don't know what's gotten into you, but it's an embarrassment to me and it needs to stop," said Daryl, not willing to mask his disappointment any longer.

"I'm sorry okay? I'm just emotional about being here. I saw Evita earlier, and she's not feeling well," Anya replied.

Daryl wasn't letting up so easily. "So what? I don't need her problems jumping on my wife."

"She passed out in the middle of the room!"

"Did she pass her problem onto you when she did?" Daryl's hands moved from his pockets as he folded his arms across his chest. "You had no right treating Tati that way."

"I said I was sorry..."

"It's time you start separating sisterhood from wifehood, especially when it comes to business. Tonight was unacceptable. Don't *ever* embarrass me like that again."

Daryl's voice carried the terse monotone of man on his last thread. Anya wanted to burst into tears. This was a side of him she never experienced before. She'd dealt with him as a bossy perfectionist, but never the side of him that was impatient and brute. Void of compassion.

"But that's my family."

Daryl moved in, staring down at her with hard dark eyes, a tense mouth and tightened jaw. "No, I'm your family! And it's *our* business at stake. Now let's fuckin' network like we've never networked before." He paused to collect himself, realizing that he must've looked like the aggressor those in the foyer who stared at them with concerned eyes that said as much.

He straightened his tie. "Go make nice with the board member wives. You'll be seeing a lot more of them in the future."

Anya had beaten him to the ballroom doors, leaving a trail of silent tears along the way. But Daryl hesitated in the foyer, wondering how deeply he'd hurt his wife's feelings.

Perhaps he was too tough, too indifferent to Anya's emotional plight. After years of managing her emotions, Daryl was starting to feel the aches and pains of love in places he had not before. Things that once upon a time didn't bother him suddenly got his lack of patience.

Surely these were the woes of marriage that would fade away with the dawn of every new morning. And yes, those typical marital quarrels both pacified and magnified by big money. Quarrels that his marriage hadn't seen, but felt like it was about to.

And suddenly, Daryl found himself empathizing with his brother in law.

Thirteen
June 20 | 10:54 pm

Mina's eyes danced head to toe over attendees, her fashion designer's eye narrowed in either approval or discontent. Some guests understood the assignment, while others fell short of the mark. She, of course, passed tonight's test, adorned in a champagne tassel cocktail dress reminiscent of prime Tina Turner. It shimmered in the dim light as she glided through the ballroom, silk-pressed hair flowing in the wind of a mean strut. She air kissed the cheeks of industry friends and loved ones and floated the floor with the favor and preference shown only to accomplished women like herself.

As well it should have been. Mina paid her dues, staying relevant and in demand as a top designer. Thirty years in, and she could name just about every producer, executive, manager, artist and content creator in the building. She would spend a good amount of the night clinking glasses with them. Celebrating the success of days past, and successes soon to come.

Mina stood outside of the Baccarat table crowd, scanning the party for a waitress. Her eyes latched on a young woman storming pass photographers and slot machines. There was a calm rage embedded in her features, and that caught Mina's attention more than anything. She recognized the face, but couldn't put a name to it.

This bothered Mina because she knew everybody. And everybody knew her. The name danced on the tip of her tongue, and served to be quite the nuisance. *Who is that girl?* The irritation would soon go away; the woman was headed straight towards her.

When they locked eyes, the name hit Mina like five shots of Hennessey on an empty stomach.

"Dreah McDonald," Mina said as she approached.

The two women looked each other over, engaging in a silent admiration of the other's dress.

"Don't you look nice?" Mina moved in first; she really did like Dreah's flapper girl number. "And I had no idea you were coming."

Dreah's eyes were cold, as was her delivery. "I was invited at the last minute."

An awkward pause passed between them. One too long for Mina's liking. Especially at a lively party that required her presence as belle of the ball.

Mina's contemplation lingered on her face as she finally asked, "So, what's up? Why you steppin' to me?"

"To let you all know that I'm going public with my story."

Mina grunted out a laugh that showed just how unbothered she was by this information. Above it really. But she had a little time to dabble in the peasantries. "And just what story are we talkin' about?"

"The one where you groomed me for industry pedophiles." Dreah watched as Mina's eyes widened, flickering across the room as the revelation took its desired effect.

"Or the one where you liked it? How dare you. You ungrateful bitch," Mina spat. She held Dreah's gaze, staring back just as intently. "Let me tell you something. You little ingrate. Most of y'all fast tailed girls were old enough to speak up if you weren't comfortable. You never said anything to me about not liking it. How many times did I ask you if you were ready? Gave you an opportunity to walk away? You had no complaints back then."

"I was fourteen!"

"And all the times you girls lied about your age to every boy who came in the building wearing a damn jersey."

Mina's words pinched a nerve in Dreah's conscience. She knew the woman was going to minimize her experience, but she didn't expect this degree of calculated coldness.

"Don't compare this to me lying about my age at 15. And I wasn't having sex outside of what you and Sam set me up to do."

Dreah's youth had been greatly skewed by her grooming as both a model and a muse, and further demented after interactions with the men Mina and Sam introduced her to. In her everyday life, when it came to platonic encounters of the opposite

98

sex, Dreah desired boys in her peer-group. Ones who saw her as a normal teen girl. Not some objectified sex slave hiding behind a teen modeling career. Behind the violation of grown men, lay an inclination to be in the presence of regular teenaged boys who could remind her that not all men used sexual gratification as a means of power and control. And that the insidious skill wasn't learned during the innocent days of boyhood. That it was something strictly confined to the men around SamStar Enterprises.

She yearned for the reassurance that she hadn't been muddied by the world of her lost hopes and dreams. A world that wasn't giving her what it promised. She could've been an It-girl actress, a serious catalog model, or a young business mogul under the proper tutelage. Instead, she walked into an industry that raped her of energy and influence. It took Dreah years to catch on to the inner workings of the foul and filthy business practices. It was an evil that saw her body being pranced and prodded beside the hand-shaking and soul-selling of men on their way to the top, with men at the top.

But there were one too many cruel faced men and women who didn't see a young girl with model dreams. Her aspirations for fame were modest, in comparison to what was around her. She desired only a dollop of popularity. As someone ready to sacrifice for causes greater than herself, Dreah was ripe for the picking. Many within the company were complicit with the rules, taking their place as a working part in what could only be described as the sex trafficking of minors.

The dark practices emerged slowly within Mina's model training camps, launched in 2004 and held at a resort in the Florida Key West.

The land itself felt like a magical faraway island to Dreah, which Sam and Mina found amusing. The young girl couldn't believe they were technically still in the United States. And there was so much more of the world to show her. At the time, Dreah was a top model for Mina's teen clothing brand, had guest-starred in popular TV shows, and thanks to the Goode Records connection, played lead video girl to several flash-in-the-pan hip hop acts.

"Wait 'til you see where we shoot!" Mina gloated to the young girls of her mentor camp.

Time at SamStar had been prosperous for the fashion designer, who rejoiced in her freedom to be creative. She was a stealthy business woman with a futuristic vision. And her eye for picking out new talent was impeccable.

But for Dreah, the training camp went beyond the 'once in a lifetime learning experience for model hopefuls' it was dressed up to be. The first year, she and three other girls bonded over their shared aspirations in the double bed hotel room. On the last night of their stay, Mina entered the room, taking a moment to speak with all four girls about their favor amongst the others. She expressed how the company saw them as the most promising models, and would be exclusively working with them going forward. The following season brought them lots of work, with Mina becoming their acting manager.

In the 2nd year of the model training camp, Mina was sneaking into the hotel room far past midnight. Her lessons had become more sinister than sisterly, ranging from inappropriate topics like pornography, sex and virginity. Dreah didn't think too much of it then. Things didn't become clearer until the next year at Dmitri Goode's party. Where Mina told Dreah about the "older guy" who wanted to speak with SamStar's most promising act.

"I still don't understand why I have to sit on his lap."

"I think they do that to check your weight, make sure you ain't too big," Mina giggled. "He wants to see you in person, finally. Just make him laugh, get him excited."

"Make him laugh?" worried the 14 year old Dreah. How was she supposed to do that?

Mina wrapped an arm around her, saying, "Tell a joke or something. Be yourself but better! You treat this like an audition. You own it. But I gotta warn you. Dmitri might get a little touchy feely. He don't mean no harm, he just gets excited around pretty girls like yourself."

"But why do I have to see him?"

"He wants to see you because you're our best talent. He's gonna put you in movies, and SamStar's gonna distribute them. But he wants to see that you'll be good to work with."

"I'm scared Mina."

"Baby that man ain't gonna hurt you. I promise you that. Just tell me and Sam if he does too much."

Dmitri's violation of her there in the party broke the last thread of innocence. Mina was quickly able to complete the corruption, twisting the trust established amongst the four girls-Dreah included. It was Mina who taught the girls how to act in the company of powerful men, reminding them that their discomfort would be just a moment in time.

Each girl was required to inform Mina when and if a man propositioned her directly for sex, and when they planned to have sex on their own accord outside of SamStar. Neither were to be done without Sam's knowledge, or approval. She took the young girls to get birth control pills (Sam's orders) and reminded them that their dream life was most likely one decision away. And babies were absolutely out the question.

Mina looked after the girls as best she could. She had seen them grow up over the years. It was hard not to care for them like a mother would her kittens, even when they were 17 and 18 years old. Far cries from the naïve little girls they came in as at 13 and 14. When the resort nights had them cackling over explicit card games, dildos and *"how to jack a guy off"* demonstrations. Mina carefully watched who was willing to let go of their inhibitions and in what order they did it. Dreah had been the last to trust her.

"Didn't you try to blackmail Sam about this a few years back? When it gets out that you took hush money, what's it gonna say about *you?*" Mina was cackling again, reminding Dreah of a witch. Her deep throaty laughter was terrifying and reeked of ridicule.

Dreah had some guts showing up tonight. But there were ways to handle problems like these. Mina had worked long enough for SamStar to see the many ways they were handled. Dreah's little rumor wouldn't follow them into the upcoming week, once Sam got a hold of it.

Mina knew Dreah was no match for the machine of media that would rip her story to shreds, assassinate her character and prove her to be another unhinged woman with mental illness of all sorts.

Dreah answered, "I'm not worried about what *it's* going to say. *I'm* going to say that SamStar was nothing more than a sex trafficking ring, and your ass led the camp."

"Led the camp? That's cute." Mina shrugged, and with nonchalant hand motions said, "Well, your receipts are also mine. You girls were damaged goods. No morals and no mothers."

Mina thought back to the conversation she had with Diondra, one that called her out on her lack of parenting skills. *"Diondra, you never had a chance to be you, to figure out who you are as a woman. Let us help you raise her, as an extended family. Being a young single mother is hard. You need a village. Trust me, I know. My mother went through hell and back with me. If you're not careful, if you're not willing to get her the help she needs, you will lose Dreah. And we can help her, we can help you."*

"I woulda did better bouncing in and out of foster homes."

"Then it would've been broke men fucking you instead of rich ones. Listen, Dreah, you need to think long and hard before you make a bad decision that you'll regret later. I suggest you take whatever money Sam is offering you, get on your way and out of ours. Now, I'm sorry you're having a bad night, but I got a party to enjoy. Excuse me..." Mina turned on her heel.

"Are you gonna tell Evita you molested her son on his fifteenth birthday?" Dreah watched the question freeze Mina midstride. She added, "I'm gonna do something I've should've done a long time ago."

Mina's face turned upward in a devilish smirk, eyes darkening as she replied, "So am I. Goodnight."

Satisfied with her threat, Mina turned again on her heel and left Dreah standing in her defeat and emptiness. The unusual chill of the room was back. Had it been following her? Goosebumps rippled on her forearm like the waters of a running creek. She felt her momentum waning as the tiny hairs on the nape of her neck rose yet again. She looked down at her feet, now swelling in her heels and aching at the balls of her feet.

But Dreah put one foot in front of the other, and mucked through a storm that seemed to have only gained in intensity.

Fourteen
June 20 | 11:16 pm

Cece the Talkative saw it. In the room's dim light, she saw the moment when Mina's parting words, whatever they were, drained the color from Dreah's face. The radio show host had been watching the exchange from a slot machine a few feet away, looking back and forth between the gaming screen and the women. Due to her investment in the matter, Cece felt compelled to watch the pair in action. She couldn't hear a damn thing, but the body language and facial expressions gave her enough context clues to make out what was happening.

So she perched her drink on the machine, and faced the bar stool to the crowd, keeping her head on a swivel that turned much slower on Dreah and Mina. She almost spilled tequila on her satin black chiffon gown when the owner of Alchemia locked eyes on her. She'd been caught in the act of spectatorship.

She placed her prying brown eyes on the slot machine, its screen illuminating a chocolate brown face, lightly powdered in just enough makeup to keep her looking like the natural beauty she was. Her goddess braids were freshly done the day before, but only now were they throbbing atop her head, reminding her of the ten hours she sat in the stylist's chair. Her ass was still paying for it, literally, with a sore back and even sorer glutes.

Cece was already having the worst luck tonight, losing the $3,000 she brought to play with. She hadn't even made it to the blackjack table, where she planned to bet most of it. She got stuck at the slot machines and lost it all to the false hope of recovery. Including the complimentary $500 voucher.

The night got a wee bit worse when murmurs of a "crazy young lady" confronting the Pitts family began to stalk their way around the ballroom. She ran into the whispers at the craps table, while cheering on a local reporter with a hot hand. Nobody was sure what lay at the core of the arguments, but Cece had an idea. She wondered if the podcast tease jumpstarted her need to stir up controversy. Then, she wondered how the hell Dreah ended up at the gala in the first damn place. She immediately backed away from the table after eavesdropping on the nearby conversation between two loud guests.

Cece decided to grab a drink and walk the floor to find Dreah, but Mina had her first. After that confrontation ended, Cece and her red bottoms clicked over to Dreah, who saw her coming. She greeted the radio host with an exasperated eye roll. Not quite the response Cece expected, since she was someone who knew the truth behind her turbulent history with the company.

Dreah was the subject of her podcast's premiere season. It was appropriately named Out & Industry; a safe space for those who made it out the industry, had intimate new details to the murder, scandal and/or conspiracy, and were willing to tell their story.

Back in March, her intentions about the project brought her to Alchemia, a store whose aesthetically pleasing Instagram posts caught her eye. The store's beautiful owner guided her on the best crystals to have as she manifested a new career path.

While she didn't make her radio dreams come true in larger markets like DC, New York, and Philly- she was grateful to make them happen in her hometown. Since the arrival of mogul Samuel Pitts, more opportunities had become available to those working in entertainment and media. The same opportunities provided her a press pass into the gala, working as a radio correspondent.

When the Old Dominion grad wasn't hosting her daytime radio show, a 10 a.m. to 2 p.m. time slot, she was buried deep in newspaper articles and crime documentaries. Naturally, this led to new business ideas, like the unique podcast pitch that won over the MysterPodcast Network execs.

Out & Industry was Cece's brilliance, her baby, and she was less than two weeks away from its launch. After being greenlit by the network, Cece felt compelled to share the news with Dreah. After all, the woman was wise beyond her years, with eyes that held not just her pain, but her power. Dreah seemed to be the master of her journey, and that's the type of opinion Cece preferred to hear. Maybe she'd give her an intuitive reading and tell her how prosperous this would be. Well, that's what she expected; she had no idea Dreah would drop a story of her past that fit perfectly into the theme of her podcast.

Over several brunches and dinners, and with MysterPodcast Network's best equipment, Cece listened and recorded Dreah's tales of debauchery and scandal surrounding SamStar Enterprises; including a boxer with a flair for transgender women, a photographer who caught them in the act, a CEO who may have ordered a hit, and young girls being trafficked for sex behind the scenes. This type of talk didn't come across her ears often, and it was right on target with the kind of stories she wanted to tell.

Now, it was her time to turn on the journalism charm, as the gala was sure to turn up a wealth of information as to how the business operates today. But Dreah's was the last face she expected to see.

"I've never seen you like this. What's going on? Have you been drinking?" Cece quickly walked her to the other side of the room to an empty table. She needed all the clarification Dreah could provide. She honestly deserved it.

"I only had two drinks, relax Cece. What are *you* doing here?"

"I should ask you the same thing!" Cece cocked her head to the side. "I just wrapped up a video for the radio app. And yes, I'm running a little investigation for the podcast. Your turn."

Dreah folded her arms across her chest, appearing embarrassed at having to have to explain herself. Especially to the woman who'd been her closest ally in what had been a lonely fight. Someone with whom she could revisit her past, sorting through the emotions and instances with no judgment. It seemed like all she ever needed was a friend to hear her side of the story.

"I came to put Sam and Mina on notice. I'm going public, and I'm gonna talk to a lawyer to see if charges can be pressed," she announced.

It was the first Cece heard of Dreah wanting to take legal action. Not that she didn't agree, but Dreah seemed to have conquered her past in ways that didn't require the law; she had an ability to speak open and honestly about her time with SamStar Enterprises.

"Wait just a minute. This is very brave of you, and I'm happy you're doing what you feel is right. But, what about the podcast? Are we still moving forward with it next month?"

Dreah sucked her teeth, almost dismissive of her now. "Damn a podcast!"

"I'm not trying to make it all about that, but I have to explain to producers that you went public. We'll have to give disclosures every-"

"I don't know what to tell you about that Cece."

"Shock value goes down when other outlets pick this up."

"Well, I gave you another exclusive..."

"You'll be giving a deposition the same thing once lawyers get involved. Should we even do a podcast?"

"I'm not trying to knock your hustle, but right now, what happened to me is bigger than that. I'm going to the authorities."

Cece kept her poise as she replied, "And you told them that? Why would you come here instead of just going to straight to law enforcement?"

Dreah rolled her eyes and removed the photo from her clutch. It was battered, but still served its purpose as proof of her assault.

"Because I have proof! And here it is, so *you* can see that I'm not lying about this shit."

Cece took a long moment with the photo. "I didn't need to see a photo. I always believed you." She handed it back to Dreah and said, "Put that away. Don't lose it."

Dreah put the photo back in her clutch and said, "This shit isn't entertainment anymore. This is my real life."

"Well what if we document that too? For season two? C'mon Dreah, you know I'm on your side with this. You deserve to be vindicated, and this whole operation needs to be shut down. But what if we do this in a way that allows us to still move forward with the series? MysterPodcast has us lined up for so many advertisements and sponsors. You can get paid to tell your story."

Cece thought about all the money the company had thrown into her, from setting up the downtown recording studio to paying her graphic designer for the podcast's cover art.

"This will never be about money. Never. And you ought to consider that. Sam is a powerful man. Unless he's already under reasonable suspicion, he'll crush your podcast before episode two. It's best you don't get associated with this yet."

"Dreah please don't give up on us. We've done so much work, and we planned to change women's lives. Please." Cece would beg if she had to. "You understand my point, don't you?"

Dreah regarded her, saying, "I don't need a fictitious name or an altered voice to tell my story. It's nothing personal, but at the same time it is. I have to do this a different way." She paused, looking around the room until her eyes met Cece's again. "I know this is sudden... I'm sorry for that. I owe you big time. You're podcast has been the catalyst for me to heal. You were a safe place for my pain."

Cece would rest in that comfort, knowing their connection was genuine. She would also respect Dreah's desire to take her wounds to the surer doctors Law and Order.

"I can never repay you Cece."

"Sure you can. Just wait until after July 2nd to go public."

The women laughed. Dreah's soul felt a little lighter now that she'd seen Cece. This had been yet another purposeful discussion between friends that granted her the opportunity to face fears she used to pretend weren't there.

"You'll be fine," Dreah reminded her.

Cece frowned, suddenly uncomfortable with the way the conversation had turned. It felt like a goodbye, one too firm and final. She asked, "Where are you going?"

Dreah shrugged and answered, "Not sure yet."

"But you are leaving Richmond? Hold that thought."

Cece peered over Dreah's shoulder as a young lady approached them, looking like she had much to say.

Fifteen

June 20 | 11:31 pm

Her smile was wide and a bit too pleasant.

Fake as fuck, Cece thought, especially given the confrontations earlier in the night. Who was this happy to see Dreah? And why?

"I'm sorry to interrupt ladies. Dreah, can I borrow you a moment?" Pia tossed friendly eyes between the two women.

Dreah looked down at the Jimmy Choo stilettos, up the white halter evening gown with a high split, and into Pia's soft face. She turned back to Cece and said, "This is Pia, Kenny's assistant. Am I right?"

"You remembered!" Pia beamed with approval and shimmied her shoulders. "Happy you both could make it."

Somebody on payroll. Cece waved and said, "Hi, I'm Cece. From 104.3."

"I'm familiar. Glad to have you here. You enjoying yourself? Didn't the theme come together?"

Cece gestured around them. "Yes, it's magnificent."

Pia accepted that with a respectful nod and appreciative grin, her go to move. She had plenty of practice with it tonight. She spent hours moving through the party, matching the good vibes of those decent enough to talk to, and avoiding the presence of those who were not. The gala was crowded with celebrities and Richmond's movers and shakers. Young and old, a variety of ethnicities and backgrounds, and a whole lot of money. She spent most of the night making sure guests wanted for nothing, and softening the concerns of those who'd seen Dreah in action.

A part of Pia wanted to give Dreah a piece of her mind. One assistant to a former one. She had been looking forward to the success of her hard work, and spent weeks stressing over every detail of the gala. How dare Dreah come to the gala with plans to ruin it with her victimhood? There was a time and place, and this gala should have been neither.

Pia stumbled into the world of personal assistance back in Miami, working under a startup finance and credit repair company, whose owner had her making grilled cheese sandwiches at 5 a.m. when she couldn't fetch it from a restaurant. After the feds saw to the company's dismantling in the court of law, Pia followed through with plans to move on and forward, far beyond the criminal investigation that soured her life back home in Miami. This career as Kenny's assistant was a godsend, and she'd tolerate nothing and no one screwing with what she was responsible for.

"You mind if I borrow Dreah for a moment?"

Cece gave a look to Dreah, one that asked if she was okay to be without her. Dreah answered it with a sure nod, grabbed her clutch off the table and followed Pia to the edge of the black and white dance floor. It was yet unoccupied as guests were still held bound in the grips of gambling.

Pia heard about the previous commotions earlier in the night, and wanted to be seen as a safe and neutral party. "I know this has been an *eventful* night for you. I talked to Kenny briefly."

"Briefly?" Dreah was dubious of that.

"Woman to woman, I don't give a damn about the business when it comes to shit like this. Had I known that was your experience, I would've never let Tati give you that invitation. I honestly don't know what Evita was thinking."

"Evita didn't know," Dreah replied. "And I didn't know she would pass out when I told her."

Pia stifled a smile. "She's fine now, by the way. You know, I don't have any personal connection to the family, so I don't really have a dog in this fight."

"Best you keep it that way."

"But I do have questions," Pia began. "And if you don't want to answer them, so be it."

"You don't believe it's true?"

"Most women don't lie about that type of trauma, so I'm *inclined* to believe you. I just want to know why this way? At their gala, of all places."

"As it turns out I spoke to everyone I needed to speak to."

"Aren't you afraid of what they'll do?"

"Should I be afraid? I've always been afraid. Afraid of men, afraid of them, afraid of not being believed." Dreah folded her arms across her chest. She had a better question now. "You think LeVario was afraid?"

"I haven't worked for SamStar long enough to answer that question," Pia replied, an honest retort. She didn't know what the Pitts were capable of. Just days ago she had just been propositioned by Evita for a sexual encounter, so she would put nothing past the couple. She continued, "When I met you at your store, you were so poised and controlled. A woman with her shit together. What happened tonight with you and the Pitts?"

"That picture I took from you in my store wasn't about Hendrik and Zsarina." She took the photo from her clutch and showed it to Pia. "There in the top corner, you'll see me in the lap of the man with the fur on."

"Dmitri Goode?" Pia knew him by his furs.

Dreah shushed her, looking around them nervously.

"If I was Evita I would've passed out too," Pia said returning the picture to her. "And Sam's been looking for you ever since he talked to Mina. You had her heated."

"I wasn't expecting things to go left. I even brought my damn selenite crystal to help me stay composed." She dug into her clutch for the stone. When she realized it wasn't there, her face became tight with worry. She put the photo inside the clutch and snapped it shut. Confused, she scanned the room, wondering when it went missing. "Shit. I must've lost it earlier in the night."

Pia noticed the shift in Dreah's mood. She grabbed two champagne flutes off an approaching waiter's tray and handed one to her. "Well, what's done is done. It's over now. I just want to make sure you're okay."

Dreah took the glass. She had a desperate desire to change the subject, for once in the night, to something lighter. A conversation that didn't entail her traumas. "Where are you from?"

Pia was caught off guard, repeating the question back to her. "Where am I from? I'm a Miami girl. I moved to Richmond two years ago."

"What brought you here? Of all places?"

"I always get asked that! Let's just say I wanted something different. And when I heard SamStar Enterprises was moving its headquarters to the city, I figured I shoot my shot. I follow the whole family so I would've worked for *whoever*. I was really going for Grant but he left me on read." Pia giggled, thinking about what her job would have been like working for the younger brother.

"Kenny's way better behaved, more sense. Grant was *super* spoiled so I'm sure he's an ass. He doesn't want an assistant," Dreah noted. She took another swig. "Is Evita nice to you?"

"Very." Pia placed her hand on her chest and continued, "She's a real sweetheart. Kinda feel sorry for her though."

Dreah nodded at the answer she expected to hear. "I get it. That sadness lingers in her eyes... Tonight, I saw it was still there. If she ever confides in you, believe her."

"I figured that was a part of the job once she pulled me into organizing the gala. I've grown to adore her. Even when she dumps her emotional baggage onto me."

"She used to ask Kenny if she could borrow me for some side work, but I always refused. I didn't want to get close with her as a woman. I still needed her as a mother figure."

"You know what's interesting? Kenny never said anything about you all's childhood time together. I always thought you were some random hire. Why do you think that is?"

"He won't open up about himself unless he feels you've earned his trust. Like how you earned his mother's."

Pia wondered where the conversation was going. Did Dreah know something about Evita that she didn't? Was Dreah also on the receiving end of Evita's sexual advances?

"We all have some shit we're running from, some dark secrets we're afraid will come out. Even though you're coming for the company I work for, I have to say, I admire your bravery. It takes a lot of strength to do what you did."

Dreah grinned in reply. It was all she could do. The conversation had ended up right where she didn't want it to. Pia noticed her empty champagne flute and pointed to the resizable charm bracelet at the base of the glass.

"Don't forget to take the bracelet."

Dreah looked at the jewelry and smiled. "Awe, a moon charm. I love it." She removed the bracelet and slid it up her wrist.

"Yeah we decided last minute to put them on some of the champagne glasses instead of inside the gift bags. We got them from a local designer in the city. I wanted RVA to show off!"

Dreah grinned, almost jealous of the woman's drive. She read her as focused and resilient. Someone who moved with purpose and would outwork the competition. It was the complete opposite of who she was as an assistant. Pia represented all the things she lacked when it came to the job requirements. The things you didn't learn in college. Either you had the will, or you didn't. Kenny was fortunate to have a hustler like Pia on his team.

The two held conversation in ways they weren't able to days before in Alchemia. Tati had come off as the friendlier (and bossier) of the two. But here, in the center of the gala, Pia's conversation moved Dreah from the dense fog of why she was in attendance, and truly made her feel welcomed. Pia had the people skills needed to work a room, and it was Dreah's turn to feel that energy. It was innovative, futuristic and focused.

"You know what I see for you?" Dreah said, pausing to review the party scene around them. "If you had a hand in all of this? You are most definitely gonna be an event manager. Set and stage design. All that! You're like a chameleon. You can do anything if you put your mind to it."

"I feel like that's the second time I've heard that this weekend. Thanks. I appreciate that, sis," Pia said, bashful now.

Neither of the women saw the security guard approaching from behind, only feeling the dread his presence caused when he stood behind them. He slapped a sturdy arm down on Dreah's shoulder.

"Aye yo' you. Party's over."

Dreah was okay with the party coming to an end, but she couldn't understand why the rain hadn't let up.

Sixteen
June 20 | 11:40 pm

The security guard was told to see Dreah out of the gala almost two hours ago. In his black dress suit, framing his triangular build, he walked the party floors with one mission. Do as Sam ordered and get the girl out of the building. For longer than he preferred, his gray eyes scanned the ballroom as he lurked through the crowds, a pensive stare holding his yellow brown face. He took his search to the balcony of the Governors room, and even to the first floor.

Just as one hour became two, he rubbed his scruffy beard and shook his dreads as fatigue set in. But he was advised to venture to the dancefloor, and that's when he saw her conversing with Kenny's assistant. Enjoying herself despite the wrath she'd brought Sam. He planned to make the exit as smooth as possible and hoped she wouldn't make it any more difficult than what it had to be. Sam was trusting him to get the job done, and he would do just that.

When Dreah saw it was the former bodyguard for Goode Records, Neville aka Ville, her jaw dropped.

"Ville?"

"It's *Neville* now. Look Dreah, I don't know what you said to Sam and I don't care. But I'm under strict orders to get yo' ass up outta here."

Grabbing hold of her wrist, Neville tried to pull her towards the exit. Dreah tussled with him, dropping her empty champagne glass in the process. The sound of it shattering seemed to quiet the crowd around them.

"Neville please!" Pia pleaded. "Not like this... and Dreah, don't fight him! It's over. Just go quietly."

"I'll leave when I'm ready."

She tussled with Neville some more as Pia stomped her foot and fumed with the need to exert her authority.

"Are y'all trying to make a scene on purpose? Please! Dreah, you've done enough. Sorry you're having a bad night but you need to leave."

Pia read the tangled expression on Dreah's face as her cue to exit. Before dipping back into the party, she told Neville, "Don't strong-arm her either. She can walk on her own." Then, to Dreah, "Get home safely. Good night."

Dreah could only watch as Pia floated into the crowd and out of sight. She had many questions she had, but couldn't get the words out of her throat. She blinked awkwardly, and turned back to the tables to see Cece was gone.

For the third time in the night, the hairs on the back of Dreah's neck rose. This time around, though, she knew there was nothing left to give. Her cause had been beaten to a coma at this point, and only she cared to keep it alive. Her best and only option was to get an Uber, take everything on her person and head to the airport. She'd buy the first ticket to New York and find legal representation.

Neville leaned into her and muttered, "Let's not cause a scene, ok? Now walk."

Under his strict lead, Dreah started towards the exit.

The last views of the gala flashed before her. It was full swing around them and far more crowded than before. The band kept at its triumphant blaze, now before an audience of tipsy dancing pairs. A slot machine sang with the promise of "free spins", as the player pumped a hopeful fist. The gambling tables were so crowded, she couldn't tell what was being played.

"Did Sam tell you why he wants me out?" Dreah asked when they were in the foyer. She started towards the escalator.

Neville shook his head, and rather nonchalantly reminded her, "And I already said I don't care. And the escalator's down. We're going to the elevator." He pointed to the elevator door next to ballroom C.

An insubordinate Dreah backed away from him. "You never cared. Always a yes man, never a man of your own. Sam's still ordering you to do his dirty work!"

Neville raised a curious eyebrow. "Dreah don't drag me into your bullshit. You're letting your emotions get the best of you. And you been drinking. Give it up."

"Ville, you're already in it. And you might want to get your story straight, before the police come knocking." Dreah was surprised by her own defiance and this final act of confronting another link in the SamStar chain of command. Yes, Neville was involved, and she knew just how deeply.

Dreah was leading him towards the elevators now. "How does it feel knowing you killed a man because Sam and his friends were in a sex trafficking ring?"

Two things Neville didn't like: getting into business that had nothing to do with him, and the police. These things going hand in hand froze him a moment. He wondered if he should even pick at the conversation as he punched the button for the elevator.

Her unruliness picked at him the more she went on, "I know you were the one who tossed LeVario out the window."

"Easy Dreah," he nudged her into the open elevator. "I'm not the one you have a problem with. Keep me out of it."

"Ville, you killed an innocent man!"

Dreah's words pricked him like a rose thorn. Annoyed him like a deep splinter that refused to be plucked.

Neville was defensive, freshly angered, as he replied, "You see why you're getting thrown out? Because you talk too much. And you talkin' old shit, at that. Just shut up already. Nobody's gonna help you here. Let it go."

"Murder has no statute of limitations. You think Sam is gonna cover for you when they dig into this story?"

When the doors of the elevator closed, Neville jumped on her. He grabbed her throat, forcing her to look at him.

Through gritted teeth, he said, "Listen you lil' bitch. Let me tell you something. I was 21 years old facing two felonies, one in Chesterfield County, one in Hanover. Sam's lawyer came through for me in ways only a god can. Next thing you know, my cases are dropped. I didn't ask no questions. I just fulfilled my obligations to Sam. I head fuckin' security!"

He released her, shoving her to the floor of the descending elevator. Dreah gasped for air and slowly rose to her feet.

"So *that's* your deal with the devil? We thought it was Satan himself. Whole time is was Samuel Pitts."

She heard the legend of Neville, circa 2004 when the 26 years old nephew of Sam's frat brother faced twenty years on drugs and weapons charges. Rumors not often repeated said he sold his soul to the devil while behind bars. Come 2005, he was a free man, employed by Goode Records as head of security.

"Yeah and don't think I won't snap your neck at his command." He watched as Dreah swallowed the lump of fear in her throat. "Luckily for you, that's not what he asked me to do."

The elevator doors opened onto the bare first floor. It was eerily empty, and the only lighting was that of the streetlights spilling in from outside.

Stepping out of the elevator, Dreah tripped over the threshold and almost fell on her face. She paused to gather herself and looked around them. Neville forcibly got her back up on her feet and hauled her towards the doors. She felt a woozy haze take over as they stepped onto 5th and Broad Street. Her face kissed the sultry night air, too thick with heat to be of any solace.

NeVille demanded she give him her phone so he could schedule the Uber. Dreah was feeling so intoxicated, she didn't care. She handed him the phone, nearly stumbling into him as he took it from her.

"Get yo'self together! Stand up!" He demanded as he fiddled with the Uber app. A moment later, he advised, "Five minutes away."

"NeVille, I have to vomit!" Dreah realized.

"You gotta hold it."

"Neville please. The restrooms are right there by the elevators!" She pointed into the building.

"Nah the Uber comin'."

"I'm not gonna throw up in his car. You have my phone. I promise I'll be right b-"

Dreah stopped mid-sentence as the spicy bile boiled in her throat. It was like heartburn and acid reflux at the same time. A migraine pounded at the top of her skull and sweat formed at her brow. Her body rose in temperature like a computer overheating.

"Don't make me come looking for you!" She heard Neville yell as she ran back into the building, feeling weaker with every step. Her body was rejecting every drink she had taken, every energy she'd absorbed. The room spun rapidly around her as she fought to keep the restrooms in fading eye sight.

Dreah crashed into the door like a defensive linebacker and threw herself into the first stall. She heaved and hurled the contents of her stomach into the toilet, as the world around her faded to black, and spun to a slow stop.

Seventeen
June 20 | 11:52 pm

In the privacy of the Governors room, Anya and Evita kept themselves from the rest of the party. The turn of found Evita spending most of the party on the balcony of the Governors room with her joint and lighter, and wandering the empty corridors of the convention center. There was no energy in her to laugh, smile, mingle or host. She had to sacrifice her makeup, using the face wipes in her bag to remove the beauty enhancements. Luckily, her skin was smooth and clear enough to show barefaced (even with the new cut near her chin), so the courage to do so wasn't a problem.

It was the eyes that worried her; they always gave her away. And now they were red and sore. Screaming for the moisture of eye drops. She looked in her purse for one of three bottles she normally kept at a time. She grew more frustrated the harder she looked.

"Don't you have to be on stage with Sam in ten minutes?"

"Yeah don't remind me. I'm looking for the eye drops in this never ending fucking bag." She sucked her teeth, then sighed-realizing she kept one in the pocket of the purse. "Oh! Oh thank God. Give me a second to put these in." She cooled her eyes with a few drops each and fanned the air.

"I'm glad you found your eye drops, but I'm sorry your night went like this. Sam's done a lot of things, but we never expected *this*. Are you really ready to walk out on a twenty eight year marriage?" Anya asked.

That was an eighteen year head start on her and Daryl. She had no advice to give her. Only questions to ask. In what was almost a whisper, she added, "Did you really not know he was doing this stuff?"

"I knew there were women. Women of age, of course. He's been a cheat. But sex trafficking and pedophiles? Never saw *that* fucking coming."

"What if he wasn't having sex with the girls? Just involved in the actual trafficking?" An important question.

"If he's involved it's because *he's* doing it. That's how these creeps work. Everybody wants to test the *product*." Anya couldn't bring herself to say the correct pronouns. She leaned in. "Do you believe Dreah?"

Evita leaned in too. "After Dmitri's party, she flew on the jet with them to Florida."

Anya threw her hands up and asked, "Who the hell else was on the plane? Who escorted her? And where were you?" Too many questions. "Listen Evita, I usually take your side in all things but I gotta know where you fall on this. Please."

Evita covered her jaw. Tears the only answer as the sweet memories of that old success turned rotten. The party ended on such a high note, despite LeVario's riddance. Evita made sure to smile in the faces of the artists, producers, managers and executives. She could place everyone in attendance of Dmitri's Harlem club. But she would never know who else had a hand in the unspeakable. Who Dreah was forced to interact with. She wish she hadn't fainted during their conversation. There was so much more to be uncovered.

"Hello? Do you hear me?" Anya waved her hands in front of her sister's face. "Glad to see you looking back to life but I'm asking you a question. Where were you when this young girl walked onto a jet with grown men?"

Evita closed her eyes, concentrating on the moment it all escaped her. How obvious and in plain sight it was.

"I was um... I was getting ready to take the kids to the car, get them home. But Mina said Dreah was gonna stay behind and sign some contracts the next day. Dmitri wanted to cast her in an upcoming project."

"Why is a fourteen year old doing business at an industry party?" Anya's neck rolled as she asked it. Her eyes did not hide her disappointment, nor her disdain.

"Mina was her manager, or something like it. She didn't tell me they were in Florida until the next day."

Anya appeared as if she was going to vomit and shook her head. "That bitch is involved. I never liked her. She's a devil."

Evita ran her fingers through her hair. "How did I not see this?" Questions of her own.

"Why did y'all bring this girl into your home?"

"It was Mina and Sam's idea. I honestly never wanted her there. Especially with Kenny being the same age. You know I don't play that."

"Where was her mama?"

"They said she was strung out."

"Had to be 'cause ain't no way in hell..."

Evita shook her head. Just baffled as her world shifted on its axis. She thought she knew Sam two ways, but now he was three completely different men: the wayward cheat, the loving husband, and now the closet pedophile. She was in for the fight of her life with this revelation.

Surely it was tough in the beginning. She was a fifteen year old model and muse, who worked with some of the biggest names in pop and hip hop. She was on the brink of her career when they met, during the days she played tagalong to Mina. He was 23 years of age, and every bit of tempting to her young, wild and free spirit. She was pregnant with Kenny six months into meeting Sam, set to birth Kenny a month after her 16th birthday.

There was pressure from Sam's team to legalize the relationship. Evita was quickly able to convince a needy mother with a waning Catholic faith that she wanted to do right by God, and the law, with a new baby on the way.

But Evita learned the hard way with a marriage that tested her faith in God, and her faith in Sam. His fast lifestyle only sped up; spinning as energetic as the beats he made for come-and-go rap artists. Mina styled them, and managed to keep Evita in a place where she felt protected as the wife. She was free to raise their son while Sam did his thing as a producer, with Mina playing guardian of fidelity.

But in the 2000s, Evita saw the tides turning with the birth of another baby boy. Through the years, big brother Kenny proved himself to be a rather advanced child. He'd been a privileged kid, of course. Privy to the best gadgets the tech world had to offer.

Evita, having bought one too many toys and products for both her sons, was overcome with business ideas she believed her husband (and his investment money) could execute. She convinced Sam to consider the digital world. Cell phones, palm pilots, iPods, and the ever developing World Wide Web. All opportunities to get hip hop streaming on multiple platforms while supplying the technology to do so.

Sam would scratch his head, her thoughts and ideas wildly complex, but also a reflection of her otherworldly beauty. He knew marrying her would be his blessing, more than it was his curse. A type of punishment for messing with a girl only fifteen years of age, while he, in his final years of adolescence, knew better. Still, their union endured more turmoil into a new decade.

Evita hated the infidelity the most. It took a lot of nerve and audacity to trust him again, to control her anger when a memory of their past boiled to the surface. The power to harness her emotions and not be easily triggered into a cauldron that lacked forgiveness.

And when Evita fell short of the ingredients, she was violent and foul-mouthed, with no regard for the man she said she would trust and forgive. For the man she said she loved. She found joy in freeing herself sexually, enough to enjoy other women. So much joy that she thought she could share in it with her husband on occasion. This time, she the guardian of fidelity, could make him watch, and not participate.

Now, there were instances where he had his way, indulging in multiple desserts. But Evita would always temper herself. She didn't mind satisfying his appetite, as long as he stayed near and dear to the table of what was only her love.

The allegations baffled Evita, but they were believable. She knew there was an eight year age difference between them, but she never thought of this being an actual attraction to young girls. To the degree he'd be involved in a trafficking ring that kept supply at bay. And truth or rumor, Evita would never look at him the same.

"This will be the first and final time I file for divorce."

The d-word dropped Anya into a deeper level of sorrow. She couldn't imagine if it was her husband. The shame and embarrassment she'd suffer. The blogs. The press coverage. It was all going to rip her sister apart. She felt sad for Evita all over again. Somehow the question of *"are you sure"* seemed inappropriate. For a moment, Anya couldn't believe she even thought to ask.

Evita continued, answering the question left unspoken. "I feel like I have to. What's it gonna look like if I stand by him? It's gonna look like I was complicit, or knew the whole time."

Anya was even more afraid to ask the next question. "Well, did you?"

"No!" Evita roared. "I took that girl in like a daughter, like how my husband and best friend asked me too. They hid this from me."

"That's gonna be a tough sell."

A moment of silence passed between the two before Evita found the words to say. "This will never go away. Everything we're affiliated with will be under review. The casino included."

"Should I tell Daryl?" Anya wondered. "You know he was working with Vernon Hines, some guy on the casino board."

"Tati's father. He talked Sam into investing. I think this Tati bitch did research on you and Daryl when I gave her the address list. Why the hell would she ask Daryl to get in on this? No disrespect to him, but there were plenty of other bankers available. She had to get Daryl mixed in with this dirty money."

"Ugh, don't tell me anything else. You're scaring me and the baby." Subconsciously, she brought her hand to her belly.

Evita gasped, and Anya immediately realized she'd let the secret slip.

"*Baby*? Oh my god! I knew it! You're pregnant?"

Anya surrendered to the reveal, nodding proudly. "We're gonna surprise family and friends with an announcement soon."

Evita rushed to her sister with open arms. Her problem seemed obsolete with Anya's news. "I know how bad you wanted this. I'm so happy for you. Do you know what you're having?"

"A boy," Anya said through fresh tears.

And with that, Evita held her a little tighter. "Oh finally. He's gonna be perfect."

Both the sisters took a moment to wipe their eyes. Evita graced hers with a few more drops.

"How do I look?" she asked.

"Gorgeous," Anya answered in truth. "At least you aren't vomiting every thirty minutes. Baby boy's got me experiencing morning sickness all damn day and night." Anya giggled and shook her head. "Which reminds me, I need to use the restroom."

She started for the door, and turned back to face her big sister one last time. "We'll get through this. We always do."

Evita's lips parted in a half smile as Anya left the room. She took one last look in the mirror, and decided she too better get going.

As she went into the ballroom, the first person who saw her was Mina. The stylist scurried towards her, rather congenial given the looming scandal. Evita couldn't understand that.

"There you are! I been looking for you all night. Girl, where have you been?" Mina asked, greeting her with open arms.

Evita returned the hug, just barely. "Getting myself together. I know you heard about Dreah."

Mina rolled her eyes. "Ugh, the bitch came for me tonight!"

Evita narrowed her gaze, certain that she would fan the flames of their friendship with this conversation.

"Tuh please! Dreah's crazy. Always has been. I blame her mama. The nut didn't fall far from the tree."

"Yet you convinced me to move her into my home." Evita was all hands on hips. Defensive now.

Mina whiffed at the brusque nature of her voice and looked around them. No need to put on a show. She kept her posture poised and powerful, remaining confident in her opinion of Dreah.

"You moved her in with your family out the goodness of your heart. She needed guidance. And you and Sam tried to give her that."

"We *all* gave her guidance. Some of us more than others. I heard you were some sort of madam." Evita's hard eyes were dark and suggestive. Unable to see the others around them who felt the tension as much as she did. "Do you understand how it felt to hear Dreah say *half* of what she said about you and Sam? What the fuck have you done?"

Mina raised an eyebrow. In that moment, she knew where Evita stood on the matter. But how could she convince her not to assume her guilt? "Did it ever occur to you that she wanted to do the things she did?"

"How dare you. She was fourteen!"

Guests nearby had *ooh*'d the exclamation. Evita and Mina both looked around and nodded graciously, as nosy individuals walked on by.

Mina finally continued, "Old enough to know what she was doing. C'mon Evita be real. We were once fourteen and fifteen. You remember what it was like."

"I don't remember it ever being appropriate for a fourteen year old girl to be on a jet with grown men."

"She's embellishing a lot of things."

"Something told me back then to ask more questions, but I trusted you as my friend. And this is what y'all were doing the whole time?"

"Nobody touched her on that plane! She was by my side the entire time."

"Considering what we know now, it all makes sense."

"How can you believe this shit? You were there all those years. Surely you would've seen the signs."

Evita's retort was matter-of-fact. "I saw a picture of her in Dmitri's lap."

"Oh please! A picture proves nothing! Dmitri Goode could've fondled teen pussy anywhere. He damn sure wouldn't have done it on camera at his own party," Mina snapped. She regretted the comment immediately as she regarded the disgust and heartbreak on Evita's face. "You think I'm a part of this, don't you?"

Evita's smile was pained, and her eyes were sore with the onset of new tears. There'd been too much crying already. She sighed and dabbed at the corners of her eyes. "You know we can't be friends after tonight. And I'm divorcing Sam. So you don't have to pick sides."

Mina was incredulous with hands on hips and a rolling neck. "Excuse me but we've been friends for thirty years. You're *really* doing me like that? I relocated my whole life for you, for y'all. You, of all people, know how loyal I am. Our friendship means nothing to you?"

"It meant everything to me but y'all are dead wrong. This is so foul! I don't know how I feel right now. But I wouldn't be able to live with myself if I stayed married to Sam. When this news gets out-"

"She's not gonna go public," Mina said with an exaggerated eye roll.

"What makes you so sure?" Evita folded her arms over her chest and looked her up and down.

"Because she's scared. She's not ready to challenge SamStar. And why are you so ready to divorce Sam? I heard you haven't even talked to him."

"I hadn't talked to you either!"

"I would've never come to you with a discussion like this tonight. This ain't the time for that."

"Well I don't want to discuss it later."

"Really? Fine. Rush to all the judgments you want," Mina spat with a finality that said she understood the friendship was over. She stormed off into a nearby crowd, filled with people who wouldn't question her character.

Evita was grateful the woman had walked away, as oppose to wearing her down in regret. Regret that would've made her reconsider Mina's role in the operation, keeping blame solely on her husband. She hadn't seen him since their rift earlier in the night. Even when Anya (who wasn't yet in the know) suggested she talk to him, she wouldn't dare.

Evita was still coming to grips with her new life, stirring in the distance like a hurricane. She didn't have the words for her husband.

But now, it was time to stand beside him.

She headed stage side, where Sam waited proudly. The body language of a wealthy and confident man. She joined him at the stage steps, and looked on as the Mayor continued his speech at the podium.

He spoke, rather preachy, about the benefits of the casino, the budget plans and the rest of the good it would serve Richmond. His voice echoed from the tiny microphone through the giant speakers around the room, as idle chatter filled out the rest of the space.

"I've been worried about you," said Sam.

Evita didn't look at him. She couldn't, not just yet. She knew what Sam would try to ignore. That this rumor, this tale of atrocity, would follow them forever. There was no escaping it. As swiftly as it was brought into the gala, it'd follow them into every room they entered from that day forward.

Sam blew the wind from his jaws, slightly irritated with her silent treatment. "You know you don't have to be up here."

"Oh I know," Evita retorted. "Lucky for you, right now I care more about our brand than I do our marriage."

"This will get straightened out."

Sam said it with a confidence that Evita couldn't quite understand. How was he so sure? She thought to ask him, but decided against it as the Mayor concluded his speech.

"-because we're gonna do it this Richmond! We're gonna ignite this economy! Bring in thousands of jobs! And we're gonna do it with the help of our hometown heroes! Ladies and gentlemen- put your hands together for Samuel Pitts!"

The band blared their instruments as Sam and Evita stepped on stage and joined the Mayor at the podium. They waved at the crowd and posed for quick picture snaps. The Mayor shook Sam's hand a final time, and the crowd quieted to a murmur as he began his speech.

Evita waited a few steps behind him, vetting the faces of a hopeful crowd. A respectably silent crowd who believed in Sam and what he could do for the city. They listened as he thanked SamStar Enterprises employees and affiliates for sixteen years in the business. Then, he too mentioned the partnership with Richmond's United Casino Group. After vouching for the project, he encouraged a 'Yes' vote to the roar of the crowd.

"For SamStar, this is a night sixteen years in the making. But there's something that's been at work long before we began. A union that has been ordained in the stars ever since I first laid eyes on her. I want to shout out a woman very special and dear to my heart. A woman whose stood by my side over the years and made me a better man, a better father, a better husband. She's the real hero of SamStar Enterprises. I know women don't get their props enough in this business but I'm changing that. I want to first acknowledge my wife, Evita Pitts..." He turned towards her, the warmest, most tender smile on his expression.

Evita jumped at the sudden roar of the crowd. And in that moment, she couldn't deny her husband, or their glory. She gracefully waved to the adoring crowd whose applause for her echoed throughout the ballroom. She felt her cheeks redden with a nervous blush.

After the applause subsided, Sam continued, "Evita, I want to thank you for being the absolute best mother to our sons, the kindest most patient wife to me, and a true mastermind behind the scenes of SamStar Enterprises. Without you, there is no me. And-"

The sudden turning of heads stopped him cold. What were they looking at? Mumbling about? Sam had to concentrate to hear those blood-curdling screams reverberating from the first floor. The sound crept its way up the stairs, reaching into the ballroom. The crowd murmured, some fearfully and others irritated that the party had been brought to its knees. But the terrified shrieks stayed just outside of the ballroom doors.

When Evita heard them, she immediately knew it was Anya. Angst on her face, she ran off the podium, maneuvering through the bodies of the crowd, bobbing aimlessly like zombies in the eerie muffled sound of their own voices. She nearly twisted an ankle as she skipped down the frozen escalator. Sam was hot on her trails and security guards weren't too far behind.

Now on the first level, Evita found Anya shaking her head profusely and pointing to the restroom doors. She was clearly in distress, causing Evita and Sam a great deal of panic. The worry was quickly spreading to the handful of guests who'd followed them to the pavilion.

"Anya! What's the matter? Are you alright? Where's Daryl? Daryl!!" Evita figured he was the only one who could calm her down.

"I'm right here!" Daryl said, seemingly appearing out of nowhere. He pushed his way through the small crowd and immediately went to console his wife.

It took Anya a moment to sputter the words out. "I saw her… in there. Dead! She's dead!"

"Who?" Sam asked as he moved cautiously towards the restroom door. He turned back to the room around him. The collage of faces in the crowd was overwhelming as he ran every possible scenario through his mind. There was nothing left to do but enter the restroom and see what it was that had a genuinely shaken Anya too terrified to speak.

She felt overtaken by the swarm of the growing crowd. Lost in a moment that would clearly send the party (and her family) into dark madness. Why did she have to happen upon this? She grabbed Daryl, hoping his arms were big enough to shelter her from the storm. Hammering down right about now.

"Who's dead baby?"

Anya snapped to and looked at Daryl to answer the question.

"Dreah." Sam said it first.

And with much regret.

Eighteen
June 24 | 7:57 pm

In the pink glow of her home studio, Cece signaled for her engineer to fix the positioning of a ring light. The last thing she needed was bad lighting on her Instagram LIVE with Sienna. The legendary model had promised her the conversation when they met at the gala. And for the Richmond radio personality, it'd be a good look to have first dibs on all the drama that occurred. Tongues were wagging with drool for gossip surrounding the gala, and the mysterious death of Dreah McDonald. Local media and news outlets referred to her only as a local businesswoman. None were talking of her past as a young model who was once an integral part of SamStar Enterprises. Even fewer knew why she was there at the gala. And the reason she caused quite a stir.

But Cece had a feeling after tonight's LIVE, that would change. And maybe, just maybe, new momentum around the story would encourage her to move forward with the podcast. Dreah's death had been a devastating blow to her spirit, and kept her far away from thoughts about the podcast. She wasn't ready to hear the song in her voice as it danced through stories of heartbreak and personal triumph. Endless hours of sincere chatter about what life had been like for a young girl in the entertainment industry.

Cece thought over her decision to go LIVE as she positioned her camera phone stand and gestured towards the ring light, still not at the right angle. The engineer sucked his teeth, and asked if she rather put on a filter.

"Damn, I don't look that bad Cedric," Cece said with disgust. "Just tilt it- no, right there. There you go!" She gave him a proud thumbs up.

He was more than glad to walk away to his other duties, like preparing an overhead mic for audio recording. They planned to use bits of the interview on her radio show

He pressed RECORD on a video camera mounted on its tripod.

Cece smiled as her phone pinged with a new message. "I just got the text from Sienna. She's ready. Here we go."

When the LIVE started, they waited silently and watched the viewership count rise from 22 to 99, to 253, to 676. Cece scanned through the names, searching for Sienna's handle. She spotted Sienna's request to join the LIVE, and the two women appeared on screen to what was now almost a thousand viewers- most of them alerted by Sienna's notification.

Cece's eyes widened at the sight of Sienna, done up in full face makeup and pouring a mixture of pineapple juice and tequila.

"Oh boy. We're starting early, aren't we?" Cece laughed, flashing a bubbly smile that fit the flowered wall behind her.

"We ain't spilling tea tonight. Honey, we're spilling *tequila.*" Sienna titled her head to the side with an all-knowing expression. "Pin it to the comments! It's about to go down."

Cece found herself grinning ear to ear at the extra bubbly woman. "Before we get into the goods, tell 'em who you are- for the fans who need to know."

"Now who don't know who I am? I'm your favorite vixen's favorite. Before all the Instagram models, hell- before *I* became an Instagram model, I was a pioneer in the hip hop model game. They call me Super Vixen Sienna." She cat-walked away from the phone, displaying her perfect figure in a velour short set. She posed, turned on one heel and walked back to the camera as Cece cheered her on.

Cece had a feeling this interview was going to be a juicy one. Perhaps the one she needed to get excited about her career again. It was easy to do with guest like Sienna, who brought an energy she found easy to match. A true girl's chat, and that was her specialty.

"Okay ma'am! Yes! Let us know! Where are you from?"

"I'm from LA. One of the natives, born and raised."

"I was so happy to meet you at the SamStar gala. You looked amazing, by the way."

"Thank you! You did too."

"Tell us how you met Samuel Pitts."

"As you know, I was a video girl for a lot of artists back in the day. So I knew Sam through my work as a model and just being in the industry. Then later down the line, in 2012, I signed to SamStar Publishing."

"Now, I read the book 'Super Vixen to Super Villain'-"

"-Either Way, Get Yours."

Cece suppressed a laugh and continued, "-about your time in the industry. I want to put a rumor to rest. The rumor was that although you had given him a fake name in the book, you leaked in an interview that you mention Sam Pitts in the book. Readers put two and two together, and you were later dropped from SamStar Publishing."

"Damn Cece. You go right in, don't you?"

"Well I saw you there with his son Grant, who was your date. So I just wanna know... because if so, this may be one of the few times I've seen a lady bag the daddy and the son."

"It's 2021. Anything is possible!" Sienna laughed. "But I had a little *entanglement* with Sam back in the day. At the time I wrote the book, I disguised his name out of respect."

"But this was the man who published your book! Why leak it at all?"

"I needed sales!" Sienna shrugged and took a sip of her freshly mixed cocktail.

"Were you having an affair with him when you were writing the book? No judgment. No judgments in the comments." Cece addressed the latter to the viewers.

Sienna rolled her eyes and shrugged. "Sure was. See me, back then? I was low vibrational. Not gon' lie. I was Super *Vindictive* Sienna."

"Really? I can't see that for you. You seem so nice and sweet online."

"Only believe half of what you see online. That's the golden rule," Sienna said, holding up a finger like she had said something profound.

"So did you get the book deal before or during the affair?"

"Before. I told them it was a self-help, and it was. But of course I was gonna talk about my escapades."

"And why did the affair end? Who broke it off with who?"

Sienna burst into a fit of giggles. "Oh my goodness. This is so fucked up- what I'm about to tell you. Hold on." She took another sip then set her drink down. After smacking her lips, she began.

"So he ended it before I could. And let's be clear, I definitely was going to end it because he's a married man. Guys like him don't leave their wives for girls like me. But he broke it off first, and I was so offended!"

Cece joked sarcastic with her. "Right, like how dare you?"

Sienna babbled, "And I wanted to get a *little* revenge so I lied and told his wife I was pregnant, when I actually wasn't."

"Wait a minute! You did what?" Cece heard exactly what was said, but for the shock factor it was in her interest to have Sienna repeat herself and expound.

"Yes, I lied and told his wife I was pregnant. And I feel so bad 'cause Evita is the sweetest woman ever. Most of the wives are not, but she really is a darling. She never confronted me though. Of course Sam did, and he cussed me to hell and back! But I rode the lie out. I told him I was pregnant, then, a few months later said I had a miscarriage."

Cece was left silent as all kinds of emojis and harsh comments flooded the bottom of the screen. She felt bad for the woman. "No judgments y'all! Remember this is a judgement free zone."

Sienna noticed though. "The comments are going crazy right now! I know y'all, I know. I was dead wrong for that. It's never too late to come clean though, right?"

Right now, sixty thousand plus viewers were tuned in. And the number was growing by the minute.

"So, back on the gala. Grant Pitts was your date?"

"Aht aht aht," Sienna said, wagging a finger. "I was *his* date. Be clear, Grant wanted me on his arm that night. And he's a low key gentleman. That boy flew me out, took me shopping before and after the party, and then we hopped on a jet to Miami."

"Is that where you are now?"

"Hell yeah. After the shit that went down? I ain't wanna be nowhere in Richmond! Y'all are dangerous."

"Easy Sienna, we'll get to that. Hold on a minute."

"I'm sorry girl. Drink's kickin' in."

Cece giggled. "I can tell. Okay, so Grant's got a big following. He's really transparent about his life. The kids love him! Are you gonna appear on his YouTube channel? Is it safe for his fans to see all that body?"

"It was safe for Grant to see it!" Sienna said suggestively. "And you damn right he's popular with the kids. Like, they love this lil' dude. The kiddos to the teenagers. I don't get this generation, but I can dig it for the right amount. Everywhere we go, they recognize him. I kinda like that popularity though!"

"And how long have you all been dating?"

"Eh, maybe a month. Since like, end of May?"

"Oh this is still fresh. Well, is it serious?"

"Not as serious as his coke habit!"

Cece's eyes widened and looked to her engineer. Another exclusive. "Coke habit? Come again."

Sienna nodded as if Cece should've known this. "Girl, after the things I seen partying with Grant- I assume all the youngsters do it. That vial around his neck, there's coke in it. Literally, powder."

"I don't believe you! Not Sam Pitts' youngest son. Cocaine? For real?"

"Hand on a Bible. He's functioning though. And he only does it socially, from what I've seen. Not that it makes it any better."

"Are you with him right now?" Cece took in Sienna's hotel background. A hotel suite, no doubt.

"Yes but I made him get me a different room," Sienna answered as she looked around, almost having to make sure she was indeed alone. "We got into an argument on the jet."

"Oh no. Is everything okay over there?"

"I got his ass blocked right now. I'm sure one of his little followers are gonna show him this."

Cece watched as her engineer suppressed a chuckle. She started, "Well we pray y'all work that out. Let's move on. So, we were both in attendance of the SamStar Enterprises gala this past Sunday night. And oh what a time that was had..."

Cece and Sienna exchanged foreboding looks, neither knowing where to start first.

"Where do we even begin with this?" Cece asked the obvious question. "Ok, so let me set it up for y'all. It was a casino theme and everybody really came dressed the part. They turned the convention center out! I mean, I have never seen no shit like this in Richmond. The SamStar team really did what needed to be done to give us that vibe. I left the party feeling very excited about Richmond getting a casino. That is, if we all vote yes in November."

"Is that what you left feeling like? Cuz I left that mother fucker feeling like I was in an episode of CSI!" Sienna countered.

Cece held her head down, embarrassed. "Now Sienna..." She wasn't sure how they were going to avoid mentioning Dreah's death while recapping the gala. She watched as Sienna took another swig of her drink, and fired more shots.

"No for real! I actually knew Dreah McDonald, rest in peace, from back in the day. A lot of y'all kids don't know her but she used to be a teen model in the 2000s. So boom! I see sis at the party, and I'm thinking, what is she doing here? Especially since she doesn't work in the industry anymore."

"Okay slow down Sienna. I want to explain my involvement. As some of y'all know, I teased my Out & Industry podcast trailer last week. For season one, I worked with the young lady who sadly lost her life at the gala"

Sienna's face became meddlesome, intent on hearing Cece loud and clear.

"She told me about an industry party back in 2005, where a picture was taken of a boxer and a transgender woman."

"But that down low gay shit was nothing new. We all knew people swinging from both ends. I ain't sayin' no names." Sienna took another swig.

"We're not saying *anybody's* name. Now, I heard the photographer who took this photo- which, by the way, absolutely exist-"

"It sure as hell does. I saw it with my own two eyes."

"Days after the party, he *allegedly* commits suicide. But then, it's later discovered that the photo he took also exposes a sex trafficking ring that can be linked to Goode Records."

"I'm not surprised. It's a real thing," Sienna co-signed.

"So I'm working with this girl for my podcast. I see her at the party, and then boom. She turns up dead!" Cece threw up her hands in an ultimate sign of surrender. "What the hell Sienna?"

She took sip of the dwindling cocktail and replied, "Well I was the first person she talked to about it that night. And I'm not gon' lie, sis was there to blow up the spot. She had to get some shit off her chest. When I last saw her, she was talking to the *wife* who passed out during the conversation. I was so embarrassed for her, I just grabbed Grant and went to shoot craps."

"I don't want to speak too much on her death, but, do you think she was murdered?"

Sienna rolled her eyes. She wasn't too inebriated to know she shouldn't accuse anyone of murder, but she'd say enough to let minds wonder. "I mean, it could be anything. She came there on a mission. We don't know what she was going through earlier that day. We don't know her drug history either. Maybe she overdosed. It might not be murder. But, and that's a *big* but, if she was killed- the resources were certainly available to men as powerful as the ones in the gala. That's all Imma say."

"Do you think the people in power, the ones in charge, had this young lady killed?"

"No ma'am. You save that for Out & Industry podcast."

"Oh c'mon! You got it started. What do you think?"

"I think this isn't the first time something like this happened, and it won't be the last."

Cece paused to check the amount of viewers. They were at roughly 100,000 people. She swallowed the lump in her throat, feeling the strong urge to end the LIVE.

"I'm scared. It's definitely time to go." She giggled, but it was the nervous kind. "Sienna, it's been so good talking to you. You are beautiful, and full of energy. Thank you for talking with me tonight. Y'all be sure to shop her boutique and support her business."

"And thank *you* Cece. It's been fun!"

"You go me shook AF. I still love you though. No, I love you even more. Take care."

And with that, the LIVE promptly ended, leaving her viewers (and Cedric) ghastly on edge.

Nineteen

Heavy drops of rain pierced through the thick air of Monday morning, finished by a dusty blue sky with a smattering of charcoal gray clouds. Evita appreciated it, as rain was always her sign of cleansing and renewal. One needed after a long week of juggling detective investigators, and dodging Sam and the scandal. In that effort to distance herself from Sam and media interest, she decided to pack up her life at the homes she shared with him.

Her marriage and everything it represented was now a cruel falsehood, a storybook dream that she no longer believed in. The home once stood as a castle, a domain dusted with photographic reminders of their love and family over the years; but now it served as a reminder of a marriage built on sand, with a foundation falling swiftly apart.

Cece's Instagram LIVE video had been the final blow. It spent the weekend making its way on urban media outlets. Grabs of a screen record viewed millions of times over. All to Evita's embarrassment. Reporters were relentless, but she made no comment.

The revelation about Sienna faking the pregnancy was a stab to the soul. For almost a decade, Evita had been privately thankful for the mistress's miscarriage; a baby birthed outside the marriage would've forced her into divorce, a step she wasn't ready to take at the time. Deep down, she hated her bitterness towards the woman. She felt that her ill feelings had brought the miscarriage on. But, lo and behold, the woman wasn't pregnant to begin with. Hearing Sienna cackle about it before an audience of one hundred thousand viewers made the hurt even worse. How much more could she endure?

Evita picked up the pace, knowing her husband would be there any minute to save himself. She had ignored his calls since the gala, while hiding out in a downtown Omni hotel suite to sort over the mess of her life. Anya would be pulling up within fifteen minutes to take her to a NoVa condominium that sat high above the city of Alexandria, overlooking the Potomac River.

The condo was purchased fully furnished, with an ambiance that rivaled the pages of Luxe Interiors & Design magazine. A clean refreshing space with panoramic views, the finest furniture and most modern of appliances awaited her. She would make it her sanctuary, and make way for a new life free of the Pitts last name.

Or should I keep it? She wondered, peaking out the master bathroom window at the James River. A couple drifted idly in a kayak along its dark waters, seemingly unfazed by the rain picking up every ten minutes. She wondered if they found it just as invigorating as she did.

At the sound of the front door opening and closing, Evita crossed back into the bedroom. Before she could zip up the last of her luggage, Sam ran into the room and began his plead.

"Damn it Evita. Please. You don't have to do this. You won't even give me a chance to handle it."

"I have no choice. Whose gonna believe that I didn't know you were trafficking Dreah? We're screwed forever because of this. Did you think about that when you were risking your business, for fuck's sake?" Evita had practiced her response for such a confrontation. It'd been days overdue after all. "Oh wait. The business is why you did it. And now there's picture proof that you and Dmitri were up to these sick antics."

"LeVario jumped out a fucking window before he had a chance to show me anything. I'd always thought the photo was about Hendrik and Zsarina- not Dmitri feelin' up a girl who I considered a daughter. I didn't know he was into that type of shit. And if I did, do you think I would've went into business with him? I'm just as pissed as you are about this."

"I bet you are, now that you're little secret is out. But you don't get to be angry about this. Not when *I'm* the fool! And I want no parts of this marriage." Evita moved past him, crossing into the walk-in closet to pack a smaller bag of her most precious jewelry and other accessories. Some given to her by Sam, others pieces she bought herself. She already had an inkling of which ones she would sell for profit.

"Get back here and talk to me!" roared Sam. "You're my wife, damn it!"

Evita stepped out of the closet, staring wildly at him. "Don't raise your voice at me. This isn't your turn to be outraged. I have every right to leave! Do you see what you're actions have done? What they're doing to your legacy? Cece's LIVE went viral. Everybody knows now! This will be talked about *forever*!"

Sam rolled his eyes as anger balled in his fist, creeping up his bulky arms and into the veins of his neck. "Fuck everybody! I'm your husband. Why don't believe me?"

"Because I know you!" Evita countered. She turned away, suddenly unable to face him. She held her teary face in the palm of her hand and wept a decade's worth of tears. The levy to a damn finally breached. Minutes had passed before she found the words to speak.

"God, Samuel. I fought myself all these years. Hypnotized by this fame and wealth. I almost forgot you met *me* as a fifteen years old girl still finding her way in life. You knew I could've been victim to the same shit y'all put Dreah through."

Evita thought it had been obvious to him back in the early 90s. She was a teen girl who recognized the feelings that overcame her when entering certain rooms was nothing more than her intuition, warning her that she was in the presence of evil.

She continued, "I've been to those industry parties. Handlers setting up my every move. Deals and decisions being made for me on the sake of *business.* They wanted me in places and circumstances I should've never been! I was just lucky enough, I thought, to have found a man who could save me. Who genuinely loved me and wanted do right by the mistake we made."

"Our son was no mistake, Evita. You know I loved you from the start." Sam started towards her, and grabbed her in a hug which she clawed her way out of.

"You didn't love me! I just satisfied your addictions."

Evita paused, wanting so badly to strike his face with an open hand. But she wouldn't. She remembered the last time she struck him physically, and how it *was* the last time.

Many years ago, her fury got the best of her and she attacked him. After seeing a doctor the next day, it was learned that he suffered a scratch on the conjunctiva of his left eye. From that day on, Evita noticed Sam's proclivity to do things to the left. Like walking with a gait that leaned leftward. Or driving closer to the left side of a street line versus staying within the middle. Evita always believed this to be from the damage she'd done. She almost cried when it was discovered he would (all of a sudden) need glasses to read and drive at night. And though Sam assured her it was due to his maturing in age, she never quite forgave herself for putting hands on him.

"Evita-"

She held up a finger to silence him, as words caught in her throat for years flowed freely from of her mouth. "I was 15 when I got pregnant with Kenny, and I was terrified. But I wasn't terrified for me, Sam. I was terrified for *you*. If word had got out that a 23 year old producer had impregnated a 15 year old model, your career would've been over before it started. So I hid myself to protect you. And we *only* got married to save face."

"We got married because we were in love."

"Yeah once upon a time I thought that too, but I know that isn't true. We got married because there was business to handle. And despite the many times you stepped out on me, I say we played the part very well. Raised our two boys, even took in a daughter…"

Again, Sam reached her for in an embrace. This time she allowed herself to melt in his arms, burying her face deep into the chest of the man she once loved beyond herself. He held her, and for a moment, believed there was hope for their marriage after all. But Evita pulled back, and the look on her face reminded him of their sad and strange reality.

"When that little girl told me about what you did, what you said… Samuel I can't forgive it. Damn, I just can't forgive it."

"It's not true, Evita. Baby it's just not true."

"And Sienna's lying too right?" Her tone was laced thick with sarcasm.

"I was just as disturbed by that bullshit on the LIVE. I got lawyers for all that. Cease and desist letters will be out by end of the week."

"Just like you to see what piece of legislation can solve a problem. As oppose to getting your hands dirty and handling it like a real man."

"I am handling it like a man! Be clear. If I handled shit myself I'd be in jail. There are better ways to do it."

"You had someone handle Dreah."

"I won't act like I'm not offended that you think I killed her," Sam retorted.

"You orchestrated it!"

Sam banged his fist atop the dresser, finally fed up with her tears and melodrama. "That's a lie Evita! You wanna know the truth? Truth is I woulda buried Dreah so deep in legal paperwork, by time we got to court she would've been broke and unavailable. The fuck I look like killing a bitch over a lie? If you think that's the man I am, then you don't know me. And maybe it is best you get out."

"Oh fuck you Sam!" Evita snapped back, now pulling her luggage out of the bedroom. "Damn right I'm out of here. And divorce papers will be on the way."

Sam exhaled loudly in an exhausted sigh that masked the pain he was feeling from losing his wife and marriage. He thought about life without her before changing his tune, saying, "Evita, baby wait! This is bad right now, but it's gonna blow over. The cops aren't even looking at me as the one who did it. And you know I couldn't have. I was on stage with you."

"So you had someone do it."

"And is that what you're gonna tell police when they question you again?"

Evita stopped at the top of the stairs and faced him. "I don't have anything more to say to them because I'm not sure what happened to Dreah. Just know, deep down, I believe it was you."

"Evita, you're making things worse by leaving. Don't do this. I still love you and want you in my life," Sam replied. He reached for her arm but she pulled it back, appearing frightened of him. And that's when he knew it was really over.

She choked over sobs, until she was able to finally say, "I've done all I'm willing to do for us. We've raised wonderful young men. Kenny is strong, and smart. And I'm gonna get Grant some help."

The Instagram LIVE had reared its ugly head once again. Though ashamed, Sam nodded in agreement. "I want to help Grant too."

"Then you won't mind me setting up a family intervention soon, and paying for his treatment. I'll be in touch about it."

The sound of the doorbell took both of their attention. Evita dragged her suitcases down the steps, assuming it was Anya, though she told her to text when she was outside. She figured the mom-to-be had to use the bathroom.

When Evita pulled the front door open, she was startled to see Tati standing there with a folder and handbag in hand and arm. Too cheery-eyed for the turmoil she was going through. She hated to be seen in her despair by the publicist.

"Just this arrogant looking bitch," Evita muttered loud enough for Tati to hear.

The comment took Tati aback, and to a place and time she thought she'd healed from. Growing up, she found it hard to make friends due to them judging her based on her looks. The high yella' green-eyed girl no one could trust. *'You look stuck up'*. *'You look conceited'*. *'You look mean'*. Tati had heard it all, all her life, and always went out of her way to prove the voices of her teenage years wrong. But she'd have to let Evita's comment slide, and instead chose to remain professional.

"Well hello to you too. I was coming over to discuss some rebranding and image consulting. You know, in lieu of all that's-"

"Fuck off Tati!" Evita spat.

Tati's face dropped its pleasantry. She crossed her arms over her chest and leaned on one hip, wondering how much more she could take. "Is there a problem?"

"So you can fix that too? Get the fuck on, will you? I never liked you. Probably sleeping with Sam for another bonus! Is that what you're here for?"

"Is now a good time?" Tati shot a look to Sam, now appearing in the doorway.

He just nodded, then rolled his eyes behind Evita's back.

"Mrs. Pitts-"

"It's *Evita*."

"Evita, I just wanted to see if you'd be willing to work on a campaign to save face. I know Kenny's birthday is coming up. We can have you two help out a homeless shelter, the children's center. Maybe get some photographers to catch the shot..."

Evita was insulted, yet impressed, as Tati went on.

"Now's a good time to donate funds to a women's shelter. Or maybe pay off some rents in lower income areas. We just want to show the public that we *do* care about victims of sexual abuse. And as we firmly deny all accusations, we just as firmly believe in law enforcement's ability to conduct a thorough investigation."

"And here it was I thought you wanted to sleep your way to the top. No, you actually are smart," Evita scoffed, looking between Sam and Tati.

Tati moved out of the way as Evita crossed over the threshold, luggage and matching tote bag in tow. Anya was finally pulling into the driveway.

Sam motioned Tati inside, and shut the door behind them. He rushed past Tati in the foyer, leading her to the leather sofa of the living room.

"So I guess that plan is out." Tati tucked her folder under her arm and watched as Sam's leg bounced in an anxious quirk.

"How's Vernon?"

"Concerned," Tati replied.

Sam exhaled, swallowed in the great open of the living room. He started to speak, "Look Tati. Sometimes men do things they regret."

Ignoring that, Tati carried on, "Concerned for you, but not with *allegations*. What comes to the light of day by way of a courtroom is different, but as of now, there's no backing out. Vernon Hines is still very interested in your endorsement."

Sam looked up to meet her gaze as gratitude softened his chiseled features, a newfound calm turning his frown. She regarded the shift in his body language and continued.

"And as *your* publicist, I have a few different ways we can protect your family and the brand. I just need to know what you're willing to do."

"Alright Tati. Show me what you got."

Twenty

Anya would've gotten out the car to help Evita had she not been pregnant. There was no way she could haul her sister's belongings into the trunk and back seat. Not with her back pain, a new symptom of the pregnancy. She unlocked the car doors so Evita could put her luggage inside. Then, she looked to the front porch to see Sam rushing Tati into the home. Evita collapsed into the passenger seat and slammed the car door shut.

"What is Tati doing here?"

"Plans for damage control. The bitch is sick. Let's get out of here." Evita pouted and stared out the window, fighting the onset of more tears.

"Whew," Anya exhaled. "This is really happening. How does Sam feel about all this? You moving out?"

"I don't wanna talk about it."

"Okay, fine. Have you talked to investigators since last Sunday?"

"Not me. But Sam spoke with them the other night. I'm sure they'll be back once they find out he had someone kill Dreah."

"Are you sure it was Sam though? She pissed off a lot of people that night." Anya put the car in drive, and pulled away from the property.

"Sam has the most to lose. He set it up for sure."

"But can you prove that?"

"Not exactly, but I know him!"

"If it came down to it, would you testify against him? You're still his wife, Evita."

"I'm his wife *for now*. When this divorce is done, he'll regret ever meeting me. I am gonna get what's mine in the settlement," said Evita. She turned to meet Anya's frown of uncertainty. "Why are you asking me this?"

"Detectives want to talk Daryl and me again. I don't want to relive it anymore. I'm trying to forget what I saw, but I just cant." Anya shivered as the sight of Dreah's lifeless body slumped over the toilet came to mind. She steadied the car wheel on the winding backroads, driving them away from the estate grounds. "Where am I taking you? To Alexandria?"

"I have to stop by the penthouse first. Kenny's there with the truck, and Pia's gathering some belonging for me."

Anya sucked her teeth. "Now why are you bringing them two into this?"

"They're just helping me move. Relax, Anya."

And Anya did, despite her additional questions.

When they arrived on Virginia Street, Kenny was locking the door to a U-Haul cargo trailer hitched to the back of his Yukon Denali, parked at the entrance of the building.

"Where's Pia?" Evita asked him as she exited Anya's car.

"She's inside, grabbing the last of it," answered Kenny.

Evita quickly took the elevator to the floor of the penthouse, and found Pia inside the living room. The entrance interrupted the assistant, who was in deep thought as she reviewed the list of belongings she'd been ask to pack up.

"Evita! You're here. I thought we were meeting you in Alexandria," Pia said when she turned towards her. It became clear the woman had been crying.

Evita launched herself forward into Pia's embrace. She could feel every bit of confusion and hurt the woman wallowed in.

"You're gonna be okay, boss lady. You gotta know that." Pia looked her in the eyes as she said it. "This will pass over."

Evita nodded her head, wishing so desperately she could believe that. She gently patted Pia's shoulder and decided not to remind her that the storm had only just begun. Instead, she looked to the list in her hand and asked, "Were you able to get everything?"

"Just about. Last box is down the hall. Kenny says we'll have to load it up in my car, so I'll be following y'all to Alexandria."

"Thank you," Evita said in what sounded like a whisper. Then, in the same faint voice, "Did Kenny tell you if he spoke to Dreah at the gala?"

Pia appeared thoughtful, having to think it over. "Not about what. Just that they spoke."

"Does he believe her?"

Pia's eyes lowered. Of course Evita knew her son better than she ever could. She wasn't sure what to say, and mustered up an answer of, "Evita, I don't know about that."

"I know he knows. Kenny hasn't been himself since the gala. He hasn't said a thing about it, and I'm ashamed to ask if he believes in his father's guilt or innocence."

"I think Kenny wants to remain neutral, and still support you, as his mother."

"I can't imagine how this feels for him. I know he loves his dad, but I don't know if he understands my position as a woman." Evita wiped her eyes, the tears set to fall again if she didn't.

"Listen, between you and me, everybody's conflicted. Especially, those of us who haven't experienced Sam in the way Dreah said she had."

Evita winced at the visions Pia's last words gave her. Ones that she only saw in the darkness of her mind when trying to fall asleep. She was then reminded of something she'd been wanting to do, a conversation she'd been needing to have with the assistant. "That night in Atlanta-"

"Oh, don't worry about that." Pia didn't want to go there, *especially* after the events of the gala.

"-I should've never came onto you, or invited you into our bedroom. It was unprofessional and inappropriate. And I'm sorry."

Pia grinned, not sure how to accept an apology she didn't need. "You're fine. It'll stay between you and me."

Evita nodded with eyes that bounced from Pia's, to the room around them, which now felt coldly unfamiliar and unsafe.

Suddenly, Kenny barged through the door, startling both the women. He chuckled at their hunched shoulders and wide eyes, unsure of why they appeared so caught off guard.

"Geez mom! Now I'm really starting to think you wanna steal my assistant. What's going on here?"

He walked over and planted a kiss on her forehead. Evita flashed a nervous smile and tossed Pia a look.

"I was just thanking Pia for helping us out today. I'm gonna double check to make sure we got everything," Evita said. She quickly left the living room, hurrying past the kitchen towards her old bedroom.

Kenny's and Pia's eyebrows drew together in an exchange of puzzling expressions, both of them trying to pry something out of the other. Pia took the bait first.

"She's worried about you. About how all of this makes you feel."

Kenny shrugged his shoulders mechanically. "I don't know. I'm not thinking about it yet. I'm just helping my mom, as any good son would. Eh, anyways... there's some shit going down with the gaming and commission board."

Pia's expression was blank. "Really? I can't imagine why."

"I thought we dotted I's and crossed our T's on this?"

"Do you know what it's about?"

"I was hoping you did. I haven't replied to my dad's text. Or his calls. Or his emails." Kenny shrugged again as his hands pulled at the lint in his pockets. "I'll get around to it and let you know."

"You still haven't talked to your dad?" She watched as he shook his head and crossed over to the window, overlooking downtown with his hands still in his pockets. Something about his body language seemed off, and fretful.

"I don't know what to say to him. Not sure I want to hear what he has to say to me."

"You can't avoid it any longer. SamStar Enterprises needs you," Pia said, appearing behind him. She slipped her arm into his and leaned a sympathetic head on his shoulder.

"No, I need SamStar Enterprises. Pia, what if this shit destroys the business? What if they put my dad in jail for this? Then how are we supposed to recover?"

"You have parents who are divorcing, a brother in treatment and employees that need your guidance. I don't know if you should worry about that right now."

"Easier said than done. You know this culture is unforgiving of pedophiles and shit like that."

"What exactly did Dreah tell you the night of the gala?"

Kenny shook his head, adamant about something but he wasn't willing to offer up details on what was said. "That's not who my dad is. I've never seen no shit like that at SamStar Enterprises. There's no way he would risk his life or his family."

"And what about this Dmitri guy?"

"What about him? He's dead, been dead for years. And I'm quite sure his family is embarrassed they have to defend him about this."

Pia fixed her lips to ask him a question she'd been afraid to ask. She figured she'd wait for the right time, but now was as good a time as any. It might've been the only time she'd catch him so vulnerable. "Is there any chance your dad could be involved?"

"With the murder or the trafficking?" Kenny could use the clarification.

"*Both*."

An answer didn't come directly, not one that Kenny was willing to speak aloud. He tightened his jaw, thinking carefully about how he would reply. Finally, he decided on, "I think I need to talk to my dad."

"Yeah, that's a good start."

The pair piped up, noses whiffing at the smell of marijuana suddenly permeating the air. Pia looked at Kenny with curious eyes, and pointed to the hallway.

"Evita?" she mouthed. For all their time together, she never knew the woman was a user of marijuana.

Kenny nodded, answering, "Medicinal use only, let her tell it. Anxiety and depression and all that shit."

Moments later, Evita came back into the living room, looking both cheery and glassy eyed. She met the shy gazes of her son and his assistant, and quickly looked away.

"You good now mama?" Kenny said, meeting her in the middle of the room.

"Boy don't make this anymore awkward than what it already is. You know my get down." Evita concealed a smirk. "One last time in the penthouse. Alexandria doesn't offer the same vibe."

"Better strains up there, though," Pia giggled.

"That I know! Which reminds me, I need to stop by the store so I can pick up some clear eye drops. Anya's a little judgmental. The type to stare into your soul and scare you straight."

"I think I have some in my truck. You can just have mine," Kenny said as he crossed the dining room towards the bedroom door. "Hey, mama, is that box ready?"

"Yeah it is! Bring it down, will you please?" Evita instructed as she and Pia exited the penthouse.

They took the elevator down to the lobby, and stepped outside into the day. As the women walked to Kenny's Denali, a dark sedan started its slow creep down Virginia Street, lurking towards them. All eyes went to the car when its tires began to screech like a wild animal, burning rubber against the road as it suddenly dashed down the street.

Anya first spotted the Beretta M9 pointing out of the driver window. She opened her car door and screamed, "Get down!"

Both Evita and Pia turned fast eyes on the oncoming sedan as it sped down Virginia Street. When the gun (now pointed directly at them) registered to mind, the two women fell to the ground behind the SUV. Anya jumped back into the Audi as the Beretta fired a reckless shot into the sky.

Kenny, exiting the building with a large box in hand, heard the shot as it cracked the air. He heard Anya screaming in her car, still parked. Then he noticed Evita and Pia lying on the ground, hiding behind his truck. He dropped the box and ran quickly down the sidewalk to them.

"What the fuck was that?" Kenny asked. "You two okay?"

Evita and Pia rose to their feet as Anya approached.

"They pointed a gun! Whoever that was may aim and not miss next time. You think it's related to the gala?" Anya's face was plastered in worry.

Evita didn't want to speculate who she thought it could be. Her theories ranged from Sam's bodyguards to a random hoodlum. Either way, it was someone who knew where she called home. Even more reason to distance herself from Sam and the post-gala madness.

Anya continued pressing for an explanation. "Are we being followed? Evita you could've been killed! Is this something Sam would do? Because if so-"

"Hell no," Kenny muttered loud enough for her to hear. "My dad ain't behind this."

"Well then who is?" Anya was relentless.

"I don't know Auntie! But I'll find out. Ma, you alright?"

Evita tossed him a concerned look and answered, "I gotta get out of here." She didn't know what the incident was about, but it was enough to scare her right out of Richmond. She placed a hand over her chest, but her heartbeat had yet to slow. The adrenaline was still pumping through her.

Kenny looked as Anya consoled his panicked mother. She was shaken, but she wouldn't voice that to him. He delegated, "Auntie, take her straight to Alexandria. Pia, you'll have to hold a box in your lap 'cause you're riding with me."

Anya nodded, wrapped an arm around Evita and turned her towards the Audi. She looked back at Kenny, saying, "Call me when you guys are on the road."

"We'll be right behind you!" Kenny assured her.

When the two sisters were out of earshot, Pia asked him, "Where's *your* gun?"

"In the car. I wasn't expecting it to pop off here of all places," he told her.

"Well it's time you keep it on you," Pia replied, still catching her breath from the fright just moments before.

Kenny knew that, and most important of all, he knew it was time to talk to his father.

Twenty One
June 29 | 4:40 pm

Jogging was never Pia's sport, and on this evening she trailed Tati the former college track star, who cleared the Canal Walk like a gazelle in the grasslands. Pia paused to catch her breath, looking up at the rows of lamppost lining the canal. The old time architecture of downtown bridges surrounded them, swallowing Pia up in its audaciousness. The shrubs of greenery whispered gracefully with the power of the wind. Wind that very well could have been caused by Tati's wickedly fast pace.

Thirty minutes earlier, they started on the James River Trail, and it took them to the Canal Walk. This was Tati's idea and now Pia wished she hadn't come.

"This is not fair," Pia said in between big breaths. "I'm not built for this-- That's all you-- You got it sis." Then she dropped to the nearest set of steps to rest. She brought a Yeti water bottle to her lips and stared into the murky waters of the Canal.

"Couldn't we have settled for dinner at Casa Del Barco?" Pia asked as Tati trotted backwards to the steps where she sat. "Food and drinks is more my speed."

"Ah c'mon this is good for us! And what happened to being outside?" Tati laughed.

"No I meant outside, but in like... spaces where I'm not working out. Girl I coulda went to my building's gym if I wanted to sweat." Pia suddenly longed for the comfort of her high floor apartment at The Locks Tower. The building was completed in 2020 and sat right behind the Richmond Canal, only minutes from where they were. It offered views of the ever expanding Richmond skyline, a cozy balcony and open living space.

"Are you sure you don't want to take this to my place?" Pia asked with pleading eyes and prayer hands. "Better views and a minibar."

"I have burned my 700 calories for the day and I am not drinking another 500 of them," Tati said as she tapped on the screen of her iWatch. "Besides, tonight I start the damage control tour. I'm meeting with Cece. *Obviously* her LIVE brought us some unwanted attention."

"What about me? I want some attention," Pia whined with an innocent grin. "To be honest, I'm lucky to be alive today."

Tati stood hands on hips and swayed side to side. She heard about the shooting scare hours after it happened, when Pia called her from Alexandria in tears. "Scared you pretty bad. You feeling better today?"

"I was, until those detectives asked to speak with me again. Now I'm wondering if that bullet was meant to scare me."

"Really?" Tati wasn't expecting to hear that. "Why would that bullet be for you though? You're not involved in that shit from their past."

"Yeah. I think I was one of the last people she talked to."

Pia looked around them; she noticed a man taking a picture of the canal and light posts with his phone. She lowered her voice and said,

"Tati, I have something to tell you but I swear you can't say a word to anybody! This is between you and me?"

"C'mon, you know me. I'm the official keeper of secrets. But you're scaring me here. What's going on?"

"When I was in in Atlanta with the Pitts, Evita invited me into their bedroom."

Tati gasped. "No she didn't." Then, believing her, she asked, "Did you join them?"

"I was going to. No shame in my game. But she put the brakes on that at the last minute. Beats me as to why." She shrugged and moved to stretch her legs.

"You know she's insecure. And the only one worse than her is her little sister," Tati giggled with an eye roll. "But I'll be damned! Whole time she's accusing me of sleeping my way to the top, and *you* were about to do just that."

Pia gave her steely eyes. "How dare you." Then her face softened with a humored smile, lasting only seconds before she went serious again. "What if they want me silenced now that Dreah's story is out there?"

"Silenced over a threesome that never happened?" Tati stifled a laugh. "Girl please! Evita's divorcing Sam. And he's got too many other problems to count. They ain't worried about you."

"So that would mean he's after Evita."

"I wouldn't say all that-"

"Oh c'mon. Take yourself out of work mode for one minute. I'm your friend, Tati."

Tati sighed and let her hands fall to her side. She took a needed seat near Pia on the steps and looked around. They were alone. "This is serious shit. I'm actually losing sleep over this job."

"So Sam is being looked at by police?"

"Girl everybody is. But there's no way he could've done it. He was on stage and the whole party saw him. But the security guard he ordered to escort her out was found with her cell phone."

"I asked Neville about that. He said she gave him the phone as like- *collateral*. Then she went to the restroom and never came out."

"You believe him?" Tati was curious.

"I actually do. Neville made it clear that he was taking her outside. He ordered the Uber!"

"And Sam's not stupid enough to order a hit at the gala. He gives me the vibes of a man far more calculated than that," added Tati. She stood up and stretched her body as the man from earlier returned, this time to capture himself in a selfie.

A picture for sure, Tati thought. His hand was too still to be filming a video. But still, she didn't like his being there. She appeared thoughtful and continued,

"I think she knew all along she was going to stir up trouble. That morning, Alchemia's Instagram page posted a 'Be Back Soon' post. The caption said the store would be closed *until further notice*. Weird, right?"

Pia looked away, a nervous expression dropping her face. "This whole thing is strange. I'd hate to be you. But girl, if you get SamStar out of this, you'll be the best damn publicist in the country."

"Yeah don't remind me. The universe ain't making this easy." Tati shook her head and realized the job would require more work than she cared to do. "Well, this concludes our time together. You're dismissed."

"You bitch!" Pia joked. The two women exchanged playful jabs and embraced each other in a hug.

"I'll call you later!" Each promised as they departed; Pia for the big bed that stared over downtown, and Tati for her West End apartment to freshen up for her next stop.

She was scheduled to meet Cece in Shockoe Bottom, at Casa Fiesta. The underground Mexican restaurant complete with dim festive lighting, candy skull paintings and a Frida themed dining room was the perfect place to have a their conversation.

Cece watched from the bar as Tati descended the stairs into the restaurant in a pair of bedazzled crocs and a cozy jogger set. She beckoned the publicist to the empty seat beside her.

"So glad you could meet up tonight," Tati said warmly, in her friendliest business tone. "Thanks for accepting my invitation."

"I really had no choice in the matter. I'm sorry about the LIVE." Cece wouldn't delay the opportunity to address the reason they were there. "Would you like a drink?"

"No, no. I won't be long. I've got to turn in early tonight. Big weekend ahead."

Cece nodded and picked up a chip. She dipped it into the chunky house salsa and lifted it to her mouth as Tati dived head first into the conversation. She took another chip and stirred the warm queso with it.

"Listen, in today's culture, I know how it goes. I'm sure you weren't expecting things to go left on the LIVE. Sienna said Dreah's name, and that wasn't cool."

Cece knew as much when she ended the LIVE days ago. "I understand," she said before taking a long sip of her skinny girl margarita.

"Speaking of Sienna, she has been served a cease and desist letter. That's all we can do with her. Sam wants to let the law do the talking. You, however, are different."

Cece swallowed the alcohol, and the lump in her throat. She hoped she didn't appear nervous, but knew some amount of worry was fixated on her face.

"I have no real stake in this story. I'm coming to you strictly as a publicist for the company, and it's nothing personal. We've reviewed our options and would prefer *not* to take a legal route with you and the station."

"The station?"

"Yes, the radio station, whom you a subsidiary of."

"But I did that live on my personal brand's time."

"It still reflects negatively on them because you're their personality. I mean, you do have them listed in your Instagram bio, with a link to their website. Has anyone from personnel contacted you yet?"

Cece stirred the ice in her drink with a straw, choosing to remain silent.

"I'll take that as a no, and I hope we can avoid them altogether if you're willing to implement these steps." Tati pulled out a planner and thumbed to a page under the day's date. "As you know this is an active investigation and we encourage law enforcement to do their jobs. We certainly don't want some washed up video model putting mess out into the media by way of your platform. Cece, you have to know that what you two did was tactless."

Cece slammed her palm on the bar top and kept her voice low saying, "Damn it Tati. I get it. The live went left. We didn't even post it on our YouTube channel after lots of consideration."

"The damage of screen recording was already done. But that's beneath us now. Here's what we request," Tati said, looking down at her planner. "On the radio show, you can air a formal apology for the direction the live went, advising that you in no way want to compromise the integrity of what is *still* an active police investigation. You don't wish to belittle the importance of your brand by entertaining conversation that implicates anyone in SamStar Enterprises or the Pitts family."

"Will I get a copy of that?" Cece's question dripped with sarcasm as thick as the queso on her chip. She rolled her eyes as exasperation turned her features.

"I've already emailed you," Tati said with a smile.

Cece shook her head, incredulous. "You gotta be kidding me." Then, a new question came to mind, and it certainly needed to be asked. "But what if I have proof that Dreah wasn't lying?"

"Are you going to police with it? Or is this simply for the sake of podcast entertainment? And did *you* encourage her to go to the police?" Tati challenged.

She had researched everything about Cece the Talkative, including her deal with MysterPodcast Networks and her job at the local radio station. "The things Dreah accused Samuel Pitts of should have been taken to law authorities from jump; this should have never been gossip and grist for the mill. Especially in today's day and age? Accusations like this are known to destroy a man's reputation and his business. Your LIVE fueled that fire."

Cece shook her head, wishing she had stuck to topics like satanic worship in hip hop and 'Is Tupac still alive?' theories.

"Tati, listen to me. No, I didn't encourage Dreah to talk to police. I wish I did though. But I was focused on my project, one that she was a willing participant of. Do you think investigators will need to speak with me?"

"You threw yourself into the mix with the LIVE. Not to mention, your podcast. That will stir the pot." Tati shrugged her shoulders, waving her hands in a 'told-you-so' kind of flair. "If they get wind of that, I'm sure you will be spoken to. Just tread lightly, I guess. You can start by airing an apology. It'll help smooth things over with not just your job, but your conscience."

When Cece failed to reply back, Tati continued, "Cece, I like you, and your voice on RVA airwaves is refreshing. One hometown girl to another, I'm looking out for you. I'd hate for you to be wrapped up in a legal battle with SamStar Enterprises. Do you even have a lawyer?"

"Not me personally, but the radio has a legal department."

"You can consult with them if you'd like, but c'mon- you don't wanna be the girl who dragged them into this. I'm sure if

Dreah could do it all over again, she would have stayed home. Instead we found this girl dead with her neck cracked over a toilet. This is a disaster for the Pitts family, and they're working very closely with law enforcement to see it through." Tati rose from the bar and gathered her belongings. "I'll cover your bill. Save yourself and make the apology."

Cece nodded, repeating the words to herself. She took a sip of her drink as Tati placed more than enough money on the counter. She watched as the publicist ascended up the stairs, out of the restaurant and into the humid night.

Tati felt rather accomplished as she pressed along the cobblestone streets of Shockoe Bottom, towards her car parked on 13th. The stiff breeze was a reminder that summer had begun, and promised to bring all the heat with its seasonal reign. She smiled to herself, wondering if she'd ever like the season.

A pair of eyes leered at her through dark shades, watching as the young woman crossed the street towards her car. As she opened the driver side door, a sudden rush of two men from behind overtook her; a hand clasped over her mouth and a hood fell over her head as both pairs of hands held her in place.

Blinded, she struggled between them and screamed for help through the palm held tight over her mouth. When they pushed her into the driver seat, Tati felt it was best she just comply. She stopped screaming and fighting, and succumbed to the fear.

A raspy voice whispered into her ear. "Don't fuck this up for us! Watch your step bitch!"

The assailants slammed the car door shut and took off into the night. Tati ripped the hood from her head and rushed to get out of the driver's seat. She looked behind her, in the direction they had run. All she could see were the backsides of two figures dressed in all black. She cursed as they disappeared around the corner.

A moment later, Tati heard car tires screeching down the street. Her eyes widened at the sound of a backfire, followed by a motorcycle sputtering to life and roaring away. Tati jumped, startled by what sounded like a gun shot, and spooked by the out of place chill than ran through her body.

Twenty Two
June 30 | 1:03 pm

Mona's Cigar Lounge was fairly quiet for this early Wednesday afternoon, and Sam preferred it that way given the nature of the conversation he was about to have with Mina. She'd always been good to the business and a true friend to the Pitts family over the decades. Nowadays she wasn't trusting of any public spaces, but agreed to meet him at Mona's because she loved the hot wings.

Ever since the gala, they shared the uncanny feeling of being watched. Maybe even hunted. Something that went beyond paparazzi and media fascination. Sam tried to ignore the penthouse scare as just a strange coincidence. He wasn't the type to live in fear and continued on with business as usual, letting lawyers handle what they were rightfully paid to deal with.

But the events this morning changed that. After parking his car in the parking deck, Sam crossed the perfectly manicured sidewalks of the West Broad Village shopping center and headed towards Mona's. As he crossed the street, a dark blue sedan flew down Old Brick Road, nearly missing him. It would have struck him had he not ran the last bit of the crosswalk.

Inside the lounge, he secured their seats on a leather loveseat, and a hookah was propped on a dining coffee table before them. Even in the brightness of the day, the room held its warm ambiance with dim lighting and classic jazz flair. A pianist freestyled his talents, serenading the few guest with popular numbers.

Mina snaked through furniture of the lounge. Relief washed her over her when Sam embraced her with a firm hug that she needed just as badly as he.

She sat down and blew the wind from her jaws. She waited for him to be seated before saying, "Thanks for getting me the hookah. You ordered food yet?" She pulled at the hose and placed a fresh plastic tip in the mouthpiece.

"Wings and salad are on the way," answered Sam. He put a Cuban cigar to his lips and pulled. After gently exhaling the smoke into the air, he continued. "Shit is crazy right now Mina. My wife left me, my son hasn't spoken to me, and shit just got worse. We're under investigation by the gaming commission."

"What the hell? How?"

"Allegedly the employees working the tables didn't have gaming licenses, and the company funded a casino themed party where guests won *cash prizes*."

"Damn Sam. The state will always want its money."

"On top of that, some of the skill game machines weren't registered with the VABC Authority."

"They're getting rid of those things end of the month anyway. I don't understand why that's a problem."

"Well, while it's still legal, the state wants its cut."

"And the wolves sunk their teeth in," said Mina, in charismatic fashion.

Sam tossed her a shrewd glare. "Tati seems to think if we pay the penalties and fines before July, it'll go away quietly."

"And you're prepared to do that?"

"Lawyers are looking into the numbers as we speak."

"Well you know, when the casino comes to town you'll be back in good graces. This will be nothing more than a growing pain. That was a beautiful speech you and the Mayor gave at the gala. I think it was enough to win some people over for the November vote."

"I hope so. The land's been purchased and hands already shook. There's too much money to be made."

"I'm glad you're so confident. *Especially* after the gala."

"I'm not as confident as you think. Vernon's still on board, but I don't know for how long."

"Dreah's death was a bad look for us. I wasn't expecting her to pop up at the gala only to die."

"No shit. I even reached out to Diondra to send flowers. And now she wants to meet up."

"Do you think that's a good idea?"

"I don't know, but she's in town and I owe her some sort of explanation."

"Maybe you should talk to her. You can see what she knows, or what police are telling her. Get her on our side..."

"What the fuck you talkin' 'bout, Mina?"

Mina sighed, tormented by the question she was getting ready to ask. A moment passed before she found the courage to say, "Let me get straight to my question. Because you know my loyalty is not just to the Pitts family, but to SamStar Enterprises. And even if the answer is yes, you know you can trust me. Did you do it, Sam?"

"No I didn't. Do you know how much shit we got on the line with this casino? I can't afford no murder investigation."

"We can't afford scandals either. I'm not saying I'm glad the girl is dead, but sheesh! Did you hear the things she was saying? You should've heard what she said to me. No disrespect but if I knew I could get away with it, I would've offed her myself." Mina made sure to keep their voices low.

But the woman meant what she said. Dreah had some nerve bringing up Kenny's fifteenth birthday. Making it sound far worse than what it was. Sam had only asked her to feel Kenny up; get his dick hard and show him how to put a condom on. She never told Sam that his son practically jizzed himself in less than three minutes, unable to stand her game of tug and pull. And she wouldn't bring it up now.

"Don't say shit like that. This problem got worse because she turned up dead. We could've handled her allegations in a courtroom. Buried her in legal paperwork before shit even seen the light of day. Now she's dead, and this clown Sienna runs her big mouth."

Mina's eyes widened as she pulled at the hookah. "Don't even get me started. I know you got a lawyer on that. And who the hell was she even talking to? Who is the blogger?"

"She's actually a local radio host, and Tati's asked her to make an apology. She knew she was dead wrong for entertaining it. It shouldn't have been discussed on social media to begin with.

I already got these detectives and investigators in my shit. I've seen these mother fuckers at least three times in the past two days."

"What are they asking?"

"The usual. How did I know Dreah? What was our run-in at the party about? People saw this, people saw that... But they not pinning me for no murder because I didn't do it. They'll get an autopsy, and compare the time she died to when I was on that stage. *And* with our mayor. I got the mayor as an alibi, for God's sake."

"Shit. Guess I should look out for some cops showing up at my door again too. Since they're going off what people allegedly saw at the party."

"Did you do it Mina?"

"Kill Dreah? Hell nah! And if I did she wouldn't have been found in that damn stall. And what exactly happened with that? Was there blood? Was she stabbed or something?" Mina had become more annoyed by the turn of events than afraid.

"When we found her it looked like she drowned in the damn toilet bowl. Choked on her own vomit."

"Gross." Mina frowned. "So this could be an overdose?"

Sam raised his eyebrows inquisitively, an answer resting in his clenched jaw. "I heard a toxicology report was ordered on top of the autopsy, but no results yet. Thanks to all the confrontations she had that night, they're assuming its murder."

"I just can't understand why she came to the party. Who invited her in the first place?"

Sam's face lit up in a tight smirk. "Your best friend did."

"Damn it. She ain't know no better." Mina took a long pull of the hookah and appeared thoughtful. "Speaking of Evita, I'm sorry to hear what happened. She hasn't returned any of my calls. I know our friendship is over."

Sam shrugged hopelessly, saying, "Eh, you're not the only one she's ignoring. I heard she reached out to a divorce lawyer. Figured it's been a long time coming."

"I don't get it though. If she leaves you, it'll look suspicious. It'll look like you *did* have something to do with all this. Then again, if she stays, what does that say?" Mina considered the public outcry towards a woman who would stay with a man accused of sex trafficking. Evita really had no choice in the matter. "She'd be just as guilty in the eyes of the media."

"Well she already thinks I am. I guess she's doing what's best for her." Just saying the words disgusted Sam, especially knowing he wasn't the reason for Dreah's demise. "I wish I could make her believe me. Maybe she needs me to be cleared by law enforcement."

Mina surrendered a smile. "Or, maybe she needs time."

Not buying it, Sam cocked his head to the side and asked, "Would *you* stay?"

Mina winced and looked away from him. The answer was obvious. "But Evita is different. She loves love. She very well could return home and push through this. It's just scandal. You've certainly survived it before."

"No. It's different this time around." Sam paused to draw in the smoke of his dwindling cigar. "Scandal became a murder."

"What if someone's fucking with us? What if a third party killed Dreah just to bring us under investigation and slow us down?" Mina was sure she was onto something.

"Who would wanna do that?"

"I don't know. Maybe somebody from back in the day, who felt like they needed to silence her for us."

"But why do it at the gala?"

"Because it turns the heat up on us. And it worked."

"So, is this person working with Dreah or against her?"

Mina shook her head, confused now. "Fuck. I don't know anymore."

"If you ask me," Sam began. "Someone didn't want Dreah to make it out of the convention center. My thing is, who was willing to risk the heat when this went south? I even thought about Evita being involved. She's the one who invited her. Maybe she's just using this as a way to frame me."

His theories bothered Mina more than her own. She realized this when their meeting was over, as she walked to the parking garage to her Lexus truck. It just didn't make sense for

Evita to harm Dreah. If she did, why divorce Sam? Was it all just a ruse to divorce him under the right circumstance?

The shopping center was fairly busy now, with several cars lurking the parking deck for a space. A sedan started up the ramp just as she got to the crosswalk. It waved her on, and Mina took the opportunity to hurry through the crosswalk.

The same vehicle followed her slowly, almost stalkily- as if it wanted her spot. Mina, having not parked far from the entrance, turned around to motion she was leaving. Of course they could take her spot. She caught a quick glimpse of the driver, who was shielded by sun glasses and a black face mask.

Mina slowed down as she came upon the Lexus. As did the sedan, which she now realized was dark blue and heavily tinted. She quickly got into the Lexus, threw the car in drive and turned out of the space. She expected the sedan to take the spot she left vacant, but on Old Brick Road she realized it had followed her.

She looped the shopping center, just to be sure that she wasn't falsely paranoid. The sedan followed her into the next strip mall plaza and into the subdivision behind the shopping center. And when she damn near ran through a yellow light to make a right on Street, the sedan did the same thing.

Mina moved her eyes from the traffic ahead to the sedan in the rearview mirror. She was able to finagle her way from left lane to right lane, making a last second dash onto the Interstate 64 entry ramp- while the sedan was forced to stay put on Broad.

Mina sighed in relief, but her fears of being followed still lingered in every breath.

Twenty Three

June 30 | 5:12 pm

Grant's legs bounced uncontrollably with paranoia as he sat on the bench. He didn't want to pass the tick off as a symptom of his withdrawal, but it very well could have been. Since his enrollment in treatment, he'd become a shell of his former self. Learning who he was off drugs was frightening, in ways that caused him to always look over his shoulder, and provided him a profuse sweat condition. Then there were the shakes. The kind of nervous ticks that others told him would fade after detox. Only three days in, he couldn't see the forest from the trees. But he wouldn't dare disappoint his mother, who showed the most concern since his habit had been made public.

From behind him, a voice said, "Grant! You made it!"

Cece's warm and cheerful tone was almost as pleasant as the sherbet evening sky above them, and as loud as the traffic around them. A much needed pleasantry for Grant's looming depression.

They embraced underneath the Bill "Bojangles" Robinson statue, a historic landmark on the triangular corner of Leigh, Adams, and Chamberlayne Parkway, and reclined to the nearby bench where Grant had been sitting.

"Cedric was nice enough to set this up."

"I didn't know he was your engineer. Mane, that's my family. I'll do anything for bruh. Including meeting yo' ass in Jackson damn Ward! You couldn't meet me down VCU somewhere?" Grant chortled out what was a much needed laugh.

"Since my LIVE, I've been trying to keep a low profile."

"Hey I hear you. Since I started this sober shit, I been feeling like somebody's watching me. Jackson Ward though? Sure that mother fucker won't follow me here."

Cece giggled and nudged him playfully. "Nothing wrong with one of the most historic spots in the city. I just wanted to talk to you about a few things. First and foremost, I owe you a sincere apology. If I had known Sienna was gonna spill your secret on my LIVE, I would have never done it."

"The bitch is a bird. I should've known she'd sing. You just didn't know it was gone blow up like this. I did. I watched the bitch from my fake page. As soon as I saw how she was comin', I cancelled her room and her flight and got the fuck out of Miami." Grant cut his eyes to the waning traffic, livid all over again. He didn't sleep that night after the LIVE, tormented by the apology he owed his parents.

"So how you been holding up?"

"Family interventions, public opinions and a few cancelled endorsements. Never been better." Grant nodded with a smile, but it was a sarcastic one. One that masked his disappointment and sadness. His eyes were puppy dog like, big and unrested. He also looked to have lost weight thanks to sunken cheeks, quite the contrast from the full robustness of his face just a week before at the gala. Loss of appetite wasn't the only thing ailing him.

The family intervention, led by his mother, brought him to a new low. Evita's intervention talk was sympathetic and kind, but her horror hadn't escaped him. And Grant knew it never would, until he proved he could live a life free of drugs. For all the money in the world, he never fathomed what it felt like to disappoint her. The embarrassment brought to his father (on top of the scandal) bruised his pride. To hear his name associated with cocaine usage had led to a decline in fan base, and several companies pulling the plug on their collaborations.

Grant almost wished he had stayed loyal to his use of marijuana. With its newfound legalization, many had saw the drug to be minor compared to monsters like fentanyl and heroin. The ones ripping communities apart at the seams. But here he was, on a degree just as deadly. Only God knew where this supply came from, especially when he dilly-and-dallied in pills like Molly and Percocet. He too could've been a casualty in the dirty street drug world. No one knew the depravity of his addiction until the family intervention.

E.K. Robertson

"Awww Grant. I'm sorry." Cece put her arm around him and patted his back like one would when burping a baby.

Grant could sense her second hand embarrassment. "I guess it's about time I got a hold on it, before I become Pookie out here in these streets. My mom's got me at some upscale wellness center. Imma document that shit too. Let my subscribers see my downfall and my bounce back."

Cece grinned, happy to hear it. "That's how you turn lemons into lemonade."

"More like water into wine. I need a miracle, Cece. I ain't realize how far gone I was until I did an assessment with the facility. The therapist spoke on some things that woke me up. And I really wanna make my mama proud."

Cece looked into the face of the young man, and saw a scared little boy coddled by the approval of the world, yet lost in the madness of that popularity. A boy who grew up with the internet at his fingertips, the same internet that would lead to him being a millionaire in his own right. A young boy who lacked discipline, to whom the rules had never applied. Until the same internet and popularity led to his public humiliation.

"So what's this about, Cece?" Grant said, changing course. His solemnness seemed to dissipate and now he was oddly cheerful in personality.

"I wanted to apologize to you directly before I air one on the radio. Things have gotten so out of hand since the LIVE. We're trying to be respectful of the investigation and the victim's family."

"What was that girl even talking about at the gala?"

"Didn't you know her?" Cece didn't want to come across as too involved.

"I was real young when she moved in with the family. So I ain't seen nothing, and I don't know nothing," Grant said in a low voice. He wiped his sweaty palms on the knees of his skinny jeans. "All I can say is what she accused my dad of doesn't sound like some shit he would do. My father loved my mama. And I damn sure don't believe he was touchin' on teenage girls. Never heard anybody say my dad was a pedophile."

"So you believe he's innocent."

"As fuck." Grant looked at her assuredly. He saw something in her eyes that questioned what he was saying. "You think otherwise?"

Cece just shrugged, again not wanting to appear too involved. "It's no mystery that Dreah reached out to me with her story before the murder. I'm not saying your dad did it, but there may be truth to her allegations."

"Mane Cece, listen. Keep me out of it. I got my own problems. And I'm sure my dad has lawyers handling this for him," Grant said as he wiped those sweaty palms on his knees again.

"You're right. I'm sorry Grant. Listen, I-"

"I heard she accidentally drowned herself in the toilet. Like shawty OD'd or something." Grant stood up and looked towards the statue. Then, shaking his hands at his side as if questioning Mr. Bojangles directly, he said, "Where did y'all hear this was a murder?"

"Where did you hear this was a suicide?" countered Cece. "No official statements have been released. Just foul play was expected."

"That's what they all say." Grant snorted a laugh. "The typical investigation bullshit. But what if she did just accidentally kill herself? Maybe that's what this is. When the truth comes to light, my dad will be cleared as an innocent man and it'll be back to business as usual."

"And what about you, Grant?"

"Me?" He turned to her with a smirk. "I'll be clean."

Then he went to his Tiktok app and played back a draft video of himself calling out various girls names. "What's Cece short for?"

"Cecilia."

Grant smirked again, and vigorously tapped at his phone's screen. "Girls names that end in 'Uh'..." and shared his new Tiktok video.

The sound of screeching tires took their attention. Grant looked around for the source as a dark sedan flew down Adams.

It was about to cross over Leigh onto Chamberlayne Parkway when it came into their view.

"Cece get low!" Grant hollered, having spotted the Beretta hanging out the driver window.

She dropped to the ground and he jumped on top of her as the sedan flew down Chamberlayne, and bent the first left on Price Street. They heard the tires screech again and knew a drive by was imminent.

Bullets whizzed overhead, bouncing off the Bojangles statue above them as the car sped down Leigh Street on their left side.

Grant stood up and pulled out his own gun, carefully firing two shots at the car as it sped away, careening a left through the stoplight and zipping into the highway entrance lane.

He quickly put his firearm back into the waistband of his jeans as police sirens faded in from the north of them.

"Stay low," Grant ordered her.

Cece remained on the ground as Grant made a call. She wondered what he'd say to the 911 operator.

Then, his call was answered. She listened quietly as he replied to the voice on the receiving end.

"Dad? We were shot at!"

Twenty Four
June 30 | 7:56 pm

"Tati, this issue with Sam is bigger than I thought. What's this nonsense about sex-trafficking?" Daryl asked as the two stood outside the convention center, swapping the buzz of the electrifying gala for the stillness of June's night air.

He happened upon her at a bad time. She had just been made aware of the allegations Sam had been threatened with. And though she spoke assuredly, Kenny could sense the dread stirring inside her.

"It's just rumors and the business will address it both legally and professionally later this week. Certainly nothing for you to be concerned about," Tati said with confident eyes. Eyes that were also pleading for him to not walk away from the business opportunity.

But Daryl shook his head, lacking confidence and not buying hers. "Are you sure about that? This is not good Miss Hines. This is some real Jeffrey Epstein shit and I can't be associated with that. I got way too much going on as a pillar in my community. You understand my position, right?"

Tati switched her stance, and placed a hand on her hip. "Maybe I don't."

"I don't think it's a good look for me to be associated with Sam in *anything*. Whether it's true or not. Let's say it is a lie. Well, it's a damn good lie. A lie that makes people to do research. If it comes out that I helped Sam get his penthouse or we had upcoming projects in development, my name is gonna be brought up in some shit that has nothing to do with me."

"That's not how it works Daryl and you know it."

"You and I both know that's exactly how it works. They investigate Sam, they investigate us all. And in this day and age? A pedophile is the last thing I want to be doing business with. The world's not having that, and neither am I."

"I'm slightly confused. Is there something *you* need to hide?"

"No, but I value the privacy I do have."

"The entire story is absurd Daryl. Sex trafficking? And why would she come to the gala with this nonsense? I mean, seriously, who does that?"

Daryl paused and looked up at the star-filled sky. He turned to meet Tati's gaze and replied, "A very broken child."

But Daryl didn't feel all the details of his conversation with Tati needed to be provided to detectives. Instead he described their conversation as a single chat about the casino and if it would be affected by the commotion at the gala.

"We discussed the potential of me staying in business with her father. This was approaching midnight," Daryl answered the two men, one sturdy in stature and the other stout.

"Okay, and did you all go back into the building after your conversation?"

"We did. Through the 5th street doors."

"And about what time would you say that was?"

"12:10, 12:15. No later. We had to be inside for the Mayor's speech, which started at midnight. We came in a little late."

"Why was that?"

"Tati was really shaken by the allegations. I could tell she was stressed out and suggested she take a few minutes to calm her nerves."

"And it was your wife who found the body, correct?"

"She did."

"May we speak with her now?"

"Absolutely." Daryl called for his wife, yelling at the staircase, "Anya! C'mere babe!"

Anya gasped at the sound of Daryl's sudden call. She had been listening from the second floor the entire time, hiding in the upstairs hallway with an ear towards the opening of the staircase. She'd done her best to make out detectives questions and her husband's answers. All while holding Gino in her arms to keep him from yapping uncontrollably.

Anya quickly set Gino down, refastened her robe, and gracefully descended the stairs into the foyer where the detectives and her husband were standing. Gino followed her, and circled her feet as she gestured towards the living room.

"May we go in here, please?" Anya needed to sit.

The detectives followed her into the living room. She sat on the mahogany leather sofa and took Gino back into her arms.

"Hello Detective-" She said the phrase in a questioning manner, giving them time to answer with their names. "-Detective Kilgore and Detective Pratt."

Kilgore, the sturdier of the two, began. "Tell us what happened before you found the body. Did you have any run-ins with Dreah earlier in the evening?"

"I saw her with my sister when she fainted. But I didn't speak to her."

"What happens when you stumble across the body, Mrs. Carver?"

"Thanks to the pregnancy, I had been throwing up all evening, and found myself, once again, going to the restroom. But instead of going to the second floor restrooms, I decided to get some privacy on the first floor. I saw a woman slumped over the toilet in the first stall as I ran in. I relieved myself in the handicap stall-"

"You vomited?"

Anya swallowed. "I did. Then came out to wash my hands, and I could see her behind me through the mirror. That's when I noticed she was just... well, kind of still."

"And by *still*, what do you mean?" Detective Pratt's stubby fingers were furious as they scribbled on his notepad.

"Like there was no sound, no movement. I thought she was passed out. And my goodness, nobody should be face down in a toilet. No matter how drunk they are."

"Did you see the victim have a drink earlier in the evening?"

"No I didn't. I just assumed she was drunk because her vomit smelled worse than mine. I mean, the party was flowing with alcohol. Figured she did too much. Of that or something or another." Anya looked between the two men, trying to make out the next question in their eyes.

"What happened next, Mrs. Carver?"

"Well, I called out to her a few times, asked if she was okay. I didn't get any response. So I went towards her, and I saw her face was-" Anya paused to wipe the tears from her eyes, hands shaking as she did. "Her face was in the toilet, just bobbing in the water. And I lifted her up, and-"

Anya realized she'd never be able to forget it. The entire image would be a still, silent photo deeply edged in her subconscious. Only making its appearance in the most random times, and during bouts of insomnia, but it would never leave her memory as long as she lived.

At the onslaught of his wife's tears, Daryl rushed into the living room with a glass of water. He tried not to get to defensive about the line of questioning, as detectives were only doing their job, but he hated to see his wife being made emotional.

"Take your time, Mrs. Carver. When you realized the victim was dead, what did you do next?" Kilgore leaned forward, resting his elbow on his knee and his chin on a balled fist. His keen eyes narrowed with what she said next.

"I just screamed and screamed. I ran out of the restroom, up the stairs, back down the stairs, the escalator. Just screaming."

"And why'd you scream? Did you realize this was the same young lady who had gotten into it with your sister and her husband?"

Daryl and Anya looked at each other. Confused. What an odd question.

Controlling her tone, Anya answered, "I screamed because I'd never seen a dead body before. I was freaked out. Scared out of my mind."

"About what time would you say you that was?"

Anya turned to Daryl, seemingly lost. She couldn't recall the time. "I'm not sure exactly. It had to have been no later than 12:15, 12:20 maybe."

Both detectives paused to review their notepads, methodically staring at the blue ink on the pages.

"Around the time your husband was entering the building with Miss Hines?"

"Is that what he told you? I guess so." Anya caught Daryl's fleeting gaze. His eyes were now studying the two detectives, who looked at her intently. She went on, "I didn't see them. I had to vomit, for goodness sake."

Pratt pressed his glasses up the bridge of his nose. "I have a question. Were you aware that the victim lived with your sister at the time of the alleged sexual abuse?"

"That was many years ago at a time where my sister and I didn't discuss the intricacies of each other's lives. I was away at U of R, and she was a kept housewife in New York. We weren't as close then as we are now."

"Excuse me for interrupting, but is this not some freak accident? Was the young lady murdered or something?" Daryl cut in. "Because if that's the case, then it's probably best you to speak with our lawyer. For everybody's protection."

"That won't be necessary, Mr. Carver," Detective Pratt replied. "Just the standard questioning."

"The manner of death gives us reason to suspect foul play. I sense your concern, but this is very well an open investigation. Please, Mr. Carver, let us ask the questions." Detective Kilgore added a warm smile, one that Daryl couldn't tell was of concern or sheer sarcasm.

"You'll have to forgive me. It's been a lot on my sister and my family. Are you aware some members of the Pitts have been shot at since the gala?"

"We're investigating that as well. For now, this is all the questions we have," he continued. "Please, take my card. And if we have anything further, we'll be sure to follow up. Or, you can reach out if something comes to mind."

Daryl took the card and showed the men to the front door. They both gave head nods and got into a dark burgundy Buick. Anya watched from the living room window as they drove out of the driveway, and down the street. She waited for Daryl to close the front door then met him in the foyer.

"Are you cheating on me?"

The question startled her husband. She watched his face twist in anger, then bewilderment. Before he could answer, she was already regretful.

"Woman, of course not. And I'm not exactly clear on why you're asking me a stupid question like that." Daryl started for the stairs.

Anya jumped in front of him, blocking his path. "Before I went to the restroom, I looked for you. I went to the first floor because my intuition told me you'd be there. And I saw you and Tati on the sidewalk. You hugged her, and then you two came inside and went up the escalator. Didn't tell the detectives that. What was that about?"

"You were eavesdropping?" Daryl looked disappointed, but his wife could care less.

"What the fuck was that about?"

"Anya, she was upset because I told her I didn't want to do business with Sam and her father! I told her there are a thousand other people who would be glad to take the job. The hug was to make sure she knew it was no hard feelings. Nothing to it." Daryl looked her up and down and regarded her unnecessary grief. "Cheating, Anya? Really? How could you think that? You know I love you."

Anya fell silent, not sure if she was embarrassed that she assumed her husband might be cheating, or happy that he pulled out of the casino deal. One she was still vehemently against. And as he rubbed her belly, Anya collapsed into happy tears and buried her face in his chest.

"I'm sorry Daryl. I'm so sorry. I swear I'm just emotional because of this baby, and I- I just thought you could've been..." Anya couldn't bring herself to complete the sentence.

"Having an affair? Yeah right." Daryl tightened the grip on his wife, never wanting to let go.

"I ran to the restroom downstairs bathroom because it was the nearest one. That's how I ended up finding the body." She bristled at another mental image of Dreah's deep blue face bobbing in the toilet water. Her red eyes with large black pupils staring at her from a face of death.

"Oh baby, it's okay. And it's over, for now. Hopefully detectives won't be back to ask us shit." Daryl cupped her face in his hands and forced her to look at him. "Stop stressing."

Anya smiled through happy tears, satisfied that one worry had been pacified, and thankful that the fear of speaking to detectives was finally behind her.

If only Evita could share in the relief.

Twenty Five
July 1 | 11:59 am

As sporadic as the sunshine had been for the past week, no amount of it could allow Evita to see past her circumstances and into the better days ahead. The pending divorce was taking its toll, and she had only met with her lawyer three days before. There was no pre-nuptial agreement, and no clear demands on what she wanted from Sam financially.

Only thing she knew for sure was that she would not stay married to him. Evita believed Dreah's allegations, and the first thing she could do to right said wrongs was distance herself from her husband, his business and let the law handle it from there. She'd gladly give up the Pitts last name, especially if it meant she'd always be associated with the scandal. For all the damage control being done, Evita had an eerie feeling that the controversy would bleed a stain on the legacy. One that might fade over time, but would never be completely rid of.

Other media sources were now digging into the story, addressing accusations and crafting conspiracy theories. Both incidents, the one in 2005 and the gala, were now the subject of several YouTube and Tiktok videos

Evita did see the reaching out from Cece as odd, but agreed to meet with her under the condition that Anya was present. Anya had been her support system following the ordeal, and was the only person she could trust.

The bright Thursday afternoon brought them to the heart of downtown at Quirk Hotel, where two peach mimosas had been poured and brunch menus provided. A soft pink and gray color scheme came alive in a mesh of modern tables and chairs and vintage sofas. The vibe was sophisticated and sensual, catering to the girly girl in all of them. High arches framed the boarders, with slender lighting fixtures hanging from the ceiling. But the natural sunlight spilling in from large storefront windows lent the room its best lighting.

"You ladies know what you want?" Anya asked, after some time had passed. She realized only silence had been shared between them since the mimosas arrived.

"I'll probably do the frittata. I heard its good," Evita replied. She didn't look up from the menu to catch Anya's waiting gaze.

Cece shrugged and answered, "I think I'm going to stick with the pancakes and bacon. Can't go wrong there."

"Okay, I'm gonna do the omelet," Anya said, motioning for their passing waiter.

The ladies placed their orders and no sooner than the waiter left the table, Anya cut her eyes to Cece. It was time to get to the business of why they were there.

"You've kept us in suspense long enough. Why did you call us here today?" She grabbed for one of three waters on the table.

Cece looked back and forth between the sisters, not sure who she should be addressing. She cleared her throat and replied, "I wanted to personally apologize for the LIVE. I should've used better judgment. It got a little, hmm... what's the word?"

"Ghetto?" Anya suggested.

Cece held her smirk. "*Ghetto.* This is my apology for the way this information about your marriage and your family came out. I really do feel awful."

Evita nodded as an understanding expression pained her face. Then she shrugged her shoulders, appearing unbothered. "It's really no matter to me. The information was bound to get out, one way or another. Don't feel bad."

"Easier said than done," Cece continued. "I mean, had I known a SamStar publicist was going to contact me-"

"Contact you?" Anya asked after exchanging looks with her sister. "But why exactly?"

"Just a publicist just doing her job. I'll be airing my apology on tomorrow morning's show. It's already been approved by management," Cece answered, both sarcasm and seriousness sewn into her words.

"Is that right? Tati wasted no time at all." Evita turned to face her sister and both pursed their lips.

"She was polite, but I knew what time it was when she underhandedly threatened my job."

"I'm not surprised. She has plenty of pull in this city, thanks to her father." Evita rolled her eyes and sipped her bubbling mimosa.

"You know, Cece, I watched a playback of the LIVE. You said Dreah was helping you with your podcast series. So you knew about the accusations?" Anya asked, stirring the ice in her glass with a straw.

Cece was taken aback, and certainly didn't want to further discuss her embarrassing LIVE. Since then, she regretted getting involved in the story altogether and wish she'd never come across Dreah in Alchemia.

Evita must have read the worry on her face. She placed a gentle hand on top of Cece's and said, "Hey. This is a safe place. We can talk. No judgments."

Cece met her gaze with a sympathetic stare and nodded. She took a deep breath and began, "Yeah. But I swear, things didn't go haywire until she got the photo from Kenny's assistant. All she told me up until then was that she'd been trafficked by Sam and Mina, and she suspected him of having LeVario killed over the picture. We were just going to explore it just as a conspiracy theory. Then, at the gala, she told me she had a photo that proved her story. I swear to you, I didn't know she was gonna be there."

Evita began laughing, a wild laugh that sounded wicked at its core. "You gotta be fucking kidding me. So I basically put this shit in motion."

"What do you mean?"

"I sent Tati to Alchemia to invite her! If she never saw the photo, then what? This would've been another podcast amongst hundreds of others looking into hip hop conspiracies? I mean, you can't make this shit up." Evita shook her head, still smiling that devious smile. "And you know what? I'm not even sorry. I'm sorry Dreah lost her life, but I'm glad she took Sam down in the process."

Cece stared awkwardly between the two sisters again. She was unsure of what to say. Anya figured it was her turn to speak.

"She told you that Mina groomed her, right?"

Cece nodded it. "Said Mina taught her and the rest of the girls everything they knew about sex and pleasing men at that time. Really gross things that I'm not comfortable repeating."

Evita wasn't laughing anymore. "I had a brief conversation with Mina about it. Of course she denied everything. But if it's true that she's involved-"

"It most certainly *is* true." Anya was firm in this conviction, and needed Evita to be the same.

Evita continued, "-it wouldn't matter to me anymore. I let her go the same way I'm letting Sam go. My mind's made up on that. I'm more concerned with Sam going to jail for murdering Dreah. Isn't that what's most important here? If they get Sam, they can get Mina. Maybe they'll turn on each other."

"So you do think Sam did it? You're not buying the accidental death theory?" Cece asked.

Evita looked at Cece as if the answer was obvious.

"Damn right we're not buying that shit. *Mina* did it, and I know how," Anya said, rather matter-of-factly.

"How?" The question had come from both Evita and Cece who held her in their inquisitive stares, with big eyes begging for her next words.

"And don't be making shit up just because you don't like her," Evita warned.

Anya waited a moment and turned her nose up at them. "First of all, I have my resources. Don't forget, I am very well connected in this city. After I talked to detectives last night, I placed a call to a friend of mine who works at the Health Office of the Chief Medical Examiner. I couldn't get all the details because my girl doesn't want to be responsible for any sort of leak on what's looking like a high profile a case."

Cece was all ears. "What'd she tell you?"

"A toxicology report was done and she was poisoned with tetra-hydro something. I can't remember the name but it's the main ingredient in eye drops."

"Eye drops?" Evita's face was penciled with curiosity. She straightened up and looked at Anya more attentively.

"Yeah, like the ones you were looking for before you went on stage with Sam," Anya said, giving her sister a reminder she didn't need.

"Why are you just now telling me this?"

"Because I just spoke to Shelia last night. Girl, *Mina* probably used your eye drops to kill Dreah. Everybody knows poison is a woman's weapon of choice."

"I did leave my bag unattended most of the night but that doesn't mean Mina did it. She didn't know I was in the Governors room."

"You gotta admit that it is a weird coincidence you're eye drops went missing." Anya wasn't letting it go.

Evita cocked her head to the side, not finding her sisters newfound spunk for the case amusing. She turned to Cece and shook her head apologetically. "Forgive my sister for these theatrics. As you can see, we're both very passionate about finding Dreah's killer."

"I'm glad I'm not the only one. So is poison the cause of death?"

Anya replied, "Um, I don't know exactly."

"What about the manner of death? Is it accident, homicide or undetermined?"

"Look, Sheila was kind enough to tell me about the tetrahydro- whatever it's called, poison shit. I wasn't gonna push my luck, or hers. The autopsy will be released later this evening though, since you're interested."

"I feel like this is my fault. Like doing the podcast only hyped her up to get the story out. But when we saw each other that night, she told me she didn't want to do it anymore."

"That's exactly why you shouldn't feel like this is your fault. She would've talked regardless, and Sam would've found a way to shut her up. That's what men like him do," Evita said. Suddenly, she sniffled and began weeping, face in hands right there at the table.

Anya moved closer to her, wrapping her arms around her big sister in the way a mother would a heartbroken daughter. She rocked her back and forth, whispering for her to hold it together. They were in a restaurant where other guests were starting to appear curious. And since the penthouse debacle, both women had expressed concerns about being followed, possibly by henchmen appointed by Sam. No additional attention was preferred at this time.

"This will stay with me as long as I live. Every interview I do, anytime I speak out, they're gonna ask me did I know. And I swear I didn't know. I didn't know. Whose gonna believe me?"

Cece too almost started crying as Evita spoke the prophecy over herself. It was becoming too much, and she felt she had overstayed her time with the two ladies. Then she remembered their food had yet to hit the table. She couldn't leave just yet, but she did ask the waiter to pack her plate to go and bring her the check.

"Leaving so soon?" Anya asked, watching as Cece downed the rest of her mimosa.

"It's just best that I go. Again, I'm really sorry, Evita."

"Stop apologizing damn it!" Evita hollered, causing the idle chatter of the restaurant to cease a moment. When it picked back up, she continued, "This is not your fault."

But Cece didn't agree. She looked towards the bar, where the kitchen was located. Where was that waiter? Answering her silent prayer, a server came with their food (hers in a take-out carton) and the waiter followed up with her check.

"Thank you guys for meeting with me. I feel a lot better." Cece left more than enough cash on the table, grabbed her food and hightailed it out of the building. She eyed Jefferson Street up and down, pacing towards her Jeep parked on Grace Street.

In the safety of her vehicle, Cece unlocked her phone, and went straight to the email where her apology had been sent back to her. An approval from radio station management. She looked over the statement for the hundredth time.

To the listening family, and followers of my Instagram: One thing I pride myself on is having integrity in this business, especially when it comes to my coverage of celebrity and the entertainment industry. Last week, I acted in a less than professional manner by airing a LIVE video conversation that lacked proven facts, and complicated what is currently an active investigation. I apologize for any damage this has done to the SamStar Enterprises brand, and to the Pitts family. I also apologize to Super Vixen Sienna for allowing her to be on a platform to discuss matters pertinent to the case.

We also apologize to anyone who may have been offended given the nature of the conversation, which lacked discretion and guidance. I apologize to the family of the victim, as they grieve a life cut way too short. This Richmond radio family sends you our deepest thoughts and prayers during what is a most difficult time. We thank our listening audience for the concern expressed, and we will continue to do better in this profession.

Cece read over the words, but couldn't bring herself to say them out loud. She didn't know how she'd muster the courage to say them live on air, but knew she had an obligation. Not just to her career, but to Dreah.

Yet somehow, this apology just wouldn't suffice. She owed Dreah so much more. She looked up to see a dark sedan pulling into the parking space behind her.

It looked like and reminded her of the sedan that had shot at her and Grant the day before. She squinted to see the driver better, but couldn't see past the black mask and shades that covered their face. Ominous looking and out of place for the middle of the day. As a shiver ran through her, Cece suddenly felt she was not safe.

She immediately turned the key in the ignition and pulled onto the street, driving away from the sedan like her life depended on it.

The sedan started to pull off behind her, but ignorant to the one-way traffic approaching from behind, it side swiped an oncoming minivan.

Behind them, two vehicles cars skirted to a stop and swerved to the right of the collision. Another crashed head on into the back of the van. The driver got out, livid and cursing over the damage down to the side and back of the van. Never minding how the driver who crashed into him was doing.

Having heard the collision, an officer came out of the Richmond Police Headquarters building on the Grace and Jefferson corner.

Panicking under the unwanted attention, the sedan reversed into an adjacent parking lot and turned a dangerous right onto the one way Jefferson. To avoid the oncoming traffic, it broke a hard left and jumped back on Grace Street. It zoomed around the accident and debris, and disappeared down another one way.

Twenty Six
July 1 | 6:37 pm

And I don't understand why she chose to stay in Richmond after you fired her. I knew she was doomed back then. But she insisted on opening her store and making a life for herself out here. And now she's dead!" Diondra rambled. Her curly lace wig shook as it framed her even and mildly aged face. Her dark brown eyes were narrowed in slits, button nose deformed in a scowl as she looked Sam up and down.

She dulled the shine of the kitchen countertop with her flagrant 'talk-with-your-hands' type of gestures. Slapping and sliding them all along the black granite and clapping with every other word that ended a sentence.

The minute she crossed into the penthouse, Sam regretted his invitation to meet with Diondra. She hopped and wobbled into a kitchen stool, breathing heavily as she adjusted herself. Skinny no more, the woman was still a knockout. And a hellcat. She went in on him as soon as the conversation began.

Sam didn't know how to combat this verbal lashing, which spewed like fire from the mouth of a dragon. She berated him in the same fashion of a time long ago, before she agreed to let her daughter live with the Pitts. Only now, she regretted that decision, one she believed may have gotten her daughter killed.

Diondra rolled her neck and pointed an accusatory finger at Sam. "And to think I thought I was doing the right thing by letting her live with you! I *did* want the best for her, Sam. Even with all our drama, I always wanted better for her. I should've never left her in y'alls care."

Sam shook his head, not too pleased with himself for inviting her to his penthouse. A power move going totally rogue. Thankfully, they were in the privacy of his home and she could be as outraged as she dared to be, without embarrassing them in a public space.

Sam was 35 years old and very married when Diondra the would-be model strutted into the audition, 26 years old and desperate to be a video girl. She'd seen the fame it brought women like Super Vixen Sienna, whose modeling career she idolized, and other women who were practically begged to show up on set. Women who the almighty dollar could do anything for.

Diondra was embarrassed to admit that Dreah was her daughter. But as the gigs poured in for the teen model, and dried up for her, she felt she had no choice. The mother-daughter relationship had become far more strained than she was willing to acknowledge.

In fact, that was it. There was no mother-daughter relationship because Dreah didn't know Diondra was her mother. It was a secret held by all three women in the house, a decision made by Diondra's own mother who took on the role herself, while they all lived under her roof.

At 26, Diondra worked small gigs as a model and was able to get an apartment of her own. But living with her daughter and no guidance from her own mother was a lethal combination. Dreah, at 14, was starting to come into her own as a young model. Diondra started to view her as competition, as oppose to a young teenaged daughter having her unique experience in a shady business. The young mother was desperate to speak her peace, and first revealed her truth to Mina.

"You and Mina ain't right!" she spat.

"Diondra, this ain't what I wanted to discuss but since we're on the subject, let's talk about it. You and I both know you were way too into yourself to be a mother. You didn't just want the best for her, you wanted better for yourself. And better for you meant being a single woman free of responsibility, who could live her life on her own terms. Don't make me remind you of all the vacations we paid for, and the home we bought you. The home you're still living in 'til this day! Let's not do this, Diondra."

"Yeah I had my fun. So what? I had to watch my daughter grow up from the sidelines," Diondra said, unable to refute him. "But I never asked you to pimp her out to your friends in the fuckin' industry! And I hate myself every day for the decisions I made. Especially now that she's dead! And I shoulda known better. You been had ya' eye on her. I shoulda never let her work for y'all. All y'all going to hell."

Sam shrugged and fanned her retort. "As if I won't see you when we get there? C'mon Diondra. I didn't bring you down here to trade insults. What's done is done."

"Did you kill my daughter?"

Sam looked her firmly in the eyes and said, "I did not kill Dreah. I swear on my life, I didn't kill her."

"Well if you didn't, then who the hell did?" Diondra's cold eyes stared back into him. Oddly enough, she did believe him. But she was certain he had something to do with it.

"I don't know, but we're working with investigators to answer that question. You know if I had my hand in this, I wouldn't show it, but I also wouldn't be able to hide it in this day and age."

Diondra slammed her fist on the countertop, cursing herself. Something she had done many times before, but always with the promise of healing the broken relationship with a daughter who had long given up on a reconciliation.

"I spoke with detectives this morning. They told me the autopsy was gone be made public today. They asked me if I wanted to hear the facts now, or read 'em later. I said now." She wiped a tear from her cheek. She didn't want the rest to fall, not in front of Sam. Through blurry eyesight, she stared at the intertwining interstates outside the window. "They say her hyoid bone was broken. I ain't never heard of that shit. The fuck is a hyoid bone? They had to break it down to me. Told me somebody poisoned my baby, then strangled her."

Diondra grabbed her own neck, fighting the urge to put herself in Dreah's heels the night of the gala. She couldn't imagine the fear she experienced as she was being murdered. She was cursed to live the rest of her days as a mother who never made things right. Burying a child was its own torment, but to not have restored the relationship would be the slow end of Diondra.

A mirage of their more innocent days flashed through her mind. The moment she birthed her, the first steps, and the first day of kindergarten. And then, the course their lives took when her daughter threatened to tell Big Mama if she didn't take her to the audition.

And Diondra, who was forced to live a life where the truth hid in plain sight, was conflicted as a woman. Completely unaware that within the next two years, she would be confronted with the pain of what happens when a mother denies herself (and her child) the ability to be one.

Diondra was so lost in her deep thought, she hadn't noticed the tears now flowing freely down her cheeks.

"Diondra, whatever you need, we'll give it to you." Sam came from around the kitchen counter and embraced her in what was a truly sincere hug. "I'm sorry this happened. I really am. I know I've made mistakes in the past, but let me do what I can to make up for that. We'll cover any funeral costs and make sure you want for nothing. If that's alright with you, of course."

Diondra heard the plea in his voice. And it was as close as she would get to the truth about his abuse of her daughter, and this was as close as he'd get to her forgiveness.

"Sure. I'll reach out if I need you. To your publicist, right?"

Sam nodded.

"The car is still waiting for me out front, yeah?" Diondra reached for her purse, suddenly ready to get away.

"It is. Let me know when you get back to the Jefferson, alright?" Sam saw her to the door. He watched her disappear down the hallway and into an elevator, then returned to the solace of the city view.

The deep yellow moon was rising over downtown against the fading sunset of a lavender sky.

Sam had just a moment to clear his head before a much needed conversation with his sons. He hadn't seen Kenny since the gala, and only saw Grant because of Evita's timely family intervention.

Coincidentally, he was less concerned with Grant than he was Kenny, whose absence and silence was unusual in its way of making him wonder where the two men stood with each other.

What did Kenny know? What had he heard? It would all be revealed tonight.

Both Kenny and Grant arrived promptly five minutes before 7-o-clock. Grant waltzed in with a video camera in hand, obviously recording as he narrated,

"Just got to my dad's house. I'm about to have a much needed conversation and we'll see how it goes."

"Is he serious right now?" Sam watched as Grant set his camera on the dining table, facing it towards the living room sofas were the men were seated.

Sam and Kenny exchanged faces, both annoyed.

"Grant, you've already apologized to me. What's with the extra shit?"

"I know but I didn't record it the first time, and I want to document an apology for my channel."

"He's a YouTuber, remember?" Kenny chimed in, rolling his eyes. "I told him not to do this but he doesn't listen!"

"Okay, guys, I'm recording," Grant said as he took a seat on the ottoman beside the sofa. "Dad, you know I love you. I never meant to embarrass our family, our brand, and our business. I made a big mistake bringing the woman I brought to the gala, and I'm sorry for the shame I caused this family with my addiction."

Kenny held back a smirk as he watched his father turn uncomfortably to the camera, and back to his son.

"Thank you Grant. I'm glad you're getting the help you need and you have me and your mother's support when it comes to this monster." He waited a few moments before asking, "Can you turn the camera off now?"

Grant went to his camera and powered it off. He joined them back on the sofa and waited for the next words to come from his father.

They came from Kenny instead.

"You should stay off social media for a while. Really focus on getting clean."

"I can't do that. I'll lose fans if I don't pump this content. Besides, I wanna keep it as real as I can with so I gotta record this."

"As much as we all appreciate authenticity, social media is its own drug. I think Kenny's right. Staying off it to focus on sobriety may be the best thing," Sam concurred.

"C'mon dad. You know this is tough for me already. Going without something else that I love – wait, I'm not saying I love drugs as much as I love making content, but if I stop doing *this*, Imma lose my mind." Grant waved his cell phone at them, ending his heartfelt objection.

"That's the problem kid! You've already lost it. We're trying to help you find it." Kenny tossed a throw pillow at him.

Grant caught it and threw it back, replying, "This ain't a joke, dickhead."

"I know, cokehead!" Kenny started to throw the pillow again but Sam blocked it midair.

"Enough you two. Kenny, cut the shit." Sam turned to Grant and said, "If you want to document your journey, that's fine. But remember, ain't no pressure but the kind you apply to yourself. That's the only kind that matters. Always make sure you're doing this for you, and not just for your fans. Got it?"

With a grin, Grant replied, "I got it."

"Hey. I love you."

"Love you too dad."

"Give me and your brother a moment to catch up."

"Pool still open, right?" Grant asked. "I didn't wear my trunks for nothing."

Sam grinned, proud, as his youngest boy disappeared out of the room, and moments later, out of the penthouse.

Now that they were alone, Kenny turned to his father, asking, "What's the deal with the gaming and commission board?'

"We closed that out with a fine, and a warning. But it's a done deal. Don't sweat it," Sam answered. He regarded Kenny, who looked just as eager to get another (more necessary) conversation started. But Sam didn't know where to begin, and let the moment of silence between them linger much longer than it should have.

"Looks like I gotta strike the match." Kenny rubbed his hands together and exhaled slowly before he continued. "I'm sorry

I've been away. I just got a little weirded out after talking to detectives. It's been a lot to handle."

"Where did you go?"

"I went to Alexandria and helped mom get situated. I'm sorry that it's over for y'all. I never thought I'd see the day."

Sam shrugged as nonchalantly as his emotions would let him. "You're a man. It's life. Shit happens. Speaking of, I'm sorry about the incident a few days ago."

"What incident?"

"The one at the penthouse. Tati and I created this plan to make our family look like we were being followed and attacked."

"Wait a minute. You set that up?" Kenny was disgusted. "Mom and Auntie were scared as shit. You're lucky I didn't have my gun on me. I could've killed somebody." He paused, contemplative. "That incudes Grant too?"

"Yeah. The BB guns made it seem real."

"Grant's gun *was* real! And that's not cool pops. He coulda relapsed."

"Oh please. Let's not take it overboard. I wasn't expecting Grant to bust back. But I damn sure taught him well," Sam gloated, to Kenny's chagrin.

"He could've killed someone. And now he has the hearing for that weapons charge."

"He'll show the court his permit, pay a fine, and be done with it." Sam waved dismissively at his son. "He was defending himself. He was a victim. *We* are all victims."

But Kenny wasn't as nonchalant as he was. "Why did you think a plan like that would work? We're in some deep shit. You know I talked to Dreah at the gala. And I saw the infamous photo from 2005. I don't mean to offend you by asking this but-"

"Did I do it?" Sam rolled his eyes; he'd heard the question one too many times in the past week. "No, I *didn't* kill Dreah, Kenny."

"That's not what I'm asking." Kenny watched Sam's facial expression drop with a heavy sternness that worried him as a son. He dreaded this conversation, and it had only just begun.

There was a long pause as Sam thought through what his son was asking. "You're asking if I touched that girl. The answer is no."

Kenny flashed a weak smile. He almost believed him; nevertheless, he decided to move on. "Dreah reminded me of my 15th birthday present. Back then, I thought it was kind of cool, you know? Something I was gonna take to my grave. I never shared that with anybody. It was weird of her to bring that shit up."

He waited for Sam to meet his gaze and said, "I just want to know what that was about. Was that something your dad did for you?"

Sam blew another breath of wind from his jaws, pacing himself for what was becoming a heavier conversation than imagined. "No, it wasn't. I thought I was doing a cool thing as a dad by getting my son checked out. That's all."

There was another long pause.

"I just need you to admit it was wrong," Kenny replied. "I finally had to."

With a slow nod, Sam replied, "You're right. I was definitely wrong for that. I'm sorry."

Kenny returned a nod of his own, replying, "All's forgiven. You wanna, um, pour up a drink? The rest of the conversation's gonna need it."

Sam stood and went to his mini bar. He decided on a strong whisky and grabbed two glass tumblers. When he brought the glass to Kenny, he could've sworn he caught a tear falling down his son's face. But Kenny moved his hand to his eye, pressing it into his skin.

"What's up son?"

"Dad," Kenny said after downing the whisky. "I have to make a confession, but I want to ask you another question. And it'll make it easier on me, if you were honest."

Sam narrowed his eyes, wondering what his son had to say that earned him a slight insult. "Of course I'll be honest."

"Did you have LeVario killed?"

Sam poured them another round, and took a drink as his mind slipped back to the year 2005. A time in his life that found him at the opening gate to a world of business and entertainment he hadn't yet transcended to.

He went with the memory, explaining "Dmitri Goode invited us to a party. And this was in the startup days, when we needed all the networking we could get. We thought it'd be a good idea to invite our photographer. So we got him in, and he's doing his thing. Snapping pictures of us with celebrities... It was just a good time."

Sam paused to pour himself a third shot. "I see LeVario flash the camera at Hendrik and Zsarina. Hendrik punches the shit out of LeVario, and mans is dragged out of the party. I knew it was bad. Back then, if you were caught with a tranny, it would've killed your career. End of story. Low key, we all heard a little bit about Hendrik having a thing for transsexuals but Zsarina wasn't putting him on blast and nobody else had a reason to.

"When I got the call from LeVario about some photos he wanted to show me, I just knew it was the one of Hendrik and Zsarina. LeVario was young. He didn't understand this shit, the way this works. Hendrik Clary was the biggest sports entertainer that year. He'd just won his boxing match, came up five million. And he had a record deal with Goode Records. Pissing Hendrik off would've pissed Dmitri off. If LeVario had leaked that photo to the media, it would've ended us before we began."

"And that was a risk you weren't willing to take."

"These were wild times And I wasn't taking no chances when he said he didn't like what he saw. Said it was enough to blast the whole party. He threatened to air it out if I didn't meet with him," Sam admitted as he poured them both a fourth shot.

"You never saw the photo back then?" Kenny asked.

"I sent Neville to LeVario's to pick them up, but LeVario insisted on speaking with me and wasn't willing to turn them over. I knew he hid the photos somewhere but we never found them," Sam replied. "Neville searched that apartment up and down."

"After he threw him over the balcony."

"Before."

Sam and Kenny let a moment of silence pass.

"LeVario hid the photos in one of your offices."

Sam shrugged, saying, "We had no idea. Best place to hide something is in plain sight."

"Did you know Dmitri and Dreah were in the photo?"

"LeVario never said that to me."

Kenny nodded, having heard all he needed to hear.

"You know something Kenny? You're the only one who didn't ask me if I killed Dreah."

The men made eye contact, engaging in a silent exchange of "I know something you don't know".

"I think it's time *you* tell me what happened at the gala."

Kenny stood, crossed over to the window and revisited the view. It was beautiful, yet not enough to slow his fast beating heart, nor the sweat building in his palms. His throat was dry, despite having taken four shots of whisky. He stared down below, imagining himself to be LeVario, and the terror felt before his body slammed into the concrete.

"I saw the photo, dad. I saw Dreah sitting in Dmitri's lap. I knew if she left that party alive, we would be ruined."

"Did you-" Sam could barely get the words out. "-do something? What's going on?"

"Dad, I love you. I did this for us!"

"Kenny. What have you done?"

"Because I'd do anything for you. For this company!" Kenny's voice was powerful, but it quaked with guilt. He was too far gone in conversation now. There'd be no going backwards, but neither of the men were sure of what lay ahead.

Sam felt the room spinning around them. A sharp pain rang from his ear and sank down into his chest. He set the tumbler on the coffee table, and sat up to steady himself. "Kenny."

"I saw the photo!"

"Why did you strangle her?"

Kenny was ridden with confusion. "Strangle? I never touched her! We kept our hands clean."

"What do you mean *we*?" Sam inched towards Kenny, who backed against the window, appearing in fear of his life.

"What do you mean strangle? That was never part of the plan!"

"The plan?"

"Dad I'm sorry!" Hot tears spilled from Kenny's eyes, searing his face with more regret. "Fuck! We messed up. I'm sorry." He slid to the floor, desperate for relief from this mental anguish. His confession, the burden it was, hadn't freed his conscience, contrary to prior beliefs.

Sam grabbed Kenny's collar and shook him like a ragdoll. Like the answer to a very important question was lodged in his son's throat and needed to be rattled out.

The city view was suddenly of no comfort as Sam roared, "Who the fuck is *we?*"

Twenty Seven
July 2 | 9:51 pm

Pia couldn't believe the life she was living. Something that began as an easy lick working as Kenny's assistant had thrown her into a real life murder mystery. And for all her planning and executing of the gala, she couldn't believe she'd been one of the last people to speak to Dreah that night.

Neville was adamant that he saw her out of the convention center. He didn't think much of her trip to the restroom until the Uber arrived and she still hadn't come back outside. He went to the door of the restroom and heard her horrid retching on the other side. He figured the least he could do was give her a few more minutes to clean herself up. He went back to the Uber and asked for more time.

But more minutes ticked by, and there was no sign of Dreah. Neville started for the building again, and was surprised to see a crowd gathered in the pavilion. Dreah had been found dead in the restroom.

Pia replayed her interview with detectives. *Moved to Richmond a few years ago. Assistant to Kenny Pitts. Talked to Dreah shortly before she was found dead. Neville escorted her out of the party ...* She ran the answers back in her mind, and couldn't think of anything she said that was out of order.

That's why when Sam asked to see her, she couldn't fathom what for. Was it about the investigation? Or something more provocative, like the quickly cancelled threesome in Atlanta? She certainly couldn't say no to her boss. So, Pia invited him to her treasured apartment.

She waited impatiently, watching the clock as it drifted further and further away from the time he was due to show. Almost forty minutes later, Sam found his way to her door and she welcomed him into the living room.

"I apologize for running late," Sam said as he stepped into the condo, looking around. Her skyline view was almost as impressive as the one from the penthouse.

Pleasantly surprised, he nodded and smirked. "Nice view. Got yourself set up pretty good in Richmond. Don't you?" He chuckled and waited for her to reply.

"Be seated, please," Pia said as friendly as possible. She showed him to a tuxedo arm loveseat.

"Yes, and thank you for inviting me to your home, Pia. Or should I say Pialoma? As in Pialoma Dotson of Miami-Dade County? Federal Larceny, 2017; eighteen months, Federal Correctional Institution, Inmate #190829904."

Pia almost dropped the two bottles of VOSS water she had retrieved from the fridge. She quickly set them on the countertop and slowly walked to the living room's large ottoman. She shivered at Sam's ear to ear grin.

"You probably liked the ShaBang chips the most. You look the type." Sam chuckled, darkly, then shook his head in a tsk-tsk-tsk manner. He read the dread on her face, a self-reflecting expression rooted in torment. He had a feeling what ailed her and continued, "Kenny hired you, not me. And he still has no idea so don't worry. Your secret's safe with me."

Though embarrassment flushed through her, Pia found her voice. "How do you know this information?"

"I like to know who works for the people who work for me. Unfortunately, I didn't pass the skillset on to my son. Hence the reason you were able to finesse your way into a job as his assistant. A good paying job that earns you a view like this." He gestured to the window before them.

But the city lights glistening against the dark purple sky only dizzied Pia. Her knees buckled beneath her weight and she quickly collapsed to the ottoman. She just knew there was something more sinister attached to his visit. "What do you want?"

"I want some information. Is that alright?"

Pia relaxed her clenched jaw. "I'm listening..."

"About the night of the gala." Sam watched her expression drop, and said, "I'm listening..."

Pia poised herself and told him her side of the story. It began with Kenny's plea for her help, just moments before she was asked to get Dreah alone by the dancefloor.

When Kenny came to her, he was a desperate son seeking to protect his father, their empire, and the kingdom come of his own fortune. She had no idea just how blind to rationalism he was by a decision made in the heat of a moment. The heat of the night, rather.

Pia paused as her conversation with Kenny played itself over and over in her mind. *"She's threatened my mother, she's threatened my father, and she's threatened me. We need her out of here."*

"Kenny said he was gonna have a waitress bring us some drinks. He told me to make sure she gets the champagne flute with the moon charm on it. Mine was a star. She drank it, and soon after that, Neville came and escorted her out. All I did was get her to the dancefloor and hand her the drink."

"Did he tell you what he did?"

Pia's jaw was clenched again. "He just said he's gonna take care of everything."

Sam was disappointed to say the next words. "He dumped two bottles of eye drops in the champagne."

Pia held her breath, as if he was going to laugh and say he was joking. But nothing such followed. She looked at the floor, her head clouding with the news.

"She didn't- overdose? He poisoned her?" Pia's face was tight with concern as the jarring truth hung low in the air between them.

Sam waited for her to make eye contact, then an eerie grin parted his lips as he reminded her, "And you helped him execute this as an accomplice."

Pia wouldn't dare get upset, though the revelation certainly called for it. She had a few choice words for Kenny.

"I was just doing my job as an assistant. He just said make sure she drinks it, and that he would send Neville to where we were. He didn't say anything about *poison*. Where the fuck did he even learn that?" Pia was enraged; it was a side of her that Sam enjoyed seeing for the first time.

"He saw it on an episode of 48 Hours," Sam chuckled. "She was supposed to be out of the building by time it kicked in," Sam went on to explain. "It's actually kind of genius, if only she had made it to the Uber."

Pia's world had been flipped upside down. She went from not being involved to being the one who handed Dreah the deadly concoction. Dreah's death came by way of her hands. Kenny set her up. How was she supposed to know he was fixated on murder- unlike his father, who only wanted her out of the building?

"I swear didn't know he was gonna do that."

"You don't have to explain. Kenny did enough of that. I just wanted to check your temperature. See how you feel about all this. Your *continued* loyalty to SamStar is expected from here on out." Sam said it so firmly, it chilled Pia to her bones.

All she could do was nod at what was clearly a command, and not some request that she could refuse.

Sam continued, "I guess I need to bring you up to speed on what we know, now that you're somewhat involved. A toxicology report shows she was poisoned, but the cause of death is strangulation."

Pia gasped, bringing a hand to her open mouth. She was now certain Neville did it. "Neville!"

Sam rolled his eyes in disgust. "Knock it off."

"Sorry. I shouldn't have assumed."

"No you shouldn't have."

Pia swallowed the lump in her throat and admitted, "Detectives want to speak with me again."

"Of course they do, to reconfirm our story. Which is…"

"I was talking to Dreah when Neville came and escorted her out of the party."

"Very good. You are not to implicate my son or mention anything about a glass of champagne, under any circumstances." His voice wasn't half as intimidating as his eye contact.

"I got it," Pia muttered with a lowly expression.

He nodded. "Kenny thinks I owe you an explanation."

Her ears perked up at that.

Sam continued, "I ought to tell you the drive by at the penthouse a few days ago was just an act. Part of the campaign to spin the narrative for the family."

Pia had nothing to say. She remembered how deeply the incident terrified her. A publicity campaign? Tati had some explaining to do. But right now, she was afraid of Sam. Her breathing fell so silent, she had to cough herself into regularity.

"We do a lot of things we don't want to do in the industry. But, business is business." Sam's voice was smooth, even and skillfully calm.

He stood to his feet and removed an envelope from his coat pocket in a motion that startled Pia off the edge of the ottoman.

"Young lady, get ahold of yourself. I'm not gonna kill you!" He chuckled and handed her the envelope. "From Kenny. Final payment for your work at the gala."

Pia opened it and saw the final payout, an additional zero added on what had been owed. She nodded, understanding more clearly what the surprise bonus was for.

"I'll let myself out. Goodnight, *Pia*." Her name dripped from his lips with a flirtatious sarcasm, the kind meant to purposefully tease and intimidate.

When he made his exit, Pia bolted to the door and locked it. She sulked back into the stillness of the living room. A room so quiet, she could hear the symphony of surrounding sounds around her. The low hum of the overhead fan, the rush of cars on the expressway outside the open window, and the sound of a train chugging along the tracks in the far distance.

All of it a soundtrack to the questions lingering in the dark corridors of her mind. Questions that might relieve her conscience if she sought answers from Kenny Pitts.

Epilogue
...You Already Knew

Tati glowed radiant as the sun beamed through the Benz' windshield. It'd been just over two weeks since the gala, and her career as a publicist and fixer had been put to the test. The job was first recommended to her by a sorority sister, who turned it down to become a housewife. Once Tati found her footing as a publicist, she realized she had nothing to lose goading for the monetary affections of the wealthy on her father's behalf. And for the most part, things had been smooth sailing up until the gala.

The night had been so wonderful. Even the days leading to it. There were the time synchronicities, caught all weekend long. She rejoiced in the magic of these numerical clues, and how it showed up in her life time and time again. They had been a wink to her soul, reminding her that the path she had taken was the right one. The odds were stacked in her favor. Whatever she believed life could be, was becoming just that. She should've known it was too good to be true, though, when murder became the SamStar Enterprises headline.

Yet, Tati thrived in the face of controversy and loved when the odds were stacked against her. Through her diligent work, she managed to quell the media shit storm surrounding Dreah's accusations and subsequent death. The murder was still being investigated, but suspects had been demoted to persons of interest, and those persons were soon moved off detectives' radars entirely. Innocence had been proven many times over thanks to CCTV, the corroboration of alibis as told by those in attendance, and the timestamps of photos and videos (after serious digital forensic scrutiny).

Tati's idea to hire henchmen to employ fake intimidation tactics on the Pitts family had been fairly successful. The theatrics of gun play and using the same dark blue sedan made it all the more believable. She and Sam wanted it to appear as if the family was under attack; like they too were the victims of something greater and darker.

When Tati learned Sam was behind her run in with the henchmen outside of Casa Fiesta, she wondered if she was too.

Tati would get her revenge, telling the hired bullies to strike him the next morning. They followed him from the estate, all the way to the West Broad Shopping Center.

To make her payback even more worth it, Tati told them Sam didn't want to be told about the encounter. He needed it to be as authentic as possible. She was delightfully satisfied as he cursed her out later that evening. *Serves his ass right*, she remembered thinking.

Tati had been so spooked by her turn with the henchmen that she all but forgot about the meeting with Cece, until the apology aired on the radio the following Monday. The apology did its job when it came to healing concerns expressed by the local public, and the cease and desist letter to Sienna had served its intended purpose. The vixen even took a timely hiatus from social media.

Yes, all was well, and just as Tati planned it. She received a big bonus from SamStar Enterprises, one that she would spend investing in stocks, and the other half on a shopping spree in the Saks Fifth at Stony Point Fashion Park.

But first, there was the business of a meeting with her father at the One James Center office. He wanted an update concerning Daryl Carver's departure from the casino project. She couldn't understand how a bunch of rumors scared him out of a lucrative deal, a once in a lifetime opportunity for his hometown.

"I can fix it! I'm a publicist. That's what I do. Please don't let a rumor cause you to miss out. I'm begging you." But to her final pleas, Daryl only hugged her, and stood firmer on his decision.

Tati would have to inform her father that efforts to keep him on board were for naught. She figured his nagging wife got in his ear and scared him out of it; she hoped Daryl (and Anya) would forever sulk in that decision. Her father was Vernon Hines for goodness sake! Who wouldn't jump at an opportunity to make money with a man who'd done it tens of millions of times over?

But that was neither here nor there, as Tati had several alternatives lined up. All Vernon had to do was take his pick of the ten candidates presented in today's meeting.

The meeting was scheduled for 2:30, and she had about twenty minutes to spare. She was prepared to show up to the office early. There was this little matter of discarding a photo of Hendrik and Zsarina. It was visibly tattered, but it needed to be destroyed. She planned to shred it to pieces in the privacy of her father's office. Just in time to catch the afternoon trash sweep.

With a large Fendi leather tote in hand, Tati exited the parking garage, heading for the South State Bank entrance on 9th and Cary. Completely unaware of the pair of footsteps that shuffled behind her, hurrying to make the crosswalk. The steps picked up pace, hoping the publicist wouldn't turn around as the gap narrowed between them.

Tati wanted to look behind her, as she realized the footsteps were encroaching on her. Was Sam still up to his tricks? She turned around and came face to face with Cece. She jumped startled as the radio host stopped just short of bumping into her.

The women paused in alarm at the steps of the plaza.

"*Cece*? Are you following me?"

"No! I just wrapped up some drops for the station and decided to take a walk. I, uh, saw you crossing the street and wanted to say hello."

Tati's eyes narrowed in a stare that told Cece she didn't believe her. "Uh huh. Well hello. And I heard the apology you made on air. Thank you for that."

"Do you have a minute to talk about the gala?"

"Listen, I have a meeting to attend. Can we chat later?"

"I won't hold you long. I've been thinking about something I read in the autopsy."

"I thought we learned our lesson on letting the police do their jobs," Tati hissed.

"I know but, I'm a fan of true crime. You know that. You knew that when we met at Casa Fiesta on June 29th, before the autopsy released..."

Tati laughed. "Where the hell is this going?"

"...When you referred to Dreah being found with her neck *cracked* over a toilet. Nobody knew her neck was broken until the official autopsy released July 1st."

"Excuse me?" Tati folded her arms over her chest, the Fendi tote still in hand and ready to swing upside Cece's head. "Are you serious?"

"As serious as murder in the first..." Cece went on, "In the beginning, everyone assumed she overdosed on something. It looked... messy, being found in the stall. But I knew Dreah didn't do drugs. Of course she was poisoned. And maybe you walked in on her. Went to hold her face down in the water. To make it look like she drowned in her own filth after passing out- which would've never worked, by the way. But maybe you pushed too hard, and broke her neck instead."

The wind seemed to take Tati's ability to speak. She huffed and looked around them, incredulous. Then she pointed a firm finger at Cece saying, "Look here Cece. You got some. You better mind the business that pays you and don't look no further into this."

As Tati started to walk away, Cece called out, "Why'd you do it Tati? For SamStar? For your father?"

Tati's heels couldn't carry her into the building, not just yet; or maybe it was pride that wouldn't let her walk away. She turned around and stormed back over to Cece, a wicked smirk twisting her pretty face. "

"If you're accusing me of murder, you better be able to back it up. Because I will ruin everything you think you got going on if you fuck with me. Now if you'd excuse me, my father's legacy is on the line."

"You murdered Dreah because once those rumors got out, it'd be over for Sam's affiliation with the casino. And your father is so desperate for the SamStar endorsement that you'd do anything to keep it going."

Tati was repulsed and took a moment to calm her nerves. "Oh Cece, give it up. This was a party. Hundreds of people went in and out of that restroom so they can't use fingerprints. And let's not forget how many enemies Dreah had in that building."

"Is that what you told yourself when you killed her?"

"Let the detectives handle this Cece. You're just a radio personality. Stay in your place. You know what happens when people get too... *talkative*."

The smile on Tati's face was the most threatening of all. She looked at the time on her Shinola bracelet watch. It read 2:22 pm. She laughed, the irony of another synchronicity not lost on her, and carried on towards the building. She stopped at the doors to adjust the pyrite stone in her bra. Then she turned around to find Cece still watching her. She tossed a less than friendly wave, and went inside.

When the publicist disappeared from sight, Cece started towards her parked car on Cary Street. Crossing the stoplight, she checked to see that her phone was still recording the voice memo. She stopped the recording, and quickly got into her car where she replayed the audio, and wondered if it was enough to bring to detectives. It was quite the interrogation. Could she share it with them at all? She wasn't sure about much anymore. Not even her business relationship with MysterPodcast, who graciously gave her a few more days to decide on moving forward. If not, they certainly would be with other projects. She'd be one of few failed shows if she didn't make up her mind.

Dreah's murder had only complicated Cece's approach to the podcast, which was now deeper than the salacious rabbit hole of celebrity conspiracy it sought to cover.

Cece opened the glove compartment and thumbed through a set of photos given to her by a hired private investigator. There were only twenty of them: photos of Tati and Pia at the Canal, Sam and Mina at Mona's- taken from the bar of the lounge, Diondra arriving and leaving the penthouse, and few shots of Sam and his Cheshire cat grin as he entered the Locks Tower.

His pictures and insight never turned up anything of substance, and Cece came to the realization that she didn't need them anyway. She just so happened to find the answer through the mighty gift of gab, the art of being talkative. Tati felt so loose and comfortable, she slipped up and referenced something only the killer would know, before anyone else did.

Chills ran up her arms when Dreah's posthumous letter arrived in her mailbox the Wednesday after the gala. The night of her controversial LIVE. Upon her engineer's departure, she picked up her days old stack of mail- mostly pre-approval credit cards and different types of insurance flyers.

The letter stuck out like a 'draw four' in a freshly plucked set of Uno cards. The rest of the junk mail pile slipped from her hands. She carefully ripped off the tail end of the envelope, and pulled Dreah's handwritten letter from inside.

"This letter is dated June 20. If you received this, it's because I never made it home from the gala to remove it from the mailbox. If I am somewhere else in the country, I will reach out July 2nd after the podcast premiere. I hate that I have to write this part but, in the event of my murder, please investigate my death with all tenacity and vigor. And please delay the podcast debut until my killer is found. I'm sorry I didn't tell you that I was going to the gala. I have given you my story, and you're the only one who knows it as thoroughly as I do. Enclosed are the keys to my store. I've hidden LeVario's original photo from 2005 under the grass mat in the crystal display case. It is proof of the Hendrik and Zsarina story. It is also proof of my abuse at the hands of Dmitri Goode, under the approval of Samuel Pitts. Look in the background. Thank you for everything. You helped me more than words can express. I wish I could've told them to you face to face. Take special care. Eternally yours, Dreah."

The letter was Dreah's last form of contact, and it unnerved Cece every time she dedicated a thought to it. She started the car, immediately turning down the radio as her own voice fired off an ad for a local business.

And now, in the silence, she could hear it better. Much better. The tenacious pleas of Dreah's ghost were loud and relentless, as was that familiar hiss of the serpent's tongue, tempting her exquisite palate for all things true crime.

About The Author

E.K Robertson is a Los Angeles native residing in Richmond, Virginia. She enjoys authentic Mexican cuisine, Real Housewives of Potomac, and sporadic vacations. She lives with her fiancé, their three children, a shy pit bull and a feisty Virgo cat. She is at work on her next novel.

Contact at EKRobertson@austinhousepublishing.com